CHAPTER
∽ AND ∾
CURSE

CHAPTER
AND
CURSE

ELIZABETH PENNEY

St. Martin's Paperbacks

First published in the United States by St. Martin's Paperbacks, an imprint of St. Martin's Publishing Group.

CHAPTER AND CURSE

Copyright © 2021 by Elizabeth Penney.

For information, address St. Martin's Publishing Group, 120 Broadway, New York, NY 10271.

www.stmartins.com

ISBN: 978-1-250-78770-5

Our books may be purchased in bulk for promotional, educational, or business use. Please contact your local bookseller or the Macmillan Corporate and Premium Sales Department at 1-800-221-7945, ext. 5442, or by email at MacmillanSpecialMarkets@macmillan.com.

Printed in the United States of America

St. Martin's Paperbacks edition / October 2021

10 9 8 7 6 5 4 3 2 1

For my English aunts
and the real George Flowers

ACKNOWLEDGMENTS

First, a big thank you to Nettie Finn, my editor at St. Martin's, and Elizabeth Bewley, my agent, for their help bringing the Cambridge Bookshop Series to life. I love bookstores, especially old, atmospheric ones stuffed with literary treasures, and the setting is a return home of sorts. My mother grew up in England fairly close to Cambridge, and went to nursing school there. As a young family, we lived in England and France, wherever my American father was stationed, and I still have relatives in King's Lynn. I hope to visit them again soon. In the meantime, members from wonderful Facebook groups "Cambridge in the Good Old Days" and "Cambridge Memories" have been very helpful. A special shout-out to Keith Mansfield and Derek Smiley for their assistance and support.

Gratitude also for the publicity and marketing efforts of Sarah Haeckel and Allison Ziegler. Your enthusiasm makes all the difference. Danielle Christopher and Mary Ann Lasher did a spectacular job bringing the bookshop to life on the cover. I especially love the depiction of Puck. And

John Simko, my intrepid copy-editor—thanks for catching the goofs and errors.

A note: Many locations in the series are real, but Magpie Lane and its businesses, and the village of Hazelhurst, are fictional.

CHAPTER 1

Spring was much later than usual this year. The huge old maples in front of our farmhouse remained bare, their limbs shivering with each blast of cold northern wind. Only a few daffodils had dared to raise yellow, nodding heads, and these brave souls were soundly scolded for their impertinence when snowed upon. And inside the white farmhouse, which had hunkered low against storms and seasons and sorrows for more than two hundred years, all was quite grim.

Until the day the letter came. It was a Saturday afternoon, so I was home. The town library where I was assistant librarian closed at noon on Saturdays. But in a few more weeks, I wouldn't have a job at all. Budget cuts.

After the postal van went by, I trudged down the drive to retrieve the mail, rubber-soled boots squelching in the mud, scanning the fields and woods for even a hint that the weather was turning.

No hints were to be found, so I hunched my shoulders against the relentless breeze and opened the battered white mailbox. The lid squeaked, as it always did, and I thought about spraying it with lubricant, as I always did. *Oh, Dad.* My heart squeezed with anguish. My father had been in charge of fixing all the squeaks around here. Every hinge of every door was delightfully silent, as he would demonstrate with glee.

I dragged in a long breath and wiped away the tears that were all too frequent. Then I grabbed the bundle of mail, letters wrapped in a slick and colorful grocery flyer, and firmly shut the squeaking lid.

While slogging back to the house, I leafed through the envelopes. Electric bill, charity appeal, credit card offer—a pretty typical haul. Except for the last letter.

It was addressed to my mother, Nina Marlowe, and several clues—the postage, the cancellation stamp, and the addition of "USA" to our address told me it was from England. I peered at the cancellation stamp more closely. Cambridge, England.

Vague memories stirred. Mum was from an English village named Hazelhurst, and she had gone to college in Cambridge. Then she met Derek Kimball, a student from Vermont studying abroad, married him, and moved here. She'd gone back when her parents died, and far as I knew, only a relative or two were left over there. But despite a world shrink-wrapped by the internet, they might as well have been on the moon for all I knew of them. About the only clues to my mother's mysterious past were her accent, which everyone found charming, and the fact that I called her Mum instead of Mom.

Curiosity sparked and I began to run, bracing my legs wide so as not to slip and fall. The mud made really interesting sounds under my boots and I began to laugh, exaggerating my movements. On the side porch, I kicked off my muddy boots, then burst into the kitchen, banging the (quiet-hinged) door shut behind me.

Mum, seated at the island with her tablet, a big mug of coffee close at hand, looked up, hand to her chest. "Molly. You startled me."

"Sorry." I circled the island and dropped the important envelope in front of her. The rest went in the middle of the island, to be dealt with later. "You got a letter from Cambridge."

She put the tablet aside and picked up the letter, examined it back and front. "It must be from Aunt Violet." I hovered by her shoulder as she proceeded to open it. "Go on, sit," she said. "I promise to tell you what it says."

I grabbed a cup of coffee while she extracted several folded pages from the envelope. Then I sat on the next stool and watched her read, lips pursed slightly and a frown of concentration creasing her forehead. Mum was a poet, quite a well regarded one with several published books. But she hadn't written a word since Dad died. And it'd been almost six months.

She'd always joked that Dad, who had been a professor of literature at Thorndike College, was her muse. Maybe it hadn't been a joke. I was worried about my mother. She'd lost weight she couldn't afford, and she was fragile, easily upset, and prone to illness. This was a woman who never, ever got sick, even when I brought nasty, antibiotic-hardened germs home from school.

I sipped my coffee, a familiar gnawing feeling rolling around in my gut. Just as the landscape longed for spring to break winter's spell, we needed something equally reviving and powerful.

Mum was reading faster, a little pink coming into her cheeks. Maybe this letter would, by some mysterious magic, provide a corner we could turn.

Finally she set the pages down and looked at me, her hands clasped. Her dark eyes sparkled with interest and something that looked suspiciously like hope. "Molly, dear, how would you feel about moving to England and taking over a book-shop?"

◆◆

CAMBRIDGE, ENGLAND

Barely two weeks later, we were pulling into Magpie Lane, nestled right in the heart of Cambridge. George Flowers, a stout old chap who wore a flat cap and tweed jacket, had picked us up at the airport in Aunt Violet's vintage Ford Cortina. He'd piloted the sedan through London traffic with ease, radio set to a classic rock station, while the two of us sat numb with jet lag and exhaustion. According to Mum, George was Aunt Violet's longtime friend and general handyman. "A very good chap to know," as she put it.

The sedan crawled down the narrow cobblestone street, passing by the Magpie Tavern, Holly & Ivy Inn, Tea and Crumpets, and Spinning Your Wheels, which had racks of bicycles on the sidewalk. A slim black cat ran out from behind the tea shop, eyeing us with disdain before darting across the lane into an alley.

George braked in front of Thomas Marlowe—Manuscripts & Folios. "Bloody 'ell," he said. "They've gone and taken my spot." He thumped a meaty fist on the wheel. "Don't they know they're not allowed?" Traffic was restricted in the city's ancient center said signs everywhere, but despite the rule, a sleek BMW sat blocking the building entrance.

And what a building it was, like something out of a storybook with its timber framing and cream plaster, diamond-pane bay windows at shop level, and smaller, matching bays on the second floor. Held up with brackets, a third level overhung the others slightly. I caught my breath, my foggy head swimming with awed disbelief. This gorgeous bookshop was ours? Established in 1605, a metal plaque near the door read. More than four centuries ago.

My dazed reverie dissolved with a pop when the Cortina reversed suddenly and then lurched forward, jerking to a stop again. George had parked at a diagonal between an Audi parked in a narrow alley, the same one the cat entered, and the BMW in front of the door.

"There," he said with satisfaction. "At least we can get your bags unloaded." Neither of the other cars would be able to move, but George didn't seem to care. He swung his large body out of the driver's seat and went around to the back to open the trunk.

Mum, who was sitting in front, turned to look at me. "How are you doing back there?"

"Uh, *gobsmacked* is the word, I believe." Ever since the plane landed at Heathrow, Briticisms had come readily to mind. Maybe it was all those Enid Blyton books I'd devoured, seeking clues to my mother's origins. In my luggage was the only print book I'd brought from our extensive library, a cherished copy of *Now We Are Six* by A.A. Milne—who studied in Cambridge, by the way. Dad had read these sweet poems to me often, and I'd imagined my mother in place of Christopher Robin, thinking her childhood must have been exactly like his.

I reached for the handle and pushed the door open, then swung my legs out and stood, stretching my cramped knees. From here, looking up the lane, I could see Trinity College's main gate. Trinity College was home to the world-renowned Wren Library, which held a collection that included amazing works like an eighth-century copy of the Epistles of St. Paul, a thousand medieval manuscripts, and one of Isaac Newton's notebooks. Newton had been a Trinity fellow. Gobsmacked, indeed. I was now living in a book-lover's dream.

"Here we are, then." George thumped our large roller bags onto the sidewalk. "Where are these going? Upstairs?" He slammed the trunk lid down.

"I'm not sure," Mum said in a tentative voice, looking up at the bookshop. "It's been ages. . . . We'll have to ask Aunt Violet." She stood hunched on the sidewalk, clutching her handbag to her side, and with a sharp pang of guilt, I wondered how she was feeling. This was more than a journey to literary heaven for her—this was a homecoming. And maybe a difficult one, at that.

"Are you okay, Mum?" I whispered as George grabbed both handles and bumped the suitcases over the curb, heading toward the bookshop's front entrance.

She worried her bottom lip with her teeth. "I think so. It's all a bit strange . . . being here, leaving Vermont . . . your father . . ."

I put my arm around her shoulder. "We'll be all right. Besides, we can always go back." This was the right thing to say, but every part of me screamed *No, please no, I want to stay here.*

Her headshake was brief but decisive. "That would be giving up." She put her arm through mine. "And the Marlowe women don't give up."

Phew. I planted a kiss on her cheek. "This is going to be the best adventure, wait and see."

At the front door, George stood the suitcases up and moved aside so we could enter first. Unlike most shops, which had plate-glass entrances, Thomas Marlowe had an old-fashioned wooden door painted purple, with a brass press-down latch and an oval window.

"After you, Mum," I said. While I waited for her to open the door, I checked out the bay windows. Although old-fashioned and charming, they were filled with stacks of books in no discernable order and certainly not placed to entice sales.

A huge tiger cat was curled up in the left-hand window, sunbeams warming his fur. He must have sensed me staring because he lifted his head and regarded me with narrow eyes. Then, no doubt deciding I wasn't worth the effort, he snuggled down and went back to his nap. The "he" was an assumption, but he looked like Orson Welles in feline form. I smiled at the image.

Mum finally got the balky door open and held it for me. Bells gave a jaunty tinkle as we crossed the mat onto creaking wood floors.

Books. Everywhere. The kaleidoscope of shape and color hit me first, followed by the intoxicating aroma of paper and ink, leather and cloth, base notes of old wood and dust floating beneath. I breathed deep as I took it all in, my pulse racing.

Built-in shelves lined all four walls, and tall bookcases here and there formed their own alcoves. In the center were tables holding yet more stacks of books but low enough to give a view of the long, curved service desk in the middle of the shop. This was backed with glass-fronted shelves, giving it an enclosed feel, like a kiosk. I guessed the more valuable books were kept there.

The five people in the shop turned to look at us. Three were business types in expensive navy blue suits, two men and a woman. Each held a smartphone.

The fourth was a middle-aged man with receding red hair and fleshy cheeks. He wore a fine wool sweater and slacks, polished loafers on his feet, but despite this careful refinement, something about him screamed gold chains and pinky rings. With crossed arms, he appraised us with cold blue eyes.

From behind the desk a slight figure rose to her feet, adjusting a pair of owlish eyeglasses. White hair was piled high on her head, two pencils and a pen poking out of the hive. A huge smile broke across her face, crinkling her papery cheeks, but before she could say anything, the redheaded man sauntered toward us.

"Nina? Is it really you?" He took her hand between his. "Clive. Clive Marlowe, your cousin." He laughed, a hearty rumble. "Second or third, never can remember how that goes."

Behind us, George horsed the bags through the door with a grunt. As he stood them near us, I noticed him eyeing Clive with barely veiled animosity.

"Oh yes. Clive." Mum pulled her hand free. "I'm sorry . . . it's been a while." George edged past us and went to talk to Aunt Violet. That had to be her behind the desk.

Clive raked those cold eyes up and down Mum's body. "Seems like only a moment, it does. Lovely as ever."

As Mum stuttered a reply and I restrained myself from kicking his shins, I noticed the suits gathered in a huddle, conferring. Now they moved toward us, one man in front, his two companions trailing behind.

"Mr. Marlowe?" the man said with a plummy accent. "Thank you for the tour." He thrust out a hand. "It looks very promising. Promising, indeed."

Clive shook the man's hand with a hearty grip. "Good, good. We'll be in touch then, mate?" Clive's accent wasn't nearly as polished and I saw the man wince. But maybe it was the strength of our cousin's handshake.

"We'll be in touch," the man agreed, wiggling his fingers. "Shall we?" He held the door open for the others.

"I'd better move the car," George muttered, exiting the shop on their heels.

"Who were they?" I asked once the trio was safely out on the sidewalk, getting into the BMW. They hadn't bought any books I'd noticed, and what was this about a tour?

Clive adjusted his gold watch, a satisfied smile tugging at his lips. "They're potential buyers, they are. From Best Books."

I had heard of Best Books, a chain of sleek bookstores located all over the UK, like a British version of Barnes & Noble. Cold shock washed away the clinging remnants of jet lag. If Best Books planned to buy Thomas Marlowe, then what were we doing here? Had we closed the Vermont chapter of our lives only to face a blank page?

CHAPTER 2

Aunt Violet lifted a huge kettle and set it on the cream-colored AGA range. "I'm sorry you had to experience such a rude welcome," she said. "Clive popped in on me with those people, uninvited."

We were in Aunt Violet's kitchen behind the shop, a spacious room featuring flagstone floors, blackened beams, and a sitting area near tall windows overlooking a walled garden. The fat tiger cat was now ensconced in a green velvet armchair, next to which sat a basket of knitting, pretty pink needles thrust through dove gray yarn. His name was Clarence, we had learned. As for the shop, Aunt Violet had put up a sign that read Gone to Lunch.

"What's going on, Aunt Violet?" Mum asked, her fingers toying with the silk scarf knotted around her neck. She and I were seated at a long pine table. "What does Clive have to do with the bookshop?"

Aunt Violet turned on the gas then adjusted the flame. "Nothing, really. I'm the owner but—" She broke off, fluttering over to the refrigerator, an older unit with a rounded top. "What would you like for lunch?" She opened the door and poked her head inside. "I've got ham and cheese and some lovely crusty rolls . . ." Her voice trailed off as she began pulling bottles, jars, and packets out of the fridge.

Mum looked at me, her eyebrows raised. Her steady look assured me we'd get to the bottom of this. "Do you want some help?" she asked.

"No, no." Aunt Violet waved off the suggestion. "You must be exhausted after that long journey." She clucked her tongue. "Traveling over three thousand miles in a single day. I'll never get over being amazed by that."

We sat pinned to our seats in exhaustion while she bustled about, setting stoneware plates laden with thick sandwiches and pickles in front of us, pouring steaming cups of tea, and dispensing glasses of icy, delicious water from a pitcher in the fridge.

I inhaled that sandwich, chasing it with quantities of hot tea. To me, my body clock still set to Vermont time, it was five in the afternoon and I was starving. We'd flown overnight from Boston, crossing five time zones, and landed early in the morning.

Once every delicious bite was gone, Mum wiped her mouth with a napkin. "Thank you. That was wonderful." She leveled a serious look at her aunt. "Now, spill."

Aunt Violet told us the story, in between running out to her files for documents and the checkbook. Clive had given her a loan late last year, when Christmas hadn't been as profitable as usual. She'd been struggling to make payments, so he'd come up with the idea of selling the shop. In fact, he was trying to pressure her into it.

"I'm just devastated," Aunt Violet said, her expression bleak. She'd propped the eyeglasses up in her hair along with the writing implements, revealing large blue eyes framed by laugh lines. She certainly wasn't laughing now. "This shop has been in the family forever and I can't bear to be the one to lose it. That's why I wrote to you, Nina. I thought you could help me turn it around, modernize things a bit." She turned to me. "You're a librarian, Molly, how perfect is that? Plus you probably know all about social media, right?"

"I do," I said. "I have tons of ideas already." The shop, even the way it was right now, in total disarray, was a social media dream. I could picture snaps of ancient tomes paired with mugs of tea, the cobblestones of Magpie Lane fuzzy in the background. As for that fat cat, Clarence? He'd be a star. Who wouldn't want to visit a quaint bookshop in one of England's most beautiful, historic cities? And if they couldn't come in person, they could purchase from us online, buying their own piece of Cambridge.

Then my vision expanded. I could take pictures of the books all over the city, themed to the various colleges and local sights. For example, a display of religious texts and Bibles in the Round Church, which was right up the road.

Knowing now was not the time, I forced myself to stop brainstorming and tune back in. "I had no idea Clive would be bringing in those corporate types so soon," Aunt Violet was saying. Her already pale face had gone even whiter and her lips trembled. "It was so humiliating. They were prodding and prying everywhere, taking notes and talking about the changes they would have to make. All while maintaining listed status, of course." She waved a hand as if cooling herself off. "What foresight we had to list this place, I tell you."

In England, I knew, landmark historic buildings were subject to many regulations aimed at preserving these treasures for future generations. Best Books couldn't just flatten the shop and put up a modern concrete box. That was a small comfort.

Mum was studying the papers, leafing back and forth, reviewing the schedule of payment. "How far behind are you?"

Aunt Violet leaped out of her chair and came around to show her. "I owe these months." She pointed to several lines on the repayment schedule.

Mum used her phone to tally the numbers up. She stared at the sum then nodded. "I can pay this for you. Get him off our backs for a while."

Hope and reluctance warred on Violet's face. "Are you sure? I hate to ask . . . it's my responsibility. . . . Maybe I—"

"I insist," Mum said. "We really don't have a choice, do we?"

Well, we did. Mum and I could fold our tents and crawl back to the States, our dream of a new start in Cambridge demolished. But I hadn't seen her so energized and . . . *alive* since Dad died. If it took the challenge of saving a bookshop on the brink of failure to get her excited, then I was all for it.

Aunt Violet stared down at her fingers, which were laced together. "I guess you're right." When she looked back up, her large eyes were wet with tears. "But how can I ever repay you? You're not just saving the store, you're saving my life."

"And you're saving mine," Mum said. She smiled at her aunt. "Give me Clive's number. And then we'll get to work."

•┨•

Male voices woke me. Soft, rumbling, *English* voices. My eyes flew open. *Where am I?*

I stared up at a low plaster ceiling then at the open diamond-pane casement window beside my bed. That's right. I was in Cambridge, England.

The events of the day before seeped into my mind little by little the way the sunlight through the curtains was slowly growing stronger. The plane ride. Our arrival at the shop. Meeting George and Aunt Violet. Our plans to outwit cousin Clive.

A roar of laughter punctuated the voices, pleasant laughter that spoke of shared confidences. I bolted upright in the brass bed, pushing aside the thick duvet and reaching for my cell phone. What time was it anyway? Mum and I had crawled up to bed around eight, hoping to sleep off our jet lag and start fresh.

Outside the window—because that is where the voices were coming from—tools clanged, followed by a muffled curse. What were they doing out there? At six *bloody* a.m., as George might say? And did, a few times when lugging our suitcases up the narrow stairs to our rooms on the second floor, which in England was the first floor, just to make things confusing. "What on earth have you got in here, love?" he'd asked, his face so red and sweaty I thought he might have a heart attack.

"Shoes," I replied with a wince, glad I'd only brought one book, and a thin one at that. *Now We Are Six* sat on the bedside table, a reminder of Dad.

Another clatter of tools was followed by the bright *bringbring* of a bell. Seriously? Laughter and chatter were fine, but this was definitely annoying. Untangling the white cotton nightgown wrapped around my legs, I pushed myself to my knees and opened the casement window wider, leaning out so I could see the sidewalk. Two men, one with longish dark hair and the other blond with a fade, were bent over a bicycle. The dark one used his thumb to set the bell off again. *Bringbring.*

"Do you mind?" I snapped. "People are trying to sleep up here." I had no idea why they were in front of this building instead of the bicycle shop next door.

Both faces looked up. The blond man was quite goodlooking but it was the dark-haired one who caught my attention. His sooty gaze took in my long dangling braid and the lace-trimmed nightdress before roaming back to my face. Our eyes locked.

"What's this?" the blond man asked. "Juliet on her balcony greeting the sun?"

It *was* funny. A giggle burst out of me and the dark one cracked a smile, one hand rubbing his square, stubbly jaw. He was gorgeous, with chiseled features, straight brows above those magnetic eyes, broad shoulders and a trim build. *He could easily play Romeo to my Juliet*, I thought fancifully.

Then he spoke. Straightening those muscled shoulders, he

said, "I run a business here, miss." He shrugged. "Sorry, but sometimes we make a little noise."

That was it? Surely that was the lamest apology I'd ever heard. "So much for being a good neighbor," I barked. I reached up and shut the casement windows with a decisive click. Then, for good measure, I drew the curtains fully closed, the curtain rings clashing.

I flopped down on the bed, hoping I could get back to sleep for at least a little while. Out on the sidewalk, the voices murmured, then faded away. Probably the blond one convinced old dark eyes that he should be more considerate. I snorted and rolled over, putting a pillow over my head for good measure.

Remorse soon crept in. To be honest, I had been rather rude myself. The bike shop owner probably hadn't known I was sleeping right above the sidewalk. Aunt Violet's bedroom was in the back of the building, on the other end. And no wonder.

I'd talk to him later, I decided, and apologize. Once I was rested.

◆◆◆

My phone informed me it was ten a.m. the next time I woke. The grogginess was gone and energy flooded my body. What was I missing on my first full day in Cambridge? I leaped to my knees and opened the curtains again.

All was quiet on Magpie Lane, with only a few people on foot going in and out of Tea and Crumpets across the way. My belly grumbled at the thought of crumpets drenched in butter. And I was dying for my first cup of coffee. A terrible thought halted me as I slid into my jeans. Could I get real coffee, not that instant stuff I'd heard was popular here? In my view, instant was for coffee emergencies only.

Dressed and washed, I made my way down the narrow stairs to the kitchen. Here too all was quiet, gentle warmth radiating from the AGA and Clarence curled in his armchair. Mum and Aunt Violet must be in the shop already. After detouring to pat the cat's silky head, which he stoically endured, I went through the door into the shop.

No one was at the desk, but I heard Mum's voice coming from the far corner so I wound my way through a labyrinth of bookcases to find them. For some reason, Mum and Aunt Violet were staring at the back wall, which was covered with shelves like the others, and the men from the bicycle shop were with them.

I froze. What were they doing here? Were they customers? But then the blond man pointed to a beam crossing the ceiling. "There's your carrier beam. So it shouldn't be a problem."

"Do you really think so, Tim?" Aunt Violet adjusted her spectacles and stared up at the beam. "I wouldn't want the place to fall down around our ears."

As I debated whether to announce myself or beat a hasty retreat, my weight shifted and a board moved under my feet, letting out a heartrending groan. My goodness.

The blond man turned and looked over his shoulder. "There's our Juliet now," he said with a grin.

The rest of them turned to look and I smiled wanly, waving my hand and not quite looking the dark man in the eye.

No, like the coward I was, my gaze skipped over his face. Just as gorgeous as I remembered. Mum looked puzzled at Tim calling me Juliet but she didn't ask.

"Hi," I said. "What are you all up to?"

Instead of answering my question, Aunt Violet said, "Did you sleep well, my dear? I can make you tea or there's coffee at the shop across the street." To the men, she said, "This is Molly, my American great-niece. The one I was telling you about."

I waved in their general direction. "I slept fine, thank you," I said, trying not to make eye contact. But out of the corner of my eye, I could see Tim grinning and his co-worker watching me with an inscrutable expression. "I think I'll go get coffee. Would anyone like anything?"

I was expecting them to say no, but Tim glanced at his friend and said, "Sure. Kieran and I will take two orders of crumpets." He dug around in his jeans pocket and pulled out a banknote. "And two large filter coffees." He handed me the money. "Thanks."

So his name was Kieran. Nice. "Be right back," I said, tucking the bill in my pocket. As I turned to leave, my foot hit that noisy board again, making heat rush to my face. If that kept happening, I was going to mark it with an X or something.

The air outside was cool, scented with something flowering from the gardens beyond the wall. Before walking across to the tea shop, I stopped to take in my new neighborhood: Trinity College's gate across the road, the jumble of quaint buildings along the lane, the ridges of cobblestones under my feet. A slim black shape darted from the alley next to the bookshop and scampered over to me. "Good morning, kitty," I said. "How are you today?"

His answer was to dart ahead to the tea-shop door, where he sat and waited. "No, you can't come in," I said, edging around him. I pushed the latch, squeezed my body through a narrow crack, and quickly shut the door. My triumph was short-lived when I saw his little triangle face peeking forlornly through the glass.

"Is that cat trying to get in here again?" the woman behind the counter asked. She was about my age, with a head of blonde curls and sparkling blue eyes. She wore a bib apron over a blue shirt, and her figure was pleasantly soft and curvy.

"Yes, he is," I said, moving across the black and white tiles toward the counter. "It was a struggle to keep him out." I glanced around, taking in the few patrons seated at the dozen or so little tables, some talking quietly to a companion, others tapping away on laptops. Just like in Vermont. The counter where the woman stood was of carved wood, display cases to both sides and the service area in the middle. On the wall behind her a chalkboard hung above racks holding baskets of bread and shelves of dishes. Coffee- and tea-making equipment was on the counter below.

"Are you American?" she asked, her face bright with curiosity. "Visiting from the States, are you?"

"I am," I admitted. "I'm from Vermont. But I'm staying at the bookshop. Violet Marlowe is my aunt."

She gasped. "Well, I never. So you're the American niece." She put out her hand for me to shake. "Glad to meet you. I'm Daisy Watson and this is my shop."

"Molly Kimball. And I'm very glad to meet you too." Aunt Violet must have mentioned me to everyone on the lane, which gave me a funny feeling. Mum never spoke of Aunt Violet or any of our relatives. There must be a reason, but I couldn't imagine what it was. Aunt Violet was wonderful. I loved her already.

"What can I get you, Molly?" Daisy asked, leaning on the counter with both hands. "We make everything fresh here, daily."

"That sounds awesome. But first, I need a cup of coffee." I scanned the blackboard in confusion. Instead of the familiar coffee lingo, the choices were "cafetière" and "filter." I had no idea what they were. "I'm sorry," I said. "But I don't understand. In America we make coffee with coffee makers. Or the espresso machine." She had one of those.

"You're not the only one asking," Daisy said. "*Cafetière* is what some people call a French press." She held one up. "*Filter coffee* means using this cone and a filter." She showed me the cone. "People are drinking so much coffee now I had to add it. Offering only tea would kill my business."

That was surprising to hear, since tea was an English tradition. But here I was, ordering filter coffee to go. "An order of crumpets too." Then I remembered. "Make that three orders of coffee and crumpets." At her raised brows, I said, "I'm picking up an order for Kieran and Tim. They're doing something at the bookshop for my aunt."

A smile tugged at Daisy's lips, revealing a dimple in one cheek. "Ooh, girl. So you've met those two. They're totally fit, aren't they?"

Fit? "Maybe," I said hesitantly. "They look like they're in shape." Then I remembered. In England, *fit* meant "attractive."

Daisy laughed. "No maybe about it. They're the best things on two legs around here. And they're not kids, either, like those college lads." She leaned closer. "Did you know that Kieran—" The front door opened and a group of chattering ladies strolled in. Daisy whirled away. "Let me get your order. We'll talk later. At the pub?"

"That sounds fun," I said, moving aside so the ladies could look at the menu. I couldn't hold back a smile as I waited by the pastry case for my order. Daisy was nice, and it looked like I had already made a friend. Plus I couldn't wait to find out what she had been going to tell me about Kieran.

A local paper lay on a nearby table and I picked it up to glance at the headlines. "Cambridge Literary Festival Next Week" read one headline. Interesting. I wondered if Thomas Marlowe participated in any events. But I didn't find us on the list of participating bookshops. That seemed like an oversight.

"Molly? Order's up," Daisy called.

∙⫶∙

When I returned to the shop with my sack of coffees and crumpets, everyone was in the kitchen, seated around the long table. Aunt Violet was pouring tea into three cups and I noticed a new face at the table, an older woman with beige poodle-permed hair and sharp features, dressed in a neat brown coat. I gave Kieran and Tim their breakfast, Tim his change, and then sat beside the newcomer, eager to dig in.

"Molly, this is Myrtle," Aunt Violet said, passing around the cups. "She's an old college classmate of mine from St. Hildegard's."

Myrtle cackled. "You can leave out the *old* part." Holding her mug in both hands, she regarded me closely with hazel eyes. "So, Molly. You're a pert one. Do you have a boyfriend?"

The coffee in my mouth threatened to spray out. With an effort, I managed to swallow while everyone around the table, including Kieran and Tim, stared at me. "No, I don't," I finally said, knowing the answer invited condescending sympathy from certain people.

Myrtle fulfilled my every expectation when she said, "That's a pity, that is. Of course it'd be hard managing a long-distance relationship with someone in the States. But a little easier with video, I would think." She sipped her tea, seeming not to realize how her comment could be construed.

At least in *my* mind. Certain my face was now beet red, I focused my attention on unwrapping the crumpet. Crumpets resemble English muffins but they're so much better. This one was toasted perfectly with butter pooled in the tiny holes on top. Yum.

"Nina," Myrtle said. "Did you have a mansion in Vermont? I've heard homes in the States are very large and posh."

Now it was Mum's turn to parry an intrusive question. "Um, no, we don't have a mansion." She curved her lips in what passed for a smile. "It's an old farmhouse, quite modest and simple." Myrtle harrumphed as though she didn't believe her.

My hunger slightly sated, I asked, before Myrtle could probe further, "So what you were you all doing, talking about carrier beams?"

"We're knocking out part of a wall," Aunt Violet said. "Well, these two strong young men are. We're going to make the old workroom into a gathering space, as you suggested, Molly. We need a way to get in there without going through the back hall."

That wasn't quite my idea, although last night I had said that Thomas Marlowe should host book events. The main problem was lack of space in the main bookshop. Aunt Violet had thought of a solution, it seemed.

"Sounds like a great plan," I said. "Where will the workroom go?" I picked up the second half of my crumpet and licked a drip of butter.

Aunt Violet pointed to the ceiling. "Upstairs in the spare room. Book repair was my brother's department." She looked sad. "We lost Tom last summer."

"Ah, yes, Tom." Myrtle shook her head. "He was a grand old chap."

Kieran and Tim grunted assent, their expressions mournful.

Another relative I hadn't known, I thought with sorrow. It was interesting that Uncle Tom had done book repair, since I had also repaired books on a small scale at the library. But those books weren't especially valuable. Making a mistake on one worth thousands of dollars would be disastrous.

"There are also boxes of odd lots in there. Mostly

children's books." Aunt Violet rolled her eyes. "Tom never could resist those. He always thought we'd stumble upon a forgotten treasure. I've been meaning to look through them but there hasn't been time."

"I'll do it." I adored vintage children's books. "And I'd like to be trained in book binding and repair, if that's possible." Then I remembered the newspaper article. "Back to the event room. Do you think we can be ready before the literary festival starts next week? We should get in on that somehow."

"I don't see why not," Kieran said. "All we need to do is take down the wall. We can do that tonight, after the shops close." He glanced at his phone. "Speaking of which, I'd better go relieve Jayde. She's got class in ten." Picking up his coffee, he pushed back his chair and stood.

"All you need is a coat of paint back there and you'll be ready to go," Tim said, crumpling the paper that had held his crumpets. "We can talk about putting shelves in later." He stood up, too, draining the last of his coffee.

Mum straightened in her chair, her face alight with excitement. "All we need for a reading are chairs and a table to hold wine and cheese. Maybe some other nibbles too."

"I can borrow a table and chairs from the parish hall," Aunt Violet said. "And Daisy will cater the food. But the bigger question is, who can we get to come on such short notice? And not just an author, but someone who will draw in the crowds."

Myrtle waved a hand. "I've got an idea." She paused until she was sure we were all properly attentive, including Kieran and Tim, who halted in the doorway to listen. "Ruth is publishing a fifty-year retrospective of Persephone's poetry. Why don't we have Persephone do a reading?"

"Are you talking about Persephone Brightwell?" Mum asked, an expression of awe on her face. She looked at Aunt Violet. "You know her?"

"Know her?" Myrtle cackled again. "She was our house-mate in college. One of the gang. Along with Ruth, who runs a publishing company called Virginia's House, and Fiona, who is a bigwig at St. Hildegard's. And *her* husband is an MP." MP was shorthand for member of Parliament. Tim and Kieran exchanged looks. I guess being married to a member of Parliament was something special.

Mum fiddled with her teaspoon, turning it over and over. "She's considered the greatest living poet in Britain. If we could convince her to read for us . . ."

She didn't need to finish the sentence. Having Persephone Brightwell appear here during the world-famous literary festival would be a slam dunk for Thomas Marlowe. We'd be back on the map with a vengeance.

"We can get her," Myrtle said with a smug smile. "I can guarantee it."

CHAPTER 3

I could barely walk by the time Daisy and I went across to the pub that evening. The renovation work in the bookshop had begun right after breakfast. I'd spent the day packing books from the shelves that were going to be removed, while George supervised a couple of men who cleared the workroom and carted everything upstairs. Protective plastic was hung, Kieran and Tim busted through a section the size of double doors, and some other men carried the debris to a rented dumpster placed in the alley. Or *skip*, as it was called here. Next up tomorrow, trim work around the opening, cleaning, and painting.

"Are you all right?" Daisy asked, holding the door open for me. "You're hobbling something awful."

I groaned a little as I sidled past her into the pub. "I moved crates of books all day. I'm so sore."

"It's exciting what you're doing, isn't it?" Daisy said. She, and everyone else on the lane, it seemed, had popped in to watch us working at one point or another. Even Susie and Steve Baker from the pub had come by. "You've brought new life to the place already."

And taken some years off mine. Hopefully a pint of beer and a warm meal, followed by a hot bath before bed, would revive me.

Inside, I paused to take in the cozy pub with its beams and wainscoting, fireplace in the corner, and leather banquettes under mullioned windows. The carved wooden bar took up a corner, lines of bottles and taps reflected in the mirror behind. At this time of night, the room was lively with chatter and laughter, every bar stool filled.

"There's a table." I pointed to an empty two-top near the fireplace and headed in that direction, dimly aware that Daisy was greeting people on the way. She seemed to know everyone.

"What do you want?" she asked, handing me a laminated card from the holder. "We order up at the bar."

Which meant getting up again. I smothered another groan and studied the menu, which had food on one side, drinks on the other. "Bangers and mash and a brown ale."

"Good choice," Daisy said. "I'll have the same." As I started to get up, she gestured me down. "Stay. I've got this."

"Are you sure?" I asked. "I can give you the money."

She shook her head, the blonde curls dancing. "My treat, to welcome you to the neighborhood. Next time it will be your turn."

While she made her way to the bar, I slumped back against the cushy banquette, allowing the warmth from the fireplace to seep into my bones. The patrons were a mix of students, professional types, and working-class folks. The two men who had helped move stuff at the shop were at the bar, and through a doorway I saw pool tables and dartboards. That room was crowded too. It appeared that the Magpie Pub was the place to be around here, and best of all, it was right across the lane from the bookshop.

An older woman slid off a bar stool and pulled her handbag from the clip holder below the bar. I recognized the brown coat first. Myrtle, Aunt Violet's friend. I watched as she toddled toward the front door, hoping to catch her eye. She'd promised to make a few phone calls to arrange Persephone's reading, and I wondered if she'd had any luck. But she slipped out without looking my way.

Behind the bar, Susie Baker picked up a slip, then stared after Myrtle, a puzzled look on her face. Had Myrtle left without paying? She showed it to Steve, who shrugged, before taking the slip and balling it up. Maybe he had given Myrtle a meal on the house, a generous gesture toward a neighborhood senior. The Bakers, who looked to be in their fifties, were hearty, outgoing sorts, well-suited to running a pub.

Daisy returned, holding two brimming glasses of brown beer aloft. "Guess who's here?" She set my glass on the table in front of me. "Tim and Kieran. Playing darts."

I really didn't want to budge from my warm seat, but I said, as a good friend should, "Do you want to go talk to them?" I was getting the idea that Daisy liked Tim.

She glanced toward the game room, chewing at her bottom lip, then at the bar. "Sure. I'll tell Susie and she'll bring our food in there."

Carrying our ale—after I took a good slurp to lower the level—we made our way into the back room. A cluster of men and women were hanging around the dartboard where Kieran and Tim were competing.

Cheers went up when Kieran hit the bull's-eye, one, two, three. Tim groaned, pretending to pull his hair out. "I'm going to beat you one day, mate," he said.

Kieran retrieved his darts, a gloating smile on his lips. "That's what you always say." He glanced around at his friends. "One more game before we eat? Who wants to challenge me? I'll buy the winner a pint."

"He hasn't bought anyone a pint yet," a bald man said with mock disgust. "But we've bought him plenty. You've beat all of us here, Kieran. Maybe you should find some new victims, er, challengers elsewhere."

Kieran's laughing eyes traveled the circle again, flaring briefly when he spotted Daisy and me standing on the fringe. "You're all a bunch of wimps, you are."

"I'll do it," I said, surprising myself. "If someone lends me their darts." I patted my pocket. "Forgot mine." I actually had a nice set, in storage back in Vermont. My father had taught me to play darts and we'd spent many a long winter day practicing in our basement. I hadn't played for a couple of years but my fingers itched to pick up darts again. There was something both meditative and satisfying about the game.

The bald man regarded me with exaggerated wide eyes. "And who might you be? Obviously not from around here." But he said it in a good-humored way and I didn't take offense. The others chuckled.

"I'm Molly, from Vermont," I said with pride, holding out

my palm. "Now, who has some darts I can use?" Tim gave me his.

By Kieran's swagger as he stood back to let me throw, I could tell he thought it would be a quick game. We were playing Around the World, which required each of us to score three in each number before moving on, starting at the 1 and working our way up to the 20, finishing with the bull's-eye. Hitting the triple and double rings awarded extra points.

After a couple of warm-up shots to get the feel of the well-balanced yet light darts, I put three in the 1—one, two, three—including hitting the double and triple rings. Pure showing off, I have to admit.

The room had fallen silent, even the pool players stopping their game to watch. "Oh, Vermont," Ollie, the bald man, said. "Shall I order her pint now, Kieran, to save time?"

In the lead most of the way, I choked on the bull's-eye, which meant owing Kieran a pint. But he bought me one anyway, and after two pints of English ale, a heavy meal, and the day I'd had, I was pretty wiped out by the time Daisy and I left the pub with Kieran and Tim.

Daisy and Tim walked ahead, talking quietly. I had spent most of the evening watching and listening, absorbing the dynamics in the group of friends. Besides the banter during our game, I hadn't really spoken to Kieran, and this was the first time he and I had been alone. But I was too wooly-headed and tired to be nervous and, at the same time, tipsy enough to get emotional.

"How lucky can a person be?" I stopped dead in the middle of the lane to stare at Trinity College's towers etched against the sky. Lights glowed in its tall arched windows as if welcoming those who sought knowledge and wisdom. "Pinch me, please. I'm actually in Cambridge, England, living in a four-hundred-year-old bookshop."

Vocalizing these thoughts made my voice shake, just a little, and a spritz of tears stung my eyes. Blinking, I spun on my heel and stared at the shop with its sweet, slumping roofline above the timbered walls, a building that had withstood wars, plagues, and monarchies. "I had no idea I belonged to such a long line of book-loving Marlowes."

"History puts everything in perspective, doesn't it?" Kieran said, his voice soft. "And it inspires us as well. To do better, to make a difference." His words rang with sincerity.

"I like that," I said. "Very much." I inhaled a deep breath, knowing now was the time. "And I'm sorry. I know I was rude to you this morning." Had it been only that morning? It felt like weeks ago.

I made myself look him in the eye so he'd know my apology was heartfelt. To my relief, his gaze was warm and friendly, crinkled with good humor. "And I'm sorry we were so inconsiderate. No ringing of bells until at least eight a.m. I've made a shop rule." He patted me on the shoulder. "Now it's time for bed, Vermont. Busy day ahead."

◆◆◆

The next day *was* busy, and so were the ones that came after it. Aunt Violet received a call from Ruth Orforo, who confirmed that Persephone Brightwell would indeed be happy to read at Thomas Marlowe during the festival. That news put wings on our feet as we finished the cleanup and renovations.

And then it was upon us, the bookshop's inaugural event: Persephone Reads. Who would have thought it, a poet so well known that only her first name was required, like certain pop stars? The posters—yes, we'd managed to get some printed and tacked up in prime locations—showed Persephone's aquiline features in chiaroscuro, one long braid pulled forward over a bare shoulder. Almost frightening, it was so artsy.

The last minute found us scrambling to get ready, of course. That always seemed to be the way with important events.

"In here." I gestured to the men carrying a folding table through the shop. Once again, the indispensable George had recruited helpers. "Set it up against the wall."

Daisy was on their heels, lugging a big box holding stacked trays. "Looks good in here," she said, setting it down as soon as the men put the table in place and spread the cloth I gave them. "I like the curtains and rug. Makes it cozy but classy too."

"You think so?" After whitewashing the plaster walls, we'd added red velvet drapes to the two windows and spread an antique Persian rug on the flagstone floor.

"I really do." Daisy pointed at the box. "If you put out those trays, I'll go get the next lot." She bustled away.

While I laid out a cheese tray, vegetable and fruit platter, and a board of meats and smoked fish, the helpers began setting up chairs. Mum popped in, directing Tim to set an ice-filled tub on the drinks table. Then they left to get the wine. I set out a glass jar, slips of paper, and a sign inviting people to enter a drawing. We were giving away a copy of Persephone's new book, *Words of Knowledge*, which was releasing soon.

Daisy returned with napkins, utensils, and plates. Electric candles, too, which she set out and turned on; and the finishing touch, a lush bouquet that resembled a Dutch still life. "My sister Primrose did the arrangement," she said. "She does flowers for the Holly and Ivy as part of her job there." The small hotel up the lane.

"She did a fantastic job," I said, pulling out my phone to take a shot of the table. It looked incredible, simple but elegant. Thomas Marlowe had social media pages now, and I tried to post every day. I hadn't gotten to my books-around-town idea yet but I was jotting down tons of ideas.

Daisy reached out to fluff the flowers. "Did I tell you that my great-aunt was at St. Hildegard's with Persephone and Violet? Joan Watson was her name."

I regarded her with surprise. "No, you didn't. We should have invited her."

Daisy's mouth turned down. "I wish we could . . . but she died while she was at college, back in the sixties. Not that I knew her. But my father did, when he was small."

"I'm so sorry," I said. "What a tragedy."

We heard a commotion at the doorway, and there she was—the guest of honor. Persephone Brightwell was regal in flowing purple draperies, the trademark braid thick and gray and hanging almost to her waist. With her were a slim dark-skinned woman with tidy features and knowing eyes, dressed in a tailored red suit, and a tanned and statuesque woman with a chest like the prow of a ship. She wore white wide-legged trousers and a navy double-breasted jacket, bringing to mind further nautical images.

"All us girls finally together again," the statuesque one said, her voice booming. "We've held up pretty well, I'd say."

"It's good to see you, Fiona," the woman in the red suit said. "How are Gregory and the children?"

"They're very well, thank you. I've got six grandchildren now and one great-grandchild, do you believe it?" Fiona brayed a laugh. "And how is your family, Ruth?"

Ruth was the publisher and Fiona did something at St. Hildegard's College, I remembered Myrtle saying.

Seeming not to hear her friends, Persephone drifted farther into the room, lips moving silently. Daisy and I exchanged glances, and Daisy shrugged. Maybe this was the way famous poets acted, although Mum was never quite so out there, even at her most inspired.

Ruth and Fiona stood aside so Tim could bring in the wine, watching while he put the white in ice and placed the red on the table. He then opened a bottle of white with deft movements of the corkscrew. "This is chilled, ladies, if you would like a glass."

They crowded close with coos of enthusiasm, even flighty Persephone, who perked up at the mention of wine. Daisy already had the wine glasses out and she handed them to him as he poured.

Mum brought in a pack of bottled water for the non-drinkers, trailed by Aunt Violet, who looked troubled. Instead of joining her friends, Aunt Violet came over to me. "Have you seen Myrtle? I rang her several times but she doesn't answer." She looked around the room as if her friend might be hiding behind a chair. "I can't imagine she'd miss the reading since she's the one who helped set it up."

A qualm chilled me. Myrtle was elderly, after all. "Can someone check her apartment, er, flat? Maybe she's . . . ill."

Aunt Violet's face lightened. "Good idea. I'll send George over. He's her neighbor. Her landlord, actually."

The bells over the front door tinkled and it was as if the floodgates had opened. Eager and excited people poured into the bookshop, greeting each other with air kisses and cries of enthusiasm before descending on the refreshments like a swarm of poetry-loving locusts. In the midst of it all, Persephone played with her braid as she gracefully accepted accolades, her pale skin pinking.

"Nice turnout," someone said in my ear. I turned to see Kieran, dressed in a light turquoise button-down shirt and faded jeans. He wore leather moccasins, and his aftershave was something spicy yet woodsy, like a pine forest. I was such a sucker for a great aftershave.

"Even better than I hoped." In fact, it looked like standing room only. Thinking it was almost time to start, I glanced around for Aunt Violet, since she would do the honors of introducing her old friend. Seeing her chatting in the corner with Fiona, I excused myself and headed in her direction. But before I got there, George came into the room. I clearly saw the headshake he directed at my aunt. Myrtle wasn't at home.

"I take it Myrtle isn't coming?" I asked Aunt Violet when I reached them. "We might as well get started, then."

"She wasn't in her flat, George said." Aunt Violet frowned, her eyes on the doorway. "I have no idea where she could be."

"Oh, you know Myrtle," Fiona said with that braying laugh. "She never was reliable. Always following her nose somewhere."

"Is that how you remember her?" Aunt Violet cocked her head, studying Fiona's face. "I don't. But no matter." She squared her slim shoulders. "The show must go on."

Aunt Violet made her way to the front of the room, where we'd placed a stool for Persephone to sit if she wished. She picked up a hand bell Mum had placed on a pedestal along with a glass of water and an advance reading copy of Persephone's new book. A few violent shakes of the bell drew everyone's attention. People scrambled for seats, and those who didn't find one stationed themselves along the walls. I remained standing in back, where I'd been keeping an eye on things.

"Good evening, everyone." My great-aunt's voice rang out in the quiet room. "It's my great pleasure to introduce a good friend of mine, also an alumna of St. Hildegard's College. Please welcome the talented and gracious Persephone Brightwell, declared last year to be Britain's greatest living poet."

Applause broke out as Persephone glided up the aisle, her chin lifted and eyes straight ahead. "Thank you, dear Violet," she said, whirling around to face the audience. "I'm glad to still be considered among the living, although small children can't quite believe anyone could be *this* old." Widening her eyes, she flicked that long braid behind her shoulder with a practiced gesture. Everyone laughed, and then she opened her book and began to read. "'Oh, haunted Cambridge,'" she began. The audience settled back to listen with an almost audible sigh of contentment.

The reading was a huge hit, evocative, touching, and funny in turns. She concluded with a wistful poem about the "fast fading of the days," then closed by urging her listeners to gobble life up while they could.

Taking her at her word, our guests attacked the food table again while Tim opened yet more bottles of wine. Adoring fans immediately engulfed Persephone, some asking her to autograph books they had brought with them since the new book wasn't out yet.

"I took the liberty of popping a couple of bottled lagers into your aunt's fridge, if you want one," Kieran said to me. I'd already told him I preferred beer to wine, which sometimes gave me a headache.

"Why don't we go out back?" I suggested, needing a break from the noise and excitement. Plus I wanted to savor our success in peace.

We went through the quiet bookshop into the kitchen, where Clarence was napping in his usual spot. While Kieran retrieved and opened the beers, I patted the cat, then added a few treats to his dish. We all deserved treats tonight. The event had been a smashing success.

Kieran handed me a frosty bottle and I led him out the French doors into the enclosed garden. "It's nice out here," he said, lifting his bottle in a salute. Although not a terribly big space, it was a charming retreat. A small paved patio near the door held a table and chairs, a gas grill close by. I planned to eat many meals at that table this summer. Sweet scents drifted from the flowering cherry tree in the middle, and flowerbeds edging the wall were coming into bloom.

"I love it." I stepped onto the lawn, thinking about taking my shoes off and wiggling my toes in the fresh grass. A shadow detached itself from the base of the tree and darted toward me. The little black cat, who must be a stray. "Where did you come from?" I asked him as he rubbed against my legs, purring.

"Through the gate, I bet." Kieran pointed to the rear gate, which was cracked open.

Aunt Violet and George were sticklers about closing doors and shutting gates. Had one of our guests come in that way? "Excuse me a minute." I handed my beer to Kieran and crossed the grass toward the gate, the little black kitty beside me.

It was because of the cat that I made the horrible discovery. He ran ahead of me, veering toward the shed, then halting with a plaintive mew. The streetlight in the alley beyond the garden was just bright enough that I could see him staring at me. He mewed again.

"What is it, kitty?" I pulled out my cell phone and turned on the flashlight to take a closer look.

I recognized the coat first, dull brown and knee length. Myrtle's coat. Dread tightened my chest as I stepped closer, almost afraid to look. But she appeared peaceful, lying faceup with her arms at her sides, her feet in their sensible shoes splayed outward.

She looked as if she were sleeping—except for the pink knitting needle protruding from her chest.

CHAPTER 4

I screamed and dropped the phone, which went dark. Maybe she was still alive—I threw myself to my knees and reached for her wrist.

"What is it, Molly?" Standing above me, Kieran gasped as his own light swept over the poor woman. He hunkered down on her other side, his face a mask of dismay. He swallowed hard. "Is she—?"

Not able to discern even a hint of a pulse, I gently placed her arm on the grass. Her skin was already cool. "Yes, Kieran, she is. She's . . . she's *dead*." At that terrible word, a gulp of shock rose in my throat and stuck there. "We need to get help," I managed to gargle out.

But he was already on it. Standing again, he paced back and forth, muttering to himself as he touched the screen of his phone.

I pushed myself to my feet and backed away from poor

Myrtle. There was nothing more I could do. It was up to the police now, to gather evidence and solve this crime. To discover the person who had attacked her right here, in the bookshop garden, mere feet away from a crowd of people. We must have been making too much noise to hear her cries for help. Or had she already been dead before we started the event? The thought made me shudder.

A movement in the back alley caught my eye. A dark shape moved at the edge of the streetlamp's glow, tall and bulky, wearing a cap. I screamed again, and when Kieran glanced at me, startled, I pointed. "A man. There's a man out there."

He thrust his phone into my hand and bolted across the grass and out the back gate. "Hello?" a woman's voice said from the speaker. "Is anyone there?"

I placed the phone against my ear with trembling fingers. "Yes, yes, I'm here. This is Molly Kimball. We're calling to report a murder. It looks like one, anyway. An elderly woman named Myrtle Marsh. Someone stabbed her." I couldn't remember the address, but thankfully she knew of the bookshop. She promised that someone would be there shortly. "Do you want me to stay on the phone with you, miss, until they get there?" she offered.

Did I? Kieran came running along the alley, feet thumping, arms pumping.

"No, I'll be all right, thank you. There are lots of people here." I disconnected with thanks as Kieran came through the back gate.

He shook his head. "Didn't catch him," he said between

gasps. "Either he knows the area and is hiding or he's extremely fit."

"That's too bad." But I was relieved. Despite admiring Kieran's bravery, what if the man had attacked him? "The police are on their way. Maybe they can track him down."

I gave him his phone then felt around on the grass for mine, yelping when my hand brushed something soft—something that licked my fingers and began to purr. "Oh, it's you." I picked up the black cat and cuddled him close, and a second later found my phone, thankfully right before I stepped on it.

Kieran put an arm around me. "Come sit down." He led me across the grass, his warmth a comfort, the tiny cat purring even louder. "Bloody hell." He jerked to a halt. "I just realized something. The police will want contact info from everyone who was here tonight. We'd better go tell them not to leave."

This was a problem, since people had started drifting out right after the reading ended. Then I remembered something. "Hopefully people who have left signed up for the raffle." At his puzzled look, I explained. "We're giving away a copy of Persephone's new book. People put their names and phone numbers in a jar."

"The police will be glad of that, though I doubt the murderer would have left a calling card." He pulled me close again, his voice a deep rumble in my ear. "We can tell whoever is left to stay put."

I was beyond grateful for his support, but with every step, my anxiety and trepidation grew. How was I going to break the news to Aunt Violet? I wasn't sure how close she and Myrtle had been, but they had known each other for decades. One small blessing was that Mum and I were here to help her deal with this tragedy.

We had reached the patio when the French door to the kitchen burst open and a gaggle of women spilled through, chattering. Even in the dark, I recognized them immediately. Persephone's long braid, Fiona's bosom, Ruth's quicksilver voice. They were carefree, laughing, elated over the night's triumphs—and about to be devastated.

Wall sconces on either side of the door lit up and Aunt Violet stepped outside, carrying a tray holding a bottle of wine and four glasses. "There. We'll be able to see something now." She smiled at me. "Thanks to your mum's help, I can step away for a drink and a natter."

"Violet," Kieran said, his voice grave. "We have bad news." He took the tray and set it on the table, probably afraid she might drop it.

Aunt Violet's hand went to her throat. "Bad news? What about?" Her eyes behind her glasses were frightened. The three other women moved closer together, reminding me of startled pigeons.

Kieran and I exchanged glances. "Why don't you go in and um, see what's up?" I suggested, trying to be discreet. "If anyone is still here, that is." I took a deep and bracing breath. "I've got this." *I hope.*

"Are you sure?"

At my nod, he slipped inside. I watched him go, immediately wishing he'd stayed for moral support. At least I still had the warm little cat in my arms.

"What's going on?" Persephone asked, her tone shrill. "I can't take the suspense."

"At our age, bad news is all too common," Fiona added solemnly. She widened her stance as if bracing for impact.

"Too true." Ruth nodded. "Lately it seems like we lose someone every day."

And they had tonight as well. I swallowed hard, clutching the cat so tightly he squeaked. How much detail should I give? *Not much*, a tiny voice warned. Let the police choose what to reveal.

"I'm sorry to tell you this," I said. "So sorry. But Myrtle has . . . passed. Kieran and I found her a few minutes ago."

The women gave little cries and croaks of dismay.

"It must have been a heart attack," Persephone said. "She always had a tricky ticker." She thumped her chest in demonstration.

"What do you mean, found her?" Aunt Violet glanced around wildly. "Not here, surely. Not in my garden?"

"Yes, I'm afraid so." I edged closer to Aunt Violet, wishing I could speak to her alone. "The police are on their way. Perhaps the ladies will want to wait in the kitchen?"

"Wait?" Ruth asked. "What for?" She turned to her friends. "I don't know about you, but I've lost my celebratory mood."

"So have I," Fiona said. "And Gregory is expecting me home soon."

"And since I'm staying with you," Persephone said, tossing her braid, "lead on."

"Where are you lodging?" Fiona asked Ruth.

"At the Holly and Ivy," Ruth said. "Right up the lane."

I gritted my teeth. So much for the soft-pedal approach. "Hold it," I practically shouted. They stopped moving and stared at me. "You need to stay a little longer. All the guests do. I don't think it was, um, a natural death." Not with a knitting needle in the chest.

Ruth gasped. Persephone went very still, the lift of her chin her only movement. Fiona's eyes narrowed, her brow furrowing as she cast glances at the others.

"You mean she had an accident?" Aunt Violet asked.

"Something like that," I said. "I can't . . . I can't give any more details." I put out a hand, pleading. "Please. Wait for the police. They'll be here any minute."

"Do it for Myrtle, won't you?" Aunt Violet's tone brooked no argument. She picked up the tray, glasses clinking. "I think we can all use a glass of something while we wait."

"Make mine two fingers of Scotch," Fiona said. "I need something medicinal after a shock like that." To my relief, she followed Aunt Violet into the house and the other two trailed along.

I waited where I was, still holding the cat, watching through the big windows as the guests took places around the table. Aunt Violet brought a brown bottle over along with highball glasses, and after she poured healthy slugs, the foursome lifted a toast then tossed down the drinks.

My mouth watered. I could use a medicinal drink myself, especially since my beer was now warm. Aunt Violet poured a second round for herself and her friends, then reached for another glass. To my joy, she carried that drink and her own outside.

"Here," she said, thrusting the whiskey at me. "Good for what ails you."

I gently released the cat, who jumped up onto a chair, and took the glass. Fiery, peaty, perfect, the Scotch burned a trail down my insides. I immediately felt a little better.

Aunt Violet leaned close. "Tell me what happened." Up on Trinity Street, a siren yipped then went silent, no doubt clearing the way. "Quick. Before they get here."

Stumbling over my words, I gave her the summary, including the assumed cause of death. Then I took another swig of whiskey, trying to wash away the terrible images.

"A pink knitting needle?" Aunt Violet was horrified. "But I—"

I put two and two together. "You mean it might be yours?" I don't know exactly what I had thought. That the needle was Myrtle's, maybe, carried in a knitting bag, the way so many women did. Or that the killer had used his or her own.

A police car rumbled over cobblestones and halted in the alley, blue lights flashing over the garden and the adjacent building. Doors slammed. Another vehicle arrived, then a third.

Aunt Violet didn't answer my question. "Time to face the music," she said. Finishing her whiskey, she wiped her forearm across her lips then squared her shoulders, as if going into battle.

She went out the side gate and I waited and worried, holding vigil over the crime scene. Then, overcome with curiosity, I popped into the kitchen. I wasn't going to touch anything, I promised myself, just check.

"Don't mind me," I said to the trio still sitting at the table.

They barely looked up before returning to their conversation. Something about Myrtle back in the day at St. Hildegard's, and another girl named Joan. Daisy's great-aunt?

The basket of knitting was sitting in its usual place beside Clarence's armchair. Pretending to pat him, I casually leaned over and studied the contents. A half-finished gray wool something was rolled up on top. Both needles, which I distinctly remembered as pink, were gone.

CHAPTER 5

I managed to make it back outside without having a melt-down in front of Aunt Violet's friends. "Who did it, kitty?" I asked, scooping him off the chair and holding him close. The poor thing was becoming my comfort blanket. "Who stole Aunt Violet's knitting needle?" He only blinked at me in response.

The side gate opened and my aunt walked into the garden, accompanied by several police officers. Steeling myself, I went to meet them, still carrying the cat.

"I'm Molly Kimball," I said to the man in the lead, who was wearing a suit. He was about my mother's age, trim and good-looking, with dark hair and a goatee. "I'm the one who found, um, Myrtle's body and called it in. Well, me and Kieran Scott. He owns the bicycle shop next door."

The officer's brows lifted briefly, a gesture so fast I almost missed it. "I'm Inspector Sean Ryan from the Major Crime Unit." He shook my hand, his grip firm. "Show me."

I led them across the grass toward the shed. Aunt Violet headed for the house, and I didn't blame her. "Kieran and I had come out to the garden to drink a beer," I explained, "when I noticed that the back gate was open. When I went to check it out, I . . . I found her. Right there, lying on the grass."

The uniformed officers, a man and a woman, went to Myrtle, using flashlights to get a better look. I quickly turned my back. I had done my duty and she was in their capable hands now.

"And where is Mr. Scott now?" Inspector Ryan asked.

"Inside the shop. He went in to stop the rest of the guests from leaving. We had a poetry reading tonight, you see." I had been stroking the cat's fur over and over as I spoke and now he gave a mew of protest. "Sorry," I told him.

"Smart move," the inspector said. "How many people were at this reading?"

I tried to estimate. "Fifty or sixty? Some left right after but others stayed for refreshments, including Myrtle's old school chums, who are still in the kitchen. We got most of the guest names, though, because they entered a drawing." I paused for breath, and no wonder the way I was babbling. "It could have been anyone. Even if Aunt Violet's knitting needle was used." A wave of cold mortification washed over me. Why had I said that?

He sent me a sharp glance. "Your aunt's knitting needle? How do you know?"

"It's missing," I said miserably. "I checked the knitting basket."

Inspector Ryan studied me for an excruciatingly long time. "I appreciate your honesty, Miss Kimball. Why don't you go back to the shop now? I'll circle back around later for your statement."

•◖•

Instead of going through the kitchen, where a constable was questioning Myrtle's friends and Aunt Violet, I chose the back door, an alternate route into the shop. This brought me—us, since I still had the cat—into a short hallway. A door to the kitchen was on the left, at the bottom of the stairs. On the right was a door to the new meeting room (blocked inside by chairs tonight), and straight ahead, the back entrance to the storefront, also with a door.

I stopped to consider how the killer had been able to steal the knitting needles. In this maze of an old building, there were several options.

For example, the loo, as we called the half bath just beyond the stairs, had two doors, one on this side for customer use, and one in the kitchen. We usually latched it on the kitchen side, after Aunt Violet found a customer snoozing in the armchair with a cup of tea and an empty packet of her favorite biscuits. She liked customers to feel at home, but that was a bridge too far.

Had we latched it tonight? I knocked. No one was inside, so I turned the rattling knob and went in. Narrow, with a slanted ceiling, the loo must have been a closet at one point. There was only a stained porcelain wall basin and an ancient toilet, and the walls were an ugly mustard yellow. It was on the top of my redecorating list.

Beyond the kitchen door, I heard the murmur of low

voices. I crept closer. Could I test the door without them no-ticing? Holding my breath, I tiptoed across the old linoleum floor, still clutching kitty.

The voices grew louder. "I hadn't seen Myrtle for ages." Persephone. "Her phone call the other week was our first contact in I don't know how long."

"She called me too," Ruth said. "But I hadn't seen her since an old girls day five years ago."

Those must have been the calls from Myrtle to ask Persephone to read. A terrible thought struck. Would Myrtle still be alive if we hadn't had the reading?

Light-headed from lack of air and dismay, I stumbled forward slightly, nudging the door. Which swung open on less than silent hinges. *Uh-oh.*

Five faces turned to regard me with varying expressions of surprise. "Sorry," I said. "Just using the facilities." And eavesdropping. I grabbed the door and shut it firmly.

At least I'd answered my question, but without definite conclusion, I realized. The door wasn't latched now, but one of the ladies might have used the loo. And there were two other options for access to the knitting basket—the hallway door and the French doors. And of course the direct kitchen door from the shop, the one marked Staff Only.

I thought of the man in the alley. If only we had gotten a better look at him. He might live in the area or maybe he'd been a guest who left early. A burning question was—why had he run away? I'd have to make sure I mentioned him to the inspector.

Inside the bookshop, a constable was standing at the open

door taking names and addresses from a short line of customers trying to leave. In the meeting room, Daisy, Tim, and Kieran were helping a grim-faced George stack chairs and clean up, and Mum sat behind the main desk, wearing her half-glasses and using the adding machine.

She stood, taking off her glasses. "Molly. Are you all right?"

"That was *my* question." Daisy flew out of the meeting room to my side. With a grimace, she rolled her eyes toward the constable at the door. "We heard the news. Just awful." She reached to hug me then noticed the black cat. "I see you have a new friend."

I looked down at him and laughed. "I guess so. He won't let go of me. See?" I showed her how he was clinging to my clothing.

"You'll have to name him." Her lips curved. "Or her."

If Aunt Violet—and Clarence—didn't object to me keeping the cat, that is. Clarence definitely ruled this roost.

"Molly." Kieran came over to us, and my heart leaped. Residual adrenaline, or was I developing a bit of a crush? I'd better put the brakes on. We barely knew each other beyond a few games of darts and a beer in the back garden. A beer interrupted by the discovery of a murder victim.

"Everything go all right with Aunt Violet and the ladies?" he asked.

I made a face. "Kind of. They stuck around, at least. A constable is talking to them in the kitchen now. I hope they can help, although it sounds like they weren't close to Myrtle."

"They weren't, not like us," George said, his voice glum. "I saw her every day." He shook his head. "She was a pip but despite our troubles, I'm going to miss the old girl."

"Truer words were never spoken." Tim was more serious than I'd seen him. "She used to rent our bicycles to do her shopping. Of course there was always something wrong with the one we gave her." He and Kieran shared a rueful chuckle.

Kieran reached out to rub the black cat's chin. "'That merry wanderer of the night,'" he quoted.

"Puck," I said, recognizing the quote spoken by the mischievous fairy from *A Midsummer Night's Dream*. "Perfect. Can that be a girl or boy name?"

"He's a boy," Kieran said. "Already been to the vet for his surgery, it seems. But we haven't been able to find his owner."

I clutched Puck closer, feeling protective. The poor thing had been abandoned. I had to take him in. "You have now."

A commotion near the front door caught our attention. The last guest from the reading was gone, but a young woman was trying to come in. The constable was refusing to let her. "I'm sorry, miss. The bookshop is closed for the night."

"It's not about that," she said in exasperation. Slender and fairly tall, dressed in jeans and a tank top, she had tattoos up one bare arm and spiky dark hair.

Kieran groaned. "I'd better take care of this." He turned to me. "Tell the inspector to give me a call. He's got my number. I'll be next door, at home."

This was very odd. Why would the inspector have Kieran's number? And who was the young woman? An employee? A girlfriend? As he approached the door, the young woman raised a camera and took several pictures.

"Why did you do that, Kelsey?" Kieran scolded her.

She laughed. "How else am I going to pay the rent?" He stepped outside and I heard her laugh at something he said.

"She's a pap," George said, seeing my confusion. "Works for the tabloids."

Now I got it. "But why would she—"

Before I could finish my sentence, an older man stepped through the open shop door, and to my surprise the constable didn't try to stop him. On the short side, he was slender, with thick white hair and dressed in what was obviously an expensive suit.

Daisy sucked in a breath, clasping her hands together. "Sir Jon. I was hoping he would show up tonight." Her voice was dreamy. "Bond. James Bond."

I must have looked totally lost because Tim laughed. "You haven't met our resident MI6 agent, I take it? Retired, of course. He owns the Crow's Nest Bookshop here in town. Specializing in guess what? Spy novels." He winked.

"Curiouser and curiouser," as Alice said in Wonderland. "No, I haven't met him." But I would love to. Dignified and elegant, he had a sharp glint in his blue eyes. The constable seemed to be hanging on his every word.

The door to the kitchen opened and Aunt Violet and her friends emerged in a group, accompanied by another constable. All of them looked grim and unhappy until they saw Sir Jon. Then their faces lit up and they swarmed him like fans at a rock concert.

George chuckled. "He was quite the lad in his younger

days. Maybe I should have served the Queen in that capacity myself."

Watching Sir Jon's calm charm as he greeted each one in turn, I had to admit I could understand their fascination. He had the gift of total attentiveness toward whomever he spoke with. He was also good at moving people along, and soon the three school chums were quite happily out the door and on their way.

Aunt Violet had been waiting on the sidelines, and now she threw herself into Sir Jon's arms. "You came. I'm so glad."

He hugged her in return then released her. "I was going to come earlier but I was detained in London." He put both hands on her shoulders. "I understand I missed all the excitement." His tone was sardonic, conveying that the situation wasn't exciting at all.

"I'll say." Aunt Violet removed her eyeglasses to dash tears away. "It's absolutely horrible. Poor Myrtle."

Sir Jon set his jaw. "Indeed. Where's the man in charge?" He glanced around, his electric blue eyes skimming over me. They gave me a little shock.

"I think he's out back at the scene," I said. This reminder of Inspector Ryan made my stomach knot up. I still hadn't given my formal statement.

The constable at the door spoke up. "I'll fetch him for you, Sir Jon."

"Much appreciated, old chap," Sir Jon said. "Now, Violet, please introduce me to the relatives I've heard so much about."

Another of Aunt Violet's friends who knew more about

us than we did about them. But she sure was acquainted with some very interesting people.

•◆•

A couple of hours later, statements given and police gone, we were seated around the kitchen table, mugs of (decaf) tea in hand—me, Mum, Aunt Violet, Sir Jon, and George. Oh, and Puck, who was curled on my lap, safe from Clarence's glares. The big tiger was back in his armchair, but the knitting basket was gone, along with the half-finished garment.

"I can't believe the inspector told me not to leave town." Aunt Violet leaned her chin on her hand. "As if. This is my *home*."

And why would she kill someone here at the shop? Unless it was in a fit of rage, which I couldn't even imagine. "It's ridiculous," I said. "You don't have a motive. It was because of Myrtle that we had such a successful event." Until she was killed. *What would the fallout be for the shop?* I wondered. Something else that wasn't fair about this. Myrtle's murder might well be the death knell for the struggling bookshop as well. The fact they had used Aunt Violet's knitting needle was the final nail in the coffin, so to speak.

"They don't really need a motive to arrest someone, I'm afraid," Sir Jon said. "Probable cause is enough."

"I'm glad they didn't arrest you tonight then," Mum said. "Since the weapon was yours, Aunt Violet. Or so they think." She'd been pretty quiet all night, taking everything in. Before they left, the police had questioned her as well as Daisy and George, asking mainly about people's movements, I gathered. And if they'd seen Myrtle, which they hadn't. "I did tell the inspector that you never left the reading once it started."

"None of us did," I said. "Until Kieran and I went out to the garden." I remembered something I hadn't mentioned. "We saw a man in the back alley right after we discovered Myrtle. He ran off when Kieran tried to talk to him." I shivered at the memory of that dark, hulking shape. He'd seemed so menacing.

"A mysterious stranger," Sir Jon said. "That is odd."

George shrugged. "Maybe not. A lot of people cut through that back alley. I'd probably run too if I saw that young lad bolting toward me."

"Good point," I said. "I mentioned the lurker to the inspector but he didn't seem too interested." Why would he be, with such an obvious suspect as Aunt Violet? "It also could have been someone who had just left the reading. I didn't pay attention to whoever was coming and going."

"People were popping in and out the whole time," Mum confirmed. "I told more than one person where they could find the loo."

The loo that connected from the shop side to the kitchen and the murder weapon. "Let me show you something." I picked up Puck and gently set him on my chair. Going over to the loo door, I explained how easily someone could have accessed the needle. "And it could even have happened before we started." I mimed snatching up a needle from the now nonexistent basket, which would take only a few seconds. "There were a lot of people milling around while we were getting ready." I pointed to the hall door. "They could also have come in through there. The main sticking point is this, though. They would've had to have known the needles were here, next to the chair."

"Which speaks to the killer being very familiar with this building and Myrtle's whereabouts," Sir Jon said. "Either they intercepted her or arranged a meeting in the garden. Good work, Molly." He regarded me with what looked like admiration.

I gave a little laugh, flattered. "Well we know Aunt Violet didn't do it, so I was trying to figure out who did. And how." I settled Puck on my lap again. "But I wish I knew *why*, whether or not the police care about that."

Sir Jon rubbed his chin. "I said motive doesn't cut any ice with the police, as far as their rules of investigation. But it can be a very useful tool in figuring out who did commit a crime. Very few are truly random."

In unison, we all picked up our mugs and sipped, thinking about this. "Who had a reason?" I muttered. "A *good* reason, to kill Myrtle?"

George raised his hand. "I did."

CHAPTER 6

Aunt Violet sucked in a sharp breath. She thumped her fist on the table, making a spoon clatter. "George Flowers. What are you on about?"

The rest of us were equally shocked, although Sir Jon's reaction was muted, merely a flare of his nostrils.

George hunched his shoulders, tracing a circle on the tabletop with his forefinger. "Myrtle owed me a lot of money. I'm her landlord, you see, over on Ivy Close," he said. "And she was seriously in arrears. Months, as a matter of fact. I had to threaten eviction."

"Hard to get your money if she's deceased," Sir Jon said crisply.

"True." George's lips twisted in a brief smile. "Unfortunately, she and I had a quite a row yesterday morning. I think the whole street heard it." He waved one meaty hand. "She kept promising to get caught up. 'I've got a windfall coming,' she'd say. 'I'll take care of it.' But I've got bills to pay, I told her. I can't pay them with promises." As he went on, his already ruddy complexion deepened to beet red. "And before you accuse me of cruelty to a pensioner, I know she was well-off. One look at her flat would tell you that."

Aunt Violet pursed her lips. "Interesting. She was always on about how much things cost, how hard it was to survive on her pension."

I thought of Myrtle and her free dinner. "I think she also convinced Steve at the pub that she was poor. She ate there without paying the other night."

"That sounds just like Myrtle," George said. "She could identify a soft touch at a hundred paces." His expression was chagrined. "She hit me up more than once 'til I caught on."

"You're a good man, George," Aunt Violet declared. "And no one will ever convince me otherwise."

"That's right," Mum agreed. "We need to look elsewhere."

George inclined his head, trying to hide a pleased smile. "Thank you kindly."

Sir Jon cleared his throat and we all looked at him. "I'd like to know where that promised windfall was coming from. Not to speak ill of the dead, but your Myrtle sounds a wee bit shifty. My spidey senses are tingling."

Coming from a former secret agent, that intuition meant something. "Mine too," I said. "And I think someone killed her here to implicate you, Aunt Violet. Or you, George." Resolve and determination hardened in my mid-section. "And we're not going to let them get away with it."

Sir Jon sent me an approving look. "That's the spirit." He circled a finger, including us all. "With the brains and talent

around this table, I think we can get to the bottom of this."
He lifted one shoulder in a shrug. "Not that I'm discounting
the police, mind you. But they have to follow a narrow set
of rules." His infectious grin transformed his face, making
him look decades younger. I could understand the swooning
now, for sure. "We don't have that problem."

Hope lit Aunt Violet's face and George gave a thoughtful nod. As for Mum, she glanced over at me with lifted
brows. I smiled at her, guessing what she was thinking. Our
Cambridge adventure had taken yet another twist, but it was
too late to turn back now. We had to save Aunt Violet. And
George.

•◑•

Something tickling my cheek woke me. I opened my eyes to
find Puck sitting on my chest and staring down at me, yellow eyes blinking. His whiskers twitched, as if he was saying, *Do I need to do that again?*

With a laugh, I turned to look at the clock. "Is it time to
get up?" Good. It was after seven. Not too early. Gently placing him aside, I scooted to an upright position. "I bet you
need to go out, don't you?"

I hadn't even thought about a litter box for the little guy.
Clarence had one but I didn't want to start Cat War III by
letting Puck use that.

He waited patiently while I threw on jeans and a T-shirt,
then found my sneakers under the bed. My plan today, besides helping in the shop, was to begin my Books in the
Wild project. Building off Persephone's reading last night, I

wanted to feature famous local poets in our first social media campaign. Cambridge had a slew of them to choose from, with wonderful former haunts to photograph.

My heart thumped as I remembered my most important mission—we had a murder to investigate. The St. Hildegard's friends were on my list to talk to, along with Steve at the pub. In addition, George was going to see if his other tenants and neighbors knew anything. Hopefully, as Sir Jon had assured us, one piece of information would lead to another.

I tied my sneakers and grabbed the cat, eager to begin the day. First up, feed Puck, then go get coffee.

The lane was quiet this morning, with no visible trace of the police activity last night. Puck and I crossed the cobblestones toward the tea shop, enjoying the touch of morning sun slanting down between the ancient buildings. At the pub, Susie was sweeping the entrance, and guests were enjoying breakfast in the small courtyard behind the Holly & Ivy Inn, where Ruth was staying. Aunt Violet should contact her before she went back to London.

"Good morning," Daisy greeted me as I entered the tea shop, poor Puck left on the other side of the door. Her blue eyes studied me with concern. "How are you, love?"

"I'm okay, considering." Glancing around, I noticed that the tea shop was empty for the moment, so I could speak freely. "We put a team together last night to investigate Myrtle's death. Do you want to help us?"

She paused in the middle of making me a filter coffee. "An investigation? Really?"

"Unfortunately, yes. Not to slight the police, but Aunt Violet and George are the main suspects." I moved closer to the counter, lowering my voice as I quickly told her about George's problems with Myrtle and her mention of a mysterious windfall. "So with Sir Jon's guidance, Mum, Aunt Violet, George, and I are going to see what we can find out. Maybe she owed other people money as well."

"That does sound intriguing." Daisy set my coffee on the counter. "Don't you find it odd that someone killed her during the reading, though? I mean, why then? Why not another time?"

I took the first heavenly sip. "I was wondering that myself. Was it because the reading distracted everyone? Or was the killer there *because* of the reading?"

Daisy's voice was a whisper. "Do you mean her friends from college?"

I thought about that. Could we really consider three women over the age of seventy as murder suspects? Well, why not, since Aunt Violet was already number one on the police's list. "I guess I do. Although they claimed they hadn't been in touch with Myrtle. Hadn't seen her for years, as a matter of fact."

Daisy considered that as she opened the bakery case and pulled out two blueberry cream cheese scones, using tissue. "Here," she said, putting one on a plate for me. She took a bite of the other. "Sorry. I don't usually eat behind the counter, but I haven't had breakfast yet."

My mouth already full of scone, I waved away her objection. "Your aunt's name was Joan, right?" She nodded. "They were talking about her last night, I think. In conjunction with Myrtle." I explained how I'd overheard them while checking out the knitting basket.

"Joan's trunk from college is up in the attic," Daisy said, pointing a finger at the ceiling. "Her brother, my great-uncle, used to run this bakery before I took over. He and his wife left a lot of stuff behind when they moved out five years ago, and I haven't gotten around to doing anything about most of it."

My veins tingled, a sensation I experienced whenever I was hot on the research trail, no matter how obscure. "This might sound really far-fetched"—and it did—"but there might be something useful in there. In the interest of being thorough, I think we should look."

"Me too," Daisy said. "That's why I brought it up. Although I can't imagine how anything that happened decades ago caused someone to kill Myrtle last night."

"Me neither," I admitted before stuffing the rest of the scone into my mouth. After I swallowed, I remembered something else. "I've been meaning to ask. Why did that photographer take pictures of Kieran last night?"

"You mean Kelsey Cook?" She picked up her phone and searched, then crooked her finger at me. "Take a look."

I scrolled down, seeing picture after picture of Kieran with lovely women, along with headlines like "Kieran Steps Out," "Ascot or Not," "Who Will Cambridge's Most Eligible Ask to the Ball?" Kelsey had taken quite a few of the photographs.

"I don't get it," I said. "Is he a reality show star or something?"

Daisy laughed. "Oh, he'd die if he heard that." She leaned closer. "His father is Lord Graham Scott. And his mother, Lady Asha, is a famous philanthropist. She is so gorgeous."

Which meant Kieran came from a titled family and was part of England's nobility. Everything I knew about him shifted, the pieces coming together into a new picture. Almost. "I don't get it," I said. "Why does he live here, on Magpie Lane, and run a bicycle shop?"

"He doesn't want any part of his parents' world," Daisy said. "He went to Cambridge, of course, and could have his pick of high-level positions. But as he told me, he wants a simple life. Plus he likes working for himself."

"Is he actually going to inherit a title?" My voice squeaked on the last word. I couldn't believe I was asking that about someone I knew. It was like something out of a novel.

Daisy shook her head. "No, he's got an older brother. But if something happens to him, and he doesn't have a son, then yes, Kieran is next in line." She cracked a smile. "He told me that he toasts his brother's health daily."

"That sounds like him." Noticing a group making their way into the bakeshop, I picked up my coffee. "I'd better run, but talk later? I want to take a peek at Joan's things."

❧

The bookshop was absolutely slammed from the moment we opened. I'd like to think it was because of Persephone's reading—the literary festival was still underway, after all—but I had a sneaking suspicion it was due to Myrtle's murder.

The local newspapers covered it, of course, and among the crowds browsing the bookshelves, I spotted more than one reporter. Kelsey wasn't among them, but I saw her photo of Kieran's startled face on the front page of a lurid tabloid someone left behind.

"How did we do?" Aunt Violet asked Mum after we closed for lunch. At her insistence, we were seated at the table in the back garden. Although crime scene tape was still flapping near the shed, she'd refused to be cowed. Her determination to learn the truth about Myrtle's death and put her to rest had seemed to grow stronger with every passing hour.

Mum gave her the numbers in between bites of roast beef on crusty bread with mayonnaise and pickles. Aunt Violet nodded. "We haven't had a morning that good in ages." She glanced up at the blue sky with a grimace. "It's an ill wind . . ."

The rest of the saying ran through my mind. *That blows nobody good.*

Aunt Violet put her roast beef sandwich down, exchanging it for a napkin, which she used to dab her eyes. "Oh, Myrtle, we're going to do our best by you." Mum and I murmured agreement.

"Any news from George?" I asked. We hadn't seen him yet today. I accidently-on-purpose dropped a tidbit of tender beef for Puck, who was lurking under the table.

She shook her head. "He promised to pop around later, at teatime." This was around four in the afternoon.

I had plenty of time, then. "Do either of you mind if I go out for a while this afternoon?" I asked. "I want to take pictures for our Books in the Wild social media campaign." I smiled. "I'm starting with Lord Byron and Wordsworth. When I get a chance, I'm going over to Newnham for Sylvia

Plath." Plath had attended Newnham, another women's college like St. Hildegard's.

"Great choices. Why don't we call it Poets in the Wild?" Mum suggested.

"I like that." Referencing the genre would immediately create a mental image concerning our featured books.

"Remind me what you're thinking again," Aunt Violet asked. As I hoped, the new topic distracted her from grief over her old friend. She had plenty of suggestions for me, and by the time we finished eating, I had firmed up my first two locations.

After carefully wrapping two beautiful leather-bound books, I placed them into my backpack, opened a Cambridge street map and stepped out into Magpie Lane. *And so the adventure begins.* My heart beating a little faster, as any book nerd would understand, I walked toward my first destination, Trinity College and the Wren Library.

Walking through the gate with its twin towers was like entering the portal to a castle. Immediately inside was the Great Court, a huge swath of lawn intersected by wide paths and edged with pale stone buildings. I paused to take in the leaded-pane windows, chimney pots, and ivy-covered walls, charming features of this college founded by King Henry VIII. Parts of it were even older than the bookshop.

I headed across the court, thrilled to be there and hoping I was blending in, not too obviously a non-student and a foreigner.

The library was in Nevile's Court, a smaller green surrounded by arcaded buildings. To access items in the collections, one needed a reader's pass and a recommendation, and perhaps at some point I would have a reason to get those. Today I needed permission for my photo shoot.

The woman at the reception desk looked skeptical at my request until I told her who I was. "You're Violet's niece?" Her expression dissolved into a welcoming smile. "The Marlowes have certainly helped us over the centuries. I think we can do the same for you today."

"I'll tag the library in my posts," I promised. Not that they really needed the promotion, but it couldn't hurt, right?

With a staff member looking on, I took several pictures of the book on a table, with bookshelves behind. Then he took one of me, with the book open and hiding my face, in front of Bryon's statue, which stood under a stained-glass window. Posed with a pencil to his chin, the poet looked as if deep in thought, busy composing one of his famous works.

"He used to own a bear, he did," he told me. "Kept it in his quarters."

"Really?" I couldn't tell if he was joking.

He nodded solemnly. "His response for not being allowed to keep a dog. He also spent a great deal of his time gambling, carousing, and boxing. 'Mad, bad, and dangerous to know,' one of his lady friends said."

"I guess you could call him a well-rounded student," I said, earning a wide smile. "Thank you for your help."

"Any time," he said before excusing himself to assist other visitors.

My next stop was up the street, King's College Chapel, an absolutely stunning and iconic building. With towers at each end and spires in between, the chapel featured Tudor stained-glass windows and the world's highest fan-vault ceiling. William Wordsworth called the architecture a "glorious work of fine intelligence," so the chapel was a perfect spot to photograph his book of poems. A poet of the Romantic movement like Byron, Wordsworth went to Cambridge in the late 1700s.

After gawking for a while in the main chapel, I found a smaller side chapel to take my photograph. *Wordsworth's Poems for the Young* looked beautiful standing on a ledge, a stained-glass window behind.

Like the Wren Library, this church embodied history. Sitting in the side chapel for a minute, I pictured the earliest students worshiping here, dressed in medieval garb. So much had changed since then, but the aim of pursuing knowledge and excellence had remained. How wonderful, that like these gorgeous old buildings, the work of my two poets had survived the centuries.

Rested from this break, I charged back out into the day. A patch of daffodils nodding in the sun reminded me of Wordsworth's poem about this harbinger of spring. "'I wandered lonely as a cloud.'" I recited the first line as I walked through the college gate. What came next?

"Molly?" someone said, making me jump. I spun around to see Kieran standing nearby, dressed as usual in worn but well-fitting jeans and a T-shirt. "I was hoping I might run into you."

CHAPTER 7

"Oh, hi." Tongue-tied, I stared at Kieran, a distinct change from our usual easy banter. What was wrong with me? Why did I feel all *Downton Abbey*, as if I were one of the servants and he was a Crawley? This was silly. I wasn't going to buy into all that royalty stuff. Besides, a cat can look at a king, right? Or so the old English proverb said.

"I've been visiting the colleges and taking pictures for the bookshop's social media," I explained after my tongue loosened. "For books by Byron and Wordsworth. Now I'm taking a walk."

"I just ran into your mother at the bank," he said. "She said you were out here somewhere, wandering around. Mind if I join you?" When I nodded, we fell into step. "Byron, hmm? 'She walks in beauty like the night' Byron?"

Were there any others? "That's the one," I said, my cheeks

heating. He'd sounded flirty, I was almost sure of it. But why flirt with me? I wasn't a supermodel or a member of the nobility.

I could feel his gaze on the side of my face as we made our way down the cobblestoned street, dodging students and visitors. After a few minutes of this, he stopped walking and gently pulled me out of the way, next to a red phone booth. Gosh, those were cool, with their little gold crown emblems. Then I groaned to myself. *His* people wore crowns, not mine.

"You found out, didn't you?" It wasn't a question. At my nod, he ran a hand through his hair, sighing in exasperation. "It was only a matter of time, of course, especially with Kelsey hunting me down."

"She's a pap," I said, letting him know I was up on the lingo.

"Uh-huh, and a persistent one at that." He opened his mouth, closed it, blinked, and then said, "I don't want any part of that lifestyle, Molly. But now and then it seems to find me, if you know what I mean." He ran a hand through his hair again. "Some people think I'm mad to reject it, including my parents."

"'Mad, bad, and dangerous to know'?" I inquired, looking at him from under my lashes.

He laughed, pointing a finger at me in acknowledgment of the quote. "I hope not. Anyway, I love my life on Magpie Lane, running the bike shop, and hanging out with my mates." Mates—slang for friends. He held out a crooked arm, inviting me to take his elbow. "So shall we go find a kebab? I'm famished."

"You mean shish kebab?" As I slid my arm through his, I pictured meat and vegetables grilled on a skewer.

Lips pursed, he shook his head. "Not exactly. I could explain it to you, but you'll see." He steered me down St. Mary's Passage, a narrow lane skirting Great St. Mary's church. At the end was a square with rows of market booths topped with colorful striped awnings. Before we entered the market, he stopped in front of a cute little food truck. "Do you want one?" he asked, releasing my arm and reaching for his wallet. "Or something else?"

The aromas from the truck were mouthwatering, so although I'd had lunch only two hours before, I said yes to kebab, but no to chips. He got in line and was back a few minutes later, carrying our food plus two bottled waters.

When we found a nearby bench and sat down, he handed me my lunch, wrapped in white paper. I peeled it back, my mouth watering. "What's in this?" I asked, biting into the stuffed pita. Savory meat, tangy sauce, and crisp, fresh vegetables mingled on my taste buds. Delicious.

"Grilled lamb," he said around a mouthful. "You can also get beef or chicken. But this is my favorite."

"I love it," I declared, wiping my mouth. "Yum." He handed me a bottle of water and I popped the top and drank.

Anyone looking at us would see only an ordinary—but very good-looking—young man and me, a happy American eating my first kebab. People strolled in and out of the square, stopping at the colorful booths to browse or buy.

"I want to check out the market after we eat." Reaching over, I stole one of his chips and he pretended to slap my hand. Salty, greasy goodness burst in my mouth.

"We can do that," he said. "There's been a market here since Anglo-Saxon times, you know."

Which was about the fifth century through the eleventh, I knew. I pictured the scene: fat pigs and cows in wooden corrals, heaps of silvery fish, lengths of fine wool and maybe even silk. Roast meat from a spit—kind of like kebab, come to think of it—and tankards of grog and ale. There wasn't any livestock now, but I could see a fishmonger and stalls with colorful clothing.

"St. Bene't's Church on the next street over is a thousand years old," Kieran went on. "The tower is part of the original church."

"Oh, I definitely want to see that. Can we go inside?" Glancing at Kieran, I saw he was smiling at me. "What?"

"I love your enthusiasm," he said. "Being with you is like seeing everything for the first time."

"Yeah, that's me," I said. "Enthusiastic to a fault. Like a puppy." Face it, I'd never be the aloof, ultracool type.

"I like puppies," he said. We continued eating, and after we demolished every bite, he crumpled the wrapping paper and said, "On a more serious note, is there anything new since last night?" He put his hand out for my discards and then put all the trash into a nearby can.

I thought back over everything that had happened after he left, including our roundtable discussion in the kitchen with Sir Jon. How much should I share? I mean, I liked Kieran and wanted to trust him, but it seemed wise to keep things "close to the vest," as Aunt Violet might say.

He noticed me hesitating. "I had my own issues with

Myrtle. I want to go ahead and put that on the table. Before you hear it from someone else."

"Hear what?" I asked cautiously. Surely he wasn't about to confess to something. Not here, sitting on a bench in the market square.

Kieran gnawed at his bottom lip. "How do I put this without sounding like an egotistical prat?" He shifted on the bench to a more comfortable position. "Myrtle was selling information about me to the tabloids."

That startled a laugh from me. "Seriously? That's awful. How do you know?"

He moved around again, putting one arm along the bench back before changing his mind and clasping his hands between his knees. "I don't absolutely, positively know that. But I suspect it. You see, she tried to get money from me *not* to go to them."

"Wow, that is terrible." In contrast to his nervous energy, I was limp with surprise and bewilderment. My initial impression of Myrtle was that she was nosy and prone to making embarrassing remarks, but extortion?

"Like I said, I can't prove it. But after I turned her down, there was a definite increase in paps and journos lurking around the lane. Plus they would turn up in spots, as if they knew my movements in advance."

I thought of another possibility. "Could an employee be doing it?" Besides Tim, who was full-time, a number of students worked part-time at the shop.

He thought about it, then shook his head. "No way. They're too busy with their own lives to notice what I'm doing.

Myrtle was around all the time. I thought of warning your aunt and George, but I know they've been her friends forever. The thought of doing that felt wrong." He scrunched up his nose.

It would have to me, as well. "Plus, to be honest, you might have sounded paranoid accusing an elderly woman of spying on you."

"Yeah, that too." He leaned his head back. "It gets tiring being on guard all the time. I was hoping I didn't need to do that on my home turf."

I could imagine. Notoriety was one of the downsides of being rich and famous, for sure. I glanced around, wondering if someone had sneaked a picture of Kieran eating kebab. *Stars love kebabs . . . just like us.* Ugh.

Kieran's phone rang. "Sorry. I better take this." He answered. "Yes, Mum, I saw it." His mother, the beautiful Lady Asha Scott. "No, of course not." He glanced at me, raising his brows. "They have no idea who did it." She must have called about the murder, which was understandable. "I'm not worried about that." A pause, then, "Can I talk to you later? I'm busy right now." He disconnected, muttering, "Sorry."

"No problem. If my mother hadn't been right there, I'm sure she'd be burning up the lines calling me."

He was still looking at his phone. Grunting, he tapped out a text. "Sorry again. I've got to head back to the store. One of my employees didn't show." He stood, tucking his phone in his pocket.

Disappointing, but understandable. "That's okay. Thanks

again for lunch." I thought of something I wanted to ask. "Do you know where Sir Jon's bookstore is?" Maybe I'd swing by and check it out.

Turning, he pointed to the east side of the market. "It's not far from here. On Queen's Crescent." Pulling out his phone again, he brought up a map and showed me the route. "Do you want me to send this to you?"

I shook my head. "No, I'll remember. Plus I want to wander." I adored exploring new places, even if I did get lost sometimes.

"All right, then." Back went the phone. "I'll see you later." He studied every inch of my face with those warm brown eyes, then to my surprise, leaned forward and kissed me on the cheek. "Have a nice afternoon."

I watched him go, one hand to my cheek until I realized how foolish I must look. Maybe I'd imagined the flirting, but I hadn't dreamed up that kiss. Shaking myself, I turned to study the market, doing my best to push Kieran Scott out of my mind. Where should I start?

I made a circuit of the stalls, saying hello to booth holders as I paused to admire the goods for sale and take a few photographs. I'd have to come back another day and buy some fish for dinner, along with vegetables harvested locally. Some of the crafts were nice, and I saw a notice that there was an artisans' market nearby. I'd have to swing by there at some point as well.

I did buy a bouquet of anemones, hyacinth, and peonies. Mum would love it, and it would brighten up the shop.

A middle-aged man wearing a flat cap almost bumped into

me as I was leaving the flower booth. "Excuse me, miss," he said, touching the cap brim. Steve Baker, from the pub.

"Hi, Steve," I said. When he blinked his eyes at me, confused, I said, "Molly, from the bookshop. On Magpie Lane."

His brow cleared. "Oh, Molly. Of course. Sorry, love, I didn't recognize you." He glanced at the flowers. "Doing a little shopping?"

"Very little," I said with a laugh as I slipped my change into a pocket. "But I'm having fun looking around."

"I'll leave you to it, then." With a nod, he set off again, winding through the throng. But instead of stopping at a booth, he headed for the far end of the square. That was the direction I needed to go to find Sir Jon's, so I went that way as well.

For a while, Steve was just a figure walking ahead of me, casual in his blue short-sleeve shirt and light slacks. We strolled along lanes and crossed busy streets. Then he slowed, glanced around, and ducked into a narrow alley.

How strange. Out of pure nosy curiosity, I sped up, closing the distance between us. At the mouth of the alley, I hid behind a stack of boxes, peeking out to watch as he studied the row of buildings.

If he hadn't been acting so furtive, I wouldn't have been suspicious. Entering through the back could be a short cut. He might be accessing a staircase, like our back stairs at the bookshop. Or, as I guessed, he was hiding his true destination.

Steve found the door he was looking for, and after looking around again, he slipped inside, shoulders hunched. Now I knew for sure he was up to something.

Still standing behind the boxes, I thought about following him down the alley. But it was narrow and dark and rather dingy, with that lingering garbage odor some places get. Instead I counted the doorways to be sure I could identify the right building. Four doors down.

At the corner, I turned onto a street lined with small, rather ordinary shops. The fourth building was plain yellow brick, with a simple sign that read Bet Here. Posters displaying numbers, lottery tickets, and sports totally blocked the windows.

Steve had gone into a betting shop. And judging by how he was acting, he didn't want anyone to know. Including his wife, maybe? An idea tickled in the back of my mind. Had Myrtle blackmailed Steve into giving her free meals? It sounded like something she'd do.

How could I find out for sure? I certainly didn't want to anger Steve with impertinent questions. That might get me banned from the pub.

But right now I needed to keep moving before people noticed me loitering. On to Queen's Crescent, wherever that was. Realizing I'd totally forgotten Kieran's directions, I pulled out my phone and brought up a map.

◆◆◆

Wedged between an upscale men's shop and a Boots drugstore, the Crow's Nest was tiny, with space for only one bow window. Reaching for the door handle, I paused, tempted by the idea of Boots, which I'd heard so much about. Should I go pick out an English-brand lipstick? Although I hardly ever wore makeup . . . only a detail, right?

Restraining myself, I opened the bookshop door instead. Bells jingled and I entered a bright space filled with bookcases and stacks of books. Sir Jon emerged from the back room, dressed in dark slacks and a white shirt with rolled-up sleeves.

"Hi there," I said. "I was out for a walk and thought I would stop by."

"I'm glad you did," he said. "I was just putting on the kettle." He gestured toward a reading area furnished with a red velvet sofa and armchairs. "Have a seat, and I'll be right with you."

I sat on the sofa, enjoying the ease of getting off tired feet, and placed the wrapped bouquet on a side table. My backpack went on the floor.

While I waited for Sir Jon to return, I glanced at the signs over various sections: Military History. Espionage Novels. Nautical Titles. Aviation. There was definitely a theme, and I wondered how much his personal history had played into these choices.

"Quite a bit, actually," Sir Jon said a few moments later, answering my question as he filled two china teacups. "Instead of write what you know, it's sell what you know." He handed me the cup. "Help yourself to milk."

"That makes a lot of sense." I poured a dab of milk into my tea and stirred it with a silver spoon. Everything was obviously expensive—the silver-plated service, the china, even the tray. "Do you get a lot of questions about your previous career? Not that I'm going to ask any," I added hastily, although I was curious, of course.

"A fair amount," Sir Jon said. "But I can't really talk about it. Classified, you understand." He gave me a knowing wink. "So I steer them to Ian Fleming, who worked for Naval Intelligence during the War." Ian Fleming was the author of the James Bond novels.

"I'll have to read his books for clues," I joked. The tea was strong and hot, the way I preferred it. No insipid brews here. "And speaking of clues, I just saw Steve Baker from the Magpie Pub acting sneaky."

He sat his teacup down, his expression attentive. "Do tell."

I told him about Steve and the betting shop. "I wonder if Myrtle was blackmailing him," I concluded. "She tried to blackmail Kieran, I found out today."

"You have been busy," he murmured. "What did she try with Kieran? He seems like an upright young chap."

"It's nothing he did," I explained. "It's who he is. He thinks she's been tipping off the newspapers about his movements. She tried to get money from him to not do that."

His eyes lost in thought, Sir Jon picked up his cup and drank. "Uncovering nasty truths can be an unfortunate part of a murder investigation. But I can't say as I'm totally surprised in this case."

My pulse leaped. "Were you aware of Myrtle's . . . tendencies?" I didn't know what else to call it. Blackmailing ways? Extortion habit?

He wrinkled his face and blinked. "Not exactly. I never really warmed to her, back in college. There was something . . ."

I put down my cup, excited. "You knew her in college? Did you know Aunt Violet and the others?"

His smile was reminiscent. "I certainly did. Hang on a minute." He rose from the armchair and went over to an immense carved desk that served as shop counter. He dug around in the top drawer. "I came across something the other day, and I've been meaning to share it with your aunt."

He handed me a square black-and-white photograph of several young women and a much younger—and extremely handsome—Sir Jon, all wearing silly hats. "This is Rag Day," he said. "The students dress up and raise money for charity. They still do it."

I easily recognized statuesque Fiona, adorable Ruth, and Persephone—center of attention with her snooty expression and long blonde braid. On one side of Sir Jon was a young woman with pointed features and frizzy hair. "Is that Myrtle?"

He nodded.

"And there's Aunt Violet." She was pretty and petite, with dark hair and glasses. "She looks a lot like my mother."

"She does indeed." Sir Jon smiled fondly at young Violet and I wondered . . .

"Who is this?" Another student stood near the edge of the frame. She was tall, with very straight blonde hair parted in the middle.

"Ah. Joan Watson. Now that was a sad story." He sighed. "She had so much potential . . ."

"That's Daisy's great-aunt. You know, Daisy from Tea and Crumpets. What happened to her?" Daisy had told me Joan died, but she didn't say how. And I hadn't wanted to ask her, since Joan was a relative.

"She killed herself," Sir Jon said, his expression grim. "All the pressures . . . I understood that she was brilliant, had a wonderful future ahead of her."

"Oh no," I said in dismay. "That's horrible."

"It is," Sir Jon said. "And it happens far too often."

There was one more person in the picture, a good-looking and tall young man with curly light hair and spectacles. He wore a top hat at a jaunty angle. "Who's that?" I asked. "Someone's boyfriend?"

Sir Jon's brow furrowed. "That's your Uncle Tom. Violet's older brother. Haven't you seen a picture of him before?"

I shook my head. "I didn't even know I had an uncle until recently. My mother was, um, tight-lipped about her family."

Thankfully he let it go, saying instead, "I thought you might enjoy this glimpse of us back in the day."

"I love it." I glanced around the shop, not seeing any office equipment. "Do you have a scanner? Or a copier? I'd love a copy."

"I sure do. I'll go make one for you." Sir Jon ducked into the back room and returned a minute later with a photocopy. "Not quite as nice as a duplicate photograph, but I hope it will do for now. I'll make a print for Violet when I have a chance."

"This is great, thank you." I folded the sheet and tucked it into my zippered pack pocket. Glancing at my phone, I said, "I've really enjoyed this, but I'd better get back to the shop." I was starting to feel guilty about Mum and Aunt Violet doing all the work, although they'd both encouraged me to go out and explore.

"It's been lovely having you pop in," Sir Jon said. "Please stop by again. And tell Violet to call if she needs me. I plan to stick pretty close until Myrtle's case is wrapped up."

And maybe after that? I hid a smile. It would be wonderful if Sir Jon and Aunt Violet got together. I could tell he'd had a crush on her back in college. Better late than never, right?

◆◆◆

"There you are," Aunt Violet said when I walked into Thomas Marlowe half an hour later. She was busy arranging books on a table near the door. Older true-crime titles, I noticed, biting back a laugh. Aunt Violet was certainly gutsy. "How did it go?"

"Great," I said, handing her the flowers, which she accepted with coos of delight. "After Trinity and St. John's, I went to the market. Had a second lunch with Kieran, then stopped by the Crow's Nest." She took a closer look at the bouquet, which made me add, "Those are from me." But I would certainly give Sir Jon a heads-up to bring her flowers next time he came by. I slipped the backpack straps off my shoulders. "I need to put these books back."

"I can't wait to see your photos," Mum called from the front desk.

"You've got to go see the colleges, Mum," I said while unpacking the Lord Byron and Wordsworth. "Again, I mean.

They're amazing." Sometimes I forgot that she'd lived in Cambridge—and met my father here.

As I shelved the books, I noticed that Clarence was back in his usual window—and Puck was napping in the other one. Here was progress of sorts. At least Clarence hadn't kicked him out of the shop.

The door to the kitchen opened and George strolled into the shop. "Here for an afternoon cup?" Aunt Violet asked.

"I wouldn't say no," George replied. "But I've got news. The police have finished searching Myrtle's flat. So if you lot would like to take a peek, we can go in any time."

We all exchanged glances. "Yes, we'd definitely would," Mum said. "How about after the store closes?"

"Sounds good," George said. "I'll go put the kettle on." Halfway to the door again, he called back, "Do you have any of those biscuits I like?"

"Top cupboard on the right," Aunt Violet said. "Put some on a plate."

During our tea break, I filled everyone in about Steve Baker's furtive visit to the betting shop and Kieran's revelation that Myrtle had tried to blackmail him.

"Making progress, we are," George said, dipping a McVitie's biscuit into his tea. I could understand why he loved them, since the whole-grain cookies were glazed with a nice layer of dark chocolate. "I gave the other tenants a shout but they had nothing too important to report." He shrugged. "I'm not surprised, they're quiet, pay their rent on time, and don't cause any fuss."

"They sound like good tenants to have," Mum said.

"I'm fortunate," George agreed. "I mean, I have been. Until now."

Aunt Violet peered out into the lane, which was empty of foot traffic. "I think we should close up early. It's been dead slow since three."

"Up to you," Mum said.

My aunt's answer was to turn the sign in the window and lock the door. She squared her shoulders. "Let me finish my tea and we'll go over."

With George in the lead, we cut over to Ivy Close the back way, through the alley. I couldn't help but imagine Myrtle using this route the night she died and probably many times before. It was much shorter than going up to Trinity Street, then over and down.

Ivy Close was a short, dead-end lane lined with attached brick three-story buildings. A couple near Trinity had storefronts on the ground floor, but the others all looked to be flats.

"I could never afford to buy my building now," George said, fishing for keys as he walked down the lane. "It's been in the family forever."

"Like the bookshop," Aunt Violet said. "We're very lucky, aren't we?"

"We are indeed." George unlocked a front door that opened into a square entrance hall. A wide flight of stairs led up, and there were doors on both sides. "Myrtle was on the first floor, in the back," he said. "I've got six flats total. All quite nice."

He trudged up the stairs and we all followed. Everything was sparkling clean, if old-fashioned, and our footsteps were the only sound in the thick-walled building.

Upstairs, George was about to unlock the door to Myrtle's apartment when he said. "That's odd." He gave the thick wooden door a fingertip push and it swung in, revealing a startling sight.

The place had been ransacked.

CHAPTER 8

"Flippin' 'ell," George exclaimed. "Who has gone and done this?" With a dazed expression on his face, he stepped into the flat.

We all crowded behind, careful to remain in the doorway of a spacious living room furnished with comfortable antiques. The sofa and chair cushions were on the carpet, and all the books had been removed from built-in shelves on each side of a faux fireplace mantel. Through the open door to the kitchen, I noticed white powder all over the tiled floor. Flour? Sugar? The cupboard doors in there hung open, contents pulled out onto the counters and floor.

"The police didn't leave it this way," Mum said. It wasn't a question.

"They certainly did not," George said. "I took a quick look round after they left." He pulled a mobile phone out of his trouser pocket. "I'm calling them right now."

I took a closer look, noticing that despite the dishevelment, the obvious items sought by thieves were still in place. The huge flat-screen television mounted above the fireplace. An expensive stereo system inside a glass-front cabinet. What looked to be antique and valuable paintings hanging on the walls.

"It doesn't look like they took the really good stuff," I said, pointing to Myrtle's expensive belongings. "What were they doing here, then?" Making a mess to make a point? Or looking for something that wasn't so obvious?

Aunt Violet was studying the room, her eyes huge behind her glasses. She stiffened, pointing. "What's that?"

A large piece of paper was taped to the wall over the desk in the corner, and even from here, I could read the lettering across the top: Marlowe Family Tree. Below were the typical lines used to show family relationships with descendants. "Why did she have that?" I asked. "Was she researching our family?"

A funny look crossed Aunt Violet's face. "She wouldn't," she said cryptically before marching across the room, her shoes crunching broken glass.

George was now speaking on the phone, so I looked at Mum. "Want to go see? It should be all right if we don't touch anything."

We crunched across the room, too, and joined Aunt Violet in front of the desk. She was peering up at the chart, her lips moving as she scanned the lines. Now that I was closer, I saw the chart began with Thomas Marlowe, the original founder of the bookshop.

"What's going on?" Mum asked.

"Myrtle and I are cousins," Aunt Violet said. She cracked a brief grin when we gasped. "Distant cousins." She pointed to a line showing the family in the 1700s. "Her branch was descended from another Thomas, often the name of the oldest male in a generation." *Like my uncle Tom*, I thought. "We are descended from Samuel Marlowe, his younger brother."

It took a few seconds before something clicked. "If her ancestor was the oldest, why did we inherit the bookshop? I thought property usually went to the oldest male back then." Thankfully inheritance laws had changed. I'd even heard that titles could go to females now instead of passing to the next closest male heir, like in *Downton Abbey*. If Lady Mary lived now, she would have inherited the estate instead of Matthew.

"The oldest male usually did inherit," Aunt Violet said. "Unless there was a specific will leaving the property to someone else." She shrugged. "And that's what I've always understood, that Samuel was favored for some reason."

"If there was a will, then what was Myrtle doing with this chart?" I asked. "Was she just generally interested in family history?" But even as I said that, it felt wrong. From what I'd learned of Myrtle, she never did anything casually. There was always an angle. Challenging a will three hundred years later was a bit of a stretch, though.

"She's been hinting around about something," Aunt Violet said. "But I ignored her. But come to think of it, it all started after Clive sprang the Best Books people on me. The day you saw them wasn't their first visit." Footsteps sounded in the hall and we all turned to look. Were the police here already? George had barely hung up. "Speak of the devil," Aunt Violet muttered.

Clive Marlowe stood in the doorway, car keys in hand and a stunned expression on his face. "Where's Myrtle?" he asked.

So many questions went through my mind. Didn't he know she was dead? And if not, why was he visiting her? Was he another blackmail victim—or in cahoots with her?

"Oh, Clive. Haven't you heard?" Aunt Violet quickly crossed the room to his side. "Myrtle . . . passed away. Last night."

He shook his head. "I just got back from London. Went up on business yesterday." Putting a hand to his brow, he ducked his chin, as if collecting himself. When he looked up again, his gaze roamed the ransacked room as if noticing the mess for the first time. "What's all this?" His mouth dropped open in shock. "Did someone break in and kill her?"

"No," George said. "She wasn't here when this happened." I noticed that he wasn't rushing to share the details of Myrtle's murder, either.

Mum, who had been taking all this in, asked, "What brings you here, Clive? Were you and Myrtle friends?"

I could see the thoughts flickering in his eyes. Mum had given him a very nice out. To his credit, he cleared his throat and admitted, "We weren't close, no." Then a crafty expression crept across his face and I guessed a lie was coming. "But she was a cousin, and elderly, so I kept an eye on her. Stopped by now and then."

"As you do with me?" Aunt Violet asked, her tone vinegar.

"Aren't you the noble one? No, all I heard from you are demands for money."

Clive's already ruddy complexion flushed. "Now that you bring it up, don't forget another payment is due next week." He nodded at Mum. "Thanks for bringing the loan current. Keep it that way." With that, he jingled his keys and spun on his heel. Soon we heard his footsteps lightly tapping down the stairs.

Aunt Violet clenched her fists and growled. "Oh, that man. He makes me furious."

"Don't let him get under your skin," George said. "He enjoys that." He tilted his head toward the family tree. "If you ask me, Clive and Myrtle were up to some mischief." He rested an elbow in one hand and tapped his chin with the other. "And I do wonder if he was *actually* in London last night. Inquiring minds want to know."

"George, you're a tonic." Aunt Violet swooped in and kissed him on the cheek. "Remember the man Molly saw lurking in the alley? Maybe it was Clive."

"That's right," I said. "Maybe it was. Certainly looked to be the same build." Meaning tallish but stout.

Someone rapped on the door downstairs. "There's the police now." George started toward the doorway, then halted. "If the street door is locked, how did Clive get in?" As he hurried to let the police into the building, we all knew the answer.

Clive had a key. That alone spoke to so much more than a casual, cousinly relationship. If he was lying about that, what else was he lying about? Had he killed Myrtle and planned to search her flat tonight, maybe to remove evidence of his involvement in her life—or something else entirely?

Several sets of footsteps ascended the stairs. To my surprise, Inspector Ryan was first through the door, followed by a female constable and George. I hadn't thought they would send an inspector to a break-in call, but maybe he had wanted to take it due to the murder case.

"What are you doing here?" he greeted us.

The three of us exchanged glances. "We came over at the landlord's invitation to look around," Mum said. "Our understanding was that the police had released the flat and we could enter."

Inspector Ryan acknowledged this truth with a nod. "What were you hoping to find?"

His cool manner intimidated me, which made me angry. We weren't guilty of anything nor had we been charged or arrested. "Clues to who killed her," I blurted. "Since it certainly wasn't my aunt."

The inspector's gaze flickered around the room. "This isn't your handiwork, I take it."

Now Mum was getting annoyed. I could tell by the set of her jaw. "Absolutely not. We found it this way and that's why George called you." She folded her arms and glared at him. "And speaking of clues, Clive Marlowe was just here. Apparently he has keys to this building and this flat, which I find very odd. You might want to talk to him."

Ryan glanced at the constable, who readied herself to make notes. "Clive Marlowe, your cousin?" he asked Aunt Violet "He didn't attend the event last night, did he?"

"No, he was in London," Aunt Violet said. "Or so he told us." She turned to the constable. There was a touch of smugness in her smile. "I have his contact information if you want it." How I'd love to be a fly on the wall when Clive got the call.

While the constable took down Clive's contact information, Inspector Ryan moved farther into the flat, gazing around. Halfway across the carpet, he stopped and pointed to the family tree on the wall. "That was not there earlier."

"It certainly wasn't," George said. "I took a walk through after your team left."

Which meant that whoever had broken in had taped the chart to the wall. To provide clues about Myrtle's activities—or to further implicate Aunt Violet?

Inspector Ryan inspected the family tree. "I didn't know you were related to her, Violet."

Aunt Violet returned to the desk. "As you can see, the connection was centuries ago. Our great-great-whatever grandfathers were brothers."

He didn't seem to fully understand the implications of the relationship or realize that the line of inheritance for the bookshop had come down through the younger brother. Or if he did, he didn't say anything. We certainly weren't going to point it out to him.

But my hope he'd overlook the family tree was dashed when he turned to the constable. "Take this into evidence, will you? Obviously someone wanted us to see it." He looked at us over his shoulder. "Thank you for phoning this in. If we have any further questions, we'll be in touch."

Dismissed. Our search of Myrtle's flat had come to a screeching halt. At least for now.

◂▸

"Good morning, dear," Aunt Violet said when I staggered into the kitchen the next morning, Puck padding at my heels. She was standing over a frying pan at the AGA, where something delicious was cooking. "How does an omelet sound? It will be ready in a sec."

"Perfect," I said. "Thank you." A tall cup of coffee from Tea and Crumpets already sat at my place. "Oh, you got me coffee." I sat at the table and Puck jumped up into the adjacent seat. From his usual spot in the armchair, Clarence gave him a tepid glare. Yesterday he had hissed. Progress.

My aunt shrugged. "Thought I'd save you a trip." She picked up her own cup and sipped. "It's not bad, is it?"

Aunt Violet drinking coffee? Wow. Sipping my own, I watched as she bustled about, making toast, cutting off a piece of the omelet and sliding it onto a plate, and then placing the works in front of me, along with salt and pepper shakers.

The omelet oozed cheese, sautéed mushrooms, and onions, and the toast was thick-cut homemade wheat glistening with melted butter. No calories here. I picked up my fork and set to work. "You are a fabulous cook," I moaned after my initial hunger had been slaked. "This is so good." Puck stared at me with hopeful eyes until I gave him a tidbit of egg.

She gave me a satisfied smile as she sat down with a plate. "That's what I like to see. A girl who appreciates her food." She sprinkled salt and pepper on her eggs. "I've enjoyed cooking for someone again. When Tom was alive, we often ate together."

How lonely Aunt Violet must have been when her brother died, especially since they'd worked together in the bookshop.

"I'm so sad I never got to meet him," I said. Maybe I could honor his memory by cataloging his collection of children's books. We had that in common, at least, a love of literature for young people. I'd get to that soon, I promised myself.

She nodded. "He would have loved you, Molly. You are two peas in a pod. Smart. Kind. Good with people."

My face heated at her praise. "Thanks," I muttered. "By the way, where is Mum? Still sleeping?"

Aunt Violet cut a forkful of omelet. "She's in the bookshop already, going over the books. She's determined to squeeze Clive's payment out somehow."

"If anyone can figure it out, it's Mum. She's a whiz with money." I reached for the rack of three jam pots and spread a spoonful of strawberry on my toast.

"And I am not." Aunt Violet sighed. "My brother used to take care of all that."

After swallowing a bite of toast and jam, I said, "Speaking of Uncle Tom, Sir Jon gave me a picture you need to see." I'd forgotten all about it until now. Setting down my toast, I pushed back my chair. "Hang on. I'll be right back."

My pack was hanging on a peg by the back door, along

with assorted jackets, hats, and umbrellas. Without taking it down, I unzipped the pocket and pulled out the photocopy.

"Look at this," I said, handing her the page and sitting down again. "What a great photo."

Aunt Violet smiled as she scanned the group of young faces. "I think I remember this. Rag Day."

"That's what Sir Jon told me." I resumed eating breakfast. Should I say it? Oh, why not? "I think he had a crush on you."

Her cheeks pinked. "Bosh. Why would you think that?"

Because he was staring at her with stars in his eyes, maybe. I dropped the subject. "It's neat to see all your old friends back then. Especially Joan. She was related to Daisy, you know."

"I do know." Aunt Violet's brow creased. "I'll never forget that terrible day when we found out she had died." She swallowed. "Fiona was the one to find her."

Imagining the tragic scene, I put my fork down. "Oh, Aunt Violet. That's awful." And now two of the old gang were dead, though in Myrtle's case, it was clearly murder.

She nodded. "It was. We all thought the world of Joan. Although she was shy and quiet, she would come out with the funniest remarks. She was also a real talent. Everyone was sure she'd be a famous poet someday."

"That's what Sir Jon said." Aunt Violet had placed the picture on the table and I glanced over at it. "On another note, what was up with Fiona and Uncle Tom? They look pretty cozy." The pair was standing close together, and a grinning Uncle Tom had his arm around Fiona.

"Oh, they dated for a while. We all thought they were going to get married." She shrugged. "But then she chose

Gregory instead. Gregory is all right, I suppose, but he's a real stick in the mud and a bit of a prig."

"I wonder why she married *him* instead of Uncle Tom." Uncle Tom looked like a great guy. I had enough experience with men to know that good ones were keepers.

"Her parents pressured her, I think," Aunt Violet said. "Gregory is from a wealthy family and eventually he became a member of Parliament. Not that Fiona isn't successful in her own right. She's quite high up at St. Hildegard's. So, wealthy landowner versus impoverished bookseller. You can see that Tom didn't stand a chance."

We were talking about fifty years ago, so I guessed I could see that happening. "Well, I would have picked Tom," I said stoutly. "If he wasn't my uncle, that is."

"I wish she had," Aunt Violet said. "He was pretty broken up about it for quite a while. And he never married. After Fiona, books became his life."

It seemed the same was true of Aunt Violet, and I wondered what her backstory was. But that was a subject for another time. As I cleaned the rest of my plate, I said, "I'm going to do a little digging into your St. Hildegard's classmates. After I set up an Instagram account for the store."

Aunt Violet shook her head. "I'm not even going to ask what that is." She pushed back her chair and stood. "But on behalf of Thomas Marlowe, I thank you."

Mum needed to go do a few errands, so I brought my laptop to the front desk. Business was fairly slow when we opened, so I was able to set up the social media accounts mostly undisturbed. It was such fun to see @thomasmarlowebooks on the sites I used personally.

"Come look, Aunt Violet," I called. "When you have a chance." She was on a stepladder dusting books on high shelves.

She set the feather duster on the top shelf and climbed down. "I was looking for an excuse to stop," she said with a laugh. "I hate dusting."

"Me too." I sighed. "But it's a chore that has to be done. I'll take over for you anytime."

"Oh, don't worry about it," she said. "It does me good to climb the ladder. Keeps the blood moving."

Aunt Violet pulled up a chair and I gave her a tour of the new pages. I was especially proud of the Instagram posts, where I already had likes and followers. "Is the book still available?" someone had asked on the Bryon volume. "Yes," I wrote back. "Give us a call." I included the landline number in my message.

"Now that is brilliant," Aunt Violet said. "Where is that person from?"

I checked out their profile. "London. I bet you'll get interest from the States, too. But right now they're still sleeping." The eastern United States was five hours behind, the West Coast, eight. "We really need to set up a web site."

"We do list our stock online," Aunt Violet said. She named a couple of big marketplaces. "Sell quite a bit that way."

"I'm sure." Those sites were perfect for finding books by title. "But your own site will help build a brand and customer loyalty. We'll get people interested through social media and then give them a way to check out what else you have."

Aunt Violet beamed in approval. "What a good idea. We are kind of special, aren't we?"

I snorted. "I'll say. Four hundred years worth of special. Even pictures of the building will drive interest." Who wouldn't want to buy books from such a quaint and charming shop? "I mean, seriously, would you rather shop in a sterile box or this place?"

"You know the answer to that, Molly." Aunt Violet clasped her hands in her lap. "That's why we have to fend off Clive. Best Books might keep the building the same but their stock will be exactly the same as their other stores. Which is fine, because we always need new books, but that's not what Thomas Marlowe is about."

I tapped my touchpad and brought up the Wordsworth post. That too was getting likes and comments already. "I'm planning to feature a few more poets. Sylvia Plath, for one, so I'll head to Newnham for photos. And I'd like to take a picture of Persephone at St. Hildegard's."

"Great idea," Aunt Violet said. "It's nice that you get to feature a living poet."

"Exactly." The word "living" reminded me of my plan to do some digging regarding Myrtle's murder. "I'd really like to talk to your other friends, see what they know about Myrtle."

Aunt Violet gave a shocked laugh. "Do you really think they were involved in her death?"

Oh no. Had I put my foot in it? The last thing I wanted to do was upset my aunt.

"I don't think anything yet." Which was true. "But any information we can get is more than we know right now."

"I suppose you're right." Aunt Violet plucked at her lower lip. "I do know that none of them really cared for Myrtle. But she was an old friend so we would have felt bad cutting her off."

Understandable. Except now someone had done much worse than snub her. "Can you help me get in touch with them? Last I knew, Persephone is staying with Fiona, and Ruth is staying up the street, at the Holly & Ivy. Unless they've left town again."

Aunt Violet's answer was to pick up the desk phone. "Hello, Monique," she said after someone answered. "How are you? Good, good. Listen, I was wondering if Ruth Orforo is still staying with you. She is? Can you put me through to her room?" After a brief pause, Aunt Violet said, "Good morning, Ruth. I was wondering if you'd like to stop by for a cuppa. Yes, an hour from now would be perfect. See you then." She hung up, turning to me with a smile. "One down."

"So I gathered. Yay." Although I was glad we were going to talk to Ruth, I also felt a rush of trepidation. I'd never questioned anyone regarding a murder. How to begin? No idea.

∙◆∙

Exactly an hour later, the door bells jingled and Ruth Orforo entered the shop, elegant in a yellow shift dress and matching sandals. She wore a solid gold cuff bracelet, chunky earrings, and a geometric-patterned headband that held her curly hair away from her face.

Aunt Violet swooped in for a hug, full skirt swirling. A pencil fell out of her bun. "Ruth. Gorgeous as ever."

Ruth returned the embrace, chuckling. "You're too kind."

She pulled back, hands on Violet's arms, and studied her friend's face. "How are you holding up?"

"I'm all right," Aunt Violet said with a shrug. She slipped her arm through Ruth's. "Come with me to the kitchen. Kettle's on."

I picked up the pencil, which had rolled across the floor to my feet. "Are you going to be okay here?" I asked Mum, who was sitting behind the desk.

She waved me off. "Go on." Her brows lifted as she put a hand to her mouth. "And fill me in later," she whispered.

My stomach tightened. I hoped we'd have something to report. We hadn't heard from the police this morning, which created the uneasy sense of waiting for a hammer to fall. Were they going to sweep in and arrest Aunt Violet? Or George?

In the kitchen, Aunt Violet was chattering away as she set the table for tea. "I've got lovely butterfly cakes from the bakery across the street." She opened the box, which held cupcakes scooped open and filled with jam and cream and topped with two pieces of cake shaped like wings.

Ruth clasped her hands together. "Ooh. Butterfly cakes. My favorite." She sent me a sly glance. "One of the benefits of getting older is not worrying about the occasional treat." She shook her head. "All the years I denied myself."

Aunt Violet set a cake on a plate and placed it in front of her friend. "Eat, drink, and be merry." *For tomorrow we die.* The unspoken words seemed to echo in the quiet kitchen. My aunt's mouth twisted. "Sorry. Bad choice."

"Don't give it a thought." Mischief shone on Ruth's face as she picked up the cupcake, holding it lightly. "'Life is uncertain. Eat dessert first.' Ernestine Ulner said that and I do my best to live by her words." She winked before taking a huge bite.

Aunt Violet poured from the teapot and I passed around the mugs of tea. Ruth had chosen the seat facing away from the garden, and who could blame her? From my chair opposite, I did my best to avoid looking at the shed, which reminded me of finding Myrtle.

"It's exciting that you're publishing Persephone's retrospective." I blurted out the first topic that came to mind. I figured we should work up to hashing over Myrtle's death, not dive right in. "We don't usually carry new books but we're going to stock it, of course. I'm in the middle of planning a social media campaign."

Ruth's eyes lit with interest. "Are you really?" She had whipped cream on her lip and she dabbed at it with a napkin. "Tell me more."

In between bites of butterfly cake—with tiny licks of cream going to Puck and Clarence—I filled her in about the Poets in the Wild project, which she greeted with enthusiasm and approval. "I'm hoping to connect with Persephone this week and take photos at your old college," I concluded. "Is she still in town, do you know?" My heart beat a little faster waiting for her reply. Not only did I want to photograph the poet, I hoped to question her about Myrtle and who might have motive to kill her.

"She's staying with Fiona until after Myrtle's service," Ruth said. "Have you heard if anything is scheduled?"

Aunt Violet nodded. "It's going to be held at the Round Church once the police give the go-ahead."

Meaning, released her body for burial, I guessed.

"Wonderful," Ruth said. "She loved that church. Is there a gathering planned yet?"

"Yes, at the Magpie," Aunt Violet said. "The Bakers offered to put on a big spread of food and an open bar. The mourners will be staggering away, no doubt."

"How generous of them," Ruth said. "Maybe I can do flowers."

I had to agree about the pub owners' generosity, especially since it looked like Myrtle might have been blackmailing Steve. He was definitely on the list to talk to after I saw him sneaking into the betting shop.

"I'm glad Myrtle is having a nice send-off," Aunt Violet said. "Even if"—she set her jaw—"she wasn't the easiest person."

Ruth's laugh was ironic. "*Easiest* person? That's an understatement, my dear. Did I ever tell you what she did to me?" Her features twisted in pain, and the paper napkin she held became a mangled ball. "Or tried to do, I should say. It all came right in the end. But at the time, I thought my life would end."

CHAPTER 9

Aunt Violet and I glanced at each other. "What did she do to you, Ruth?" Aunt Violet asked, her voice gentle.

Ruth ducked her head, obviously wrestling with the memories. Her fingers continued to squeeze and shred the poor napkin. Finally she tossed it onto the table with a laugh. "Guess I destroyed that." She picked up her mug and took a sip of tea, then set it down, moving it to the perfect spot. "Catherine," she said. "It was about Catherine."

Aunt Violet, guessing correctly that I was lost, whispered to me, "Her partner, in every way."

Oh. I got it. Fifty years ago attitudes were far different. Myrtle obviously had the knack of zeroing in on a person's vulnerabilities. Anger and revulsion churned in my gut. How evil.

"She threatened you," Aunt Violet said, saving Ruth from having to go into detail.

Ruth nodded, tears glittering in her eyes. "Right before my parents came to visit. She was going to tell them unless I *paid* her." Her voice rose to an offended squawk. "It wasn't as though I was rich, although I did have a bit of spending money." She swallowed. "And she wanted it all."

"What did you do?" I asked, horrified at the dilemma she had faced. Had Ruth still held a grudge against Myrtle all these years? I couldn't say as I blamed her.

Her answer surprised me. "I told them." She lifted her chin. "It took everything I had, but it went far better than I expected." Picking up the shredded napkin, she dabbed at her eyes. "They really were the best. Violet, did I ever tell you that they invested in our publishing company?" Her face glowed with satisfaction. "And when we had our first best seller, it added a very nice chunk to their retirement fund."

"How wonderful," Aunt Violet said. "The first of many bestsellers, I've noticed. And awards too."

Ruth nodded. "Catherine has a great eye. Between her taste and my business skills, we've done all right."

I picked up my phone and searched for Ruth's company, Virginia's House. The catalog was impressive, fairly small but featuring fine poetry, fiction, and memoirs. Aunt Violet was right about awards—many titles had at least one. The overall focus was on women's voices, and the description said the company name had been inspired by Virginia Woolf's famous essay, *A Room of One's Own*. Women now had a publishing *house* of their own.

Although tempted to check out some of the titles further, I set the phone aside. We needed to talk to Ruth about Myrtle while we had the chance.

"Anyone want a refill?" Aunt Violet held up the teapot, which was ensconced in a knit tea cozy shaped like a cottage.

Ruth glanced at her phone then shook her head. "I'm sorry, love, but I've got to run." She gave a little laugh. "Back-to-back meetings with potential authors."

Oh no. We hadn't even discussed the murder yet. "Before you go," I said hastily. "Did you see anything out of the ordinary the night Myrtle died? Anyone acting strangely?"

Ruth pulled her head back. "What do you mean? During the reading?"

"Or before it." I gestured around the kitchen. "Someone sneaking around the property, for instance." Aunt Violet nodded, encouraging me to go on. But since the papers only revealed that Myrtle was stabbed, I wouldn't mention the knitting needle. "Aunt Violet is their main suspect. Thankfully they haven't arrested her yet."

"That's dreadful." Ruth's hand went to her throat. "Because it happened in your garden, Vi? But there were dozens of people here that evening. Anyone could have killed her."

"We know," I said with a groan. "It makes it very complicated." A flash of insight struck. "Maybe the killer took advantage of the situation. To muddy the water." It had been a bold move, the risk of discovery high, but the murderer had pulled it off.

Our guest fiddled with her bracelet, thinking. Finally she shook her head. "I'm sorry, I really didn't see or hear anything out of the ordinary." She shrugged graceful shoulders. "I was so caught up in the reading, in the excitement of Persephone's new book." She gave Aunt Violet a small smile. "And seeing you again, of course."

Frustration slid across my aunt's features but her expression smoothed as she said, "And it's been lovely to see you. Do me a favor, though, will you? If you think of anything that sheds light on the situation, please tell the police."

"Or us," I put in, not wanting to be out of the loop. "We'll make sure Inspector Ryan gets the message."

Ruth rose from her chair. "If I remember anything odd or unusual about that night, I promise I'll let you know."

Aunt Violet stood to kiss Ruth on both cheeks. "Come by again, won't you, while you're in town?"

"I certainly will," Ruth promised. She looked around, inhaling deeply. "I adore this shop. It's a book-lover's dream." With a wave of farewell, she left, bells jingling on the door.

"I'll take more tea," I said once she was gone. "I was really shocked to hear what Myrtle did to Ruth. How hateful."

Aunt Violet set her lips in a thin line. "It really was despicable." Finished pouring, Aunt Violet set the teapot down with a clatter. "I wish Ruth had confided in me back then. I would have reported Myrtle to the head of college."

"I'm starting to see a pattern," I said. "Kieran Scott told me yesterday that Myrtle tried to blackmail him into giving her money. She said she wouldn't tip off the tabloids about his movements if he paid her."

Aunt Violet's mouth formed an O. "What cheek. Did he fall for it?"

I shook my head. "No. And guess what? The tabloids seem to know his every move." My tone was dry. "Including the night of the reading. Kelsey Cook got a picture of him leaving the shop."

Aunt Violet clucked. "I'm sure his parents loved that. Especially after Myrtle . . ." Her voice trailed off but we got the gist. Kieran at the scene of a murder was not the look his mother preferred.

"I was there when his mother called him," I said. "I gathered she wasn't very happy."

"Asha is lovely," Aunt Violet said. "But a stickler for propriety." Her lips pursed. "She certainly whipped Lord Graham into shape."

"What do you mean?" I asked, dying to know more about Kieran's family.

My aunt laughed. "He used to be a wild one, that's for sure. I know they don't approve of Kieran running the bike shop, but I think that secretly Lord Graham is envious. I always sensed that his title tethered him a little too much."

I'd had no idea that Aunt Violet knew Kieran's parents so well, and I filed away her little tidbits. But what she'd said only confirmed my doubts about my place in Kieran's life. If they didn't like him running a bike shop, then surely a bookseller would be far from suitable in their eyes. *Their loss*, I told myself. In my world, books trumped a title any day.

◀▮▶

Later that afternoon, I walked over to St. Hildegard's College to meet Persephone for a photo shoot. The college was on the other side of the river, and my route would take me down Trinity Street and into King's College, where I planned to cross the bridge.

On the phone, Persephone had sounded excited, almost

girlish. "I can't believe the interest my new book is getting," she'd said with a giggle. "I'm having a little renaissance, it seems."

I was glad for her, of course, but as I dodged the students and tourists clogging the cobblestone street, I couldn't help but wonder if Myrtle's death had boosted Persephone's profile. A tabloid headline in a newspaper stand caught my eye—and offered a possible answer to my question. "St. Hildegard's Alumnae Linked in Life—and Death," it read, over college-age headshots of Myrtle, Ruth, Fiona, Aunt Violet, and Persephone.

I reached for a copy, deciding I really should buy it. Tabloids weren't known for their accuracy, but I might glean something. When I turned, paper in hand, I almost bumped into a middle-aged man with close-cropped salt-and-pepper hair, dressed in dungarees and a T-shirt. "Sorry," I said at the same time he said, "Pardon me." We both laughed and after he moved aside, I went into the newsagent's and paid for the paper.

On King's College Bridge, I paused to look up and down the Cam. Punts floated along the river, and on the banks, people strolled or sat in the sun. Like the college inner courts, the river provided an oasis of quiet beauty in the middle of this bustling city. Putting my hands on the rampart, I inhaled air flavored with fresh-cut grass, river water, and warm stone. What a wonderful place to while away a warm afternoon.

Here on the bridge there was also a constant stream of foot traffic, with people crossing both ways. A man stopped to lean against the wall and leaf through a newspaper.

With a start, I recognized the man from the newsagent. Was he following me?

Surely not. Obviously this was a popular spot, and if I hadn't almost bumped into him, would I even have noticed him? How many of the other people on the bridge had also been walking down Trinity Street at the same time as me? I pushed these ridiculous speculations aside, realizing I needed to get moving.

After reaching the river's far shore, I followed the map to St. Hildegard's, which was a brick Victorian enclave. Not nearly as majestic and massive as the other colleges, it still had an imposing, elegant presence. I caught myself glancing over my shoulder several times, but to my relief, I didn't see the man with the newspaper again. I had been imagining things.

One section of the gate with its filigree metal screen was open, and after I walked through, I stopped to sign in with the porter. "Where is the Medieval Knot Garden?" I asked the kindly older gentleman. The garden had been inspired by the writings of the college's patron saint, St. Hildegard of Bingen, who had been an herbalist as well as a mystic, a songwriter, a theologian, and a poet. Truly a woman to admire and emulate.

He pulled out a photocopied visitor map of the college, tracing the route then marking the garden with an X. "Can't miss it," he said with a friendly smile, sliding the page toward me.

"Thank you. Have a nice day." I accepted the map and continued into the college proper, where brick Gothic Revival buildings draped with ivy were set here and there behind hedges and among flower beds. St. Hildegard's had been built in the 1870s, and the college's architecture perfectly reflected the era.

Following the map, I skirted several buildings and soon found the knot garden, featuring patterned herb and flower beds in a sunken area. A fountain adorned the center, and there, perched on the rim like a nymph, was Persephone. Today her abundant gray hair was long and loose and she wore an ankle-length gauzy dress and gladiator sandals.

She hopped off the edge of the fountain when she saw me approaching. "There you are, Molly. Isn't it a beautiful day?" Holding her arms wide, she threw her head back and inhaled deeply. "This place is magic. Inspiration is flowing, I tell you. I've written two poems already."

On the grass next to her feet was an open lined notebook, a pen resting in the crease. Seeing the notebook gave me an idea. She should pose as if penning a new poem here in the garden.

"It's definitely a special spot," I said, sliding my pack off my shoulders. Inside was Persephone's first book of poems, a slim volume published in the late 1960s. We could also use that as a prop, and she could sit under that arbor smothered in fat white roses.

Before we moved to the arbor, I took several shots of Persephone on the fountain with her first book. Pretending to read. Coyly displaying the book so the title showed. Holding it aloft in an exuberant pose, the sun sparkling on water droplets around her.

"These are great." I scrolled through the pictures, pleased that each had the elusive "wow" factor I was aiming for.

Persephone tried to look modest. "I used to do some modeling you know, back in the day. Local fashion shows, some magazine shoots, a couple of album covers."

"Really? How cool." Although she was on the short side, she was very photogenic, and judging by the old photo I'd seen, she'd had a classic Carnaby Street style that reminded me of Patti Boyd and Twiggy.

The poet stretched, preening. "What fun we had." She picked up her tote and started strolling toward the arbor. "My mother was a model too. My father, Geoffrey Brightwell, was completely smitten when he met her at a London nightclub."

Geoffrey Brightwell. His name rang a bell. Doing a quick search on my phone while we walked, I learned that he had been part of an illustrious group called the Movement, along with Philip Larkin and Kingsley Amis. Like father, like daughter, apparently.

Persephone put her tote on the grass and settled on the arbor bench. "What do you need me to do?"

"I'd love you to pretend you're writing a poem." I glanced up at the heavy, clustered blossoms, taking a deep breath of their sweet fragrance. "These roses could even inspire me to write something. They're incredible."

"Aren't they?" Persephone pulled one close for a sniff. "Going to school here was the best part of my life."

"I doubt that, though it must have been amazing," I said lightly, directing her how to sit. How sad when someone believed college or even high school was the peak. I preferred to think that the best was yet to come. Especially now, working at my dream job in this historic and charming city.

She studied me, lips pursed. "Where did you go to college, Molly? One of the Ivies?"

"The University of Vermont, for library science. UVM is one of the oldest universities in the country and a very good school." I bit my lip, annoyed at myself for adding the disclaimer. I despised the game of positioning by alma mater, all too common in some circles.

"I'm sure," she muttered, her tone condescending.

Grr. Brushing off her snobbery, I returned to the task at hand. "I'm ready when you are."

Obediently, Persephone picked up her pen and pretended to write in the notebook. The dappled pink light cast by the roses was flattering, and I quickly fired off a great series of shots.

"Take a look," I said, sitting down beside her. "Pick out your favorites." Since she was doing me a favor, I wanted her to be happy.

Heads together, we chose the best ones and I saved them in a cloud folder for easy access. "If you have time," I said. "I'd like to hear more about St. Hildegard's, for the social media posts." *And hopefully learn something to help us solve Myrtle's murder.* Maybe her demise had nothing to do with her college friends, but we had to explore this angle. Was their reunion for the reading a coincidence or an inciting factor?

"I'd love to chat." Persephone reached for her tote. "Tea and a biscuit?" She pulled out a thermos of hot tea, two mugs, and a packet of McVitie's, the kind George liked.

"Oh, I love those biscuits," I said, opening the packet at her instruction.

"Me too," she said, opening the thermos and filling a mug for me. "It already has milk. I hope that's all right."

I accepted the tea. "That's the way I take it." In between sips and bites, I pulled out my own notebook. "Were you good friends with Myrtle in college?" At her questioning look, I added, "I never got a chance to get to know her. What was she like as a young woman?"

Persephone nibbled on a biscuit. "I didn't know her really *well*. She was one of those people who hang around so much they eventually become part of the gang."

"Was she in one of your classes?" I asked, wanting to know more.

The poet shook her head. "No. We all lived in the same accommodations." She pointed to a building. "Our own study-bedrooms on different floors. Myrtle was across the hall from Joan, who was a friend of Violet's. I introduced Fiona to Violet, and then somehow we all gelled."

I'd heard the college friends talking about Joan and Myrtle in our kitchen the other night, so that fit. "Sir Jon showed me a picture of all of you at Rag Day," I said, coming at the topic sideways.

Persephone laughed. "Oh, Sir Jon. We were all in love with him. Though he wasn't a 'sir' then. That came later, when the Queen knighted him."

"He was quite handsome," I said. "Still is. So was my uncle Tom." A wistful pang hit whenever I thought of my late uncle and how I'd never get to know him.

"Tom was a love," Persephone said. "I always thought

he and Fiona . . . well, the heart is a mystery. She and Gregory have muddled along for ages now." She tilted her head, studying me with puzzled eyes. "You never met Tom? Why is that?"

I shook my head. "I didn't even meet Aunt Violet until we moved here." Shame twisted at the admission and I regretted being so honest. Mum obviously had a reason for staying away, and although I desperately wanted to know what it was, I hadn't planned to open the topic to public comment.

As I feared, she didn't drop the subject. "Odd. How about your grandparents? Did you meet them?"

My cheeks burned with embarrassment. "No, I never had the opportunity." How rude would it be if I got up and left? Maybe I could claim another appointment.

"How sad," she said, patting my arm with what felt like faux sympathy. "And quite strange, really. Maybe Americans don't place the same importance on family as we Brits do."

Why was she needling me this way? "That's not it," I said before forcing myself to stop talking. It had been Mum's decision to cut off her family, not Dad's. Plus I didn't owe this woman an explanation about family dynamics I didn't even understand yet.

When I remained silent, Persephone went on. "Myrtle was a Marlowe, you know. Well, way, way back. Generations ago. So you were cousins of sorts."

"I'm aware of that." Because of our visit to Myrtle's flat, this news didn't quite have the impact I guessed she was aiming for. I jumped up from the bench and began packing my belongings. "And now, sorry to say, I must go. Thanks for the photo shoot, I'll let you know when the posts are up. Oh, and tea was great. Much appreciated."

As I practically ran across that lovely garden, pack jostling on my back, I could sense her watching me. What an unpleasant woman she was—despite her talent.

CHAPTER 10

"Be careful," Daisy warned. "These stairs are pretty steep." She was leading me up the narrow, winding flight to the tea shop attic, where we were going to search through Joan's belongings.

She wasn't kidding about the stairs. I had to place my sneakers carefully on tapering steps obviously made for much smaller feet. This building wasn't as old as the bookshop, but it made my Vermont farmhouse look new. Some people don't like the smell of ancient dust and wood and plaster, but I breathed it in with relish, feeling strangely connected to all the generations who had gone before. Another woman had climbed these stairs when the apple fell on Newton's head. While Jane Austen was penning her novels. The year Victoria ascended the throne.

At the top, Daisy pressed the thumb latch and opened the door, releasing a gust of hot, dry air. "It's pretty stifling up here," she warned, pulling a string to turn on an overhead light. "One reason I haven't made much progress clearing it out. It's also a complete shambles."

One person's shambles was another's treasure trove. Echoing the roof, the room was steeply peaked with only a tiny window at each end, and it was jam-packed with interesting and enticing objects. On our way to Joan's trunk, I spotted a row of Toby face mugs, a stuffed badger, and a Guy Fawkes mask on a mannequin head that also held a cavalier's feathered hat.

Daisy threw a smile over her shoulder. "My great-aunt and uncle were eccentric, to say the least. He wore that mask whenever he put on those stilts"—she pointed to the long poles propped in a corner—"along with that cloak." The garment in question was black, hooded, and spangled with crescent moons and stars.

"He must have been quite the sight," I said. "Seriously, if you need help, let me know. I love looking through attics." Judging by what I'd seen so far, many wonderful finds were lurking up here.

"I might take you up on that," Daisy said. Kneeling on the floor, she threw up the lid of a black metal trunk. "As you can see, they just tossed everything from Joan's room inside."

I sat cross-legged beside her, and both of us stared into the trunk, which held a jumble of books, notebooks, loose papers, pens, a mug or two, a hairbrush, and more. I could imagine Joan's grief-stricken parents clearing surfaces and drawers, the remnants of their daughter's life of no interest without her. Or maybe they'd been gun-shy about uncovering secrets, kind of the way I felt after Persephone's insinuations about my family this afternoon.

"Where do we begin?" I asked, reluctant to paw through the late student's belongings.

Daisy sighed as she lifted out a book. "From the top, I guess. Let's sort things by category."

Together we excavated the trunk, making piles around us on the floor. In addition to textbooks, we found a number of yellowed, dog-eared paperbacks, mostly poetry and literature.

"Anything of value here?" Daisy asked me.

I took a closer look at the books. "This first edition of Wordsworth is interesting." I pulled out my phone and looked it up. "It's not super-rare—those go for tens of thousands—but probably worth around a thousand dollars. Seven or eight hundred pounds," I translated. An expensive book for a scholarship student to own, even fifty years ago. Where had she gotten it? Was it a lucky find at the Cambridge Market? Or a gift, perhaps, from a very generous friend?

"Can you get me a firm price?" Daisy asked. "I'll ask my aunt and uncle if they want to sell it. I'm sure they could use a little extra money."

"I'd be happy to." I set the book to one side. "Shall we keep going?"

"Sure." Daisy glanced at her phone. "We have about fifteen minutes." We were meeting Kieran and Tim at the pub for dinner and darts.

Next I leafed through a few photographs. One showed Joan seated at her desk, Myrtle beside her, both grinning. Another picture was of a young man standing next to the fountain in St. Hildegard's garden. The name *Gregory* was written on the back.

"Gregory. Isn't that the name of Fiona's husband?" I asked.

Daisy nodded. "Yes. Gregory Fosdyke, MP. He's in the House of Commons."

Why did Joan have a photograph of him? "House of Commons. So not a member of the nobility," I said. Parliament had two government bodies, and members of the Commons were elected by the people, not appointed or internally elected as in the House of Lords.

"He's a barrister," Daisy said, turning the pages of a notebook filled with scrawled handwriting. "Representing Cambridge. Very respected, he is."

I put the pictures down and turned to the notebooks. Most had flimsy cardboard covers and spiral binding, typical student supplies. But one was bound in leather, heavy and expensive and butter-soft. My heart beat a little faster when I flipped it open, my intuition already telling me it was special.

First day of term, St. Hildegard's, 1964

Alone. In my own room, sitting at a desk overlooking an incredible garden, the whole situation beyond my wildest dreams.

I stopped reading, knowing that I was intruding into something not meant for public consumption. "Daisy." I nudged her with my elbow. "I think this is Joan's journal. Her diary."

She took it and leafed through, each page dated and followed by entries, some long, some short. Fragments of poems, too, it looked like. Near the end, the pages were blank.

The hair on my arms stood up. Was this Joan's *last* journal? No wonder her parents had stuffed it into the bottom of the trunk.

Daisy pressed it onto my lap. "Take it, will you? Please. Read it?" Her brows drew together. "I can't. But there might be something, a clue. . . . We never understood why, why she . . . and maybe, just maybe, there's something important in there about Myrtle."

Honored by her trust, I held the notebook to my chest. "I'll take good care of it, I promise." And Joan's secrets as well.

·ı·

After leaving the notebook at the bookshop for safekeeping, Daisy and I went across to the pub. A blackboard easel sign outside the door announced, Cottage Pie Tonight.

"That's what I'm getting," Daisy said. "Susie makes the best cottage pie ever."

I wasn't quite sure what cottage pie was, but I was game to try it. Inside the pub, Kieran and Tim were already sitting at a four-top table. Kieran waved when he saw us, then stood, as did Tim. How polite. Two pints already awaited us, I noticed.

"Brown ale, right?" he asked, sitting again when I did.

Flattered he'd remembered, I grinned as I picked up my glass. "Perfect." The local ale had a slightly bitter and hoppy taste I had come to appreciate.

Tim fiddled with the menu. "We're having cottage pie. What's your pleasure, ladies?"

"Same," we said simultaneously, then laughed.

Tim got up, tapping the table. "I'll order."

"I'll go with you," Daisy said. "I need to talk to Susie."

After the pair went up to the bar, Kieran and I sipped beer in silence for a long moment. Ridiculously, I felt totally tongue-tied, like a teenager. Was it because I found him so devastatingly attractive? Or did his notoriety and family background intimidate me? *Buck up, Molly,* I told myself. *This isn't the Middle Ages.*

"What have you been up to?" Kieran finally asked. He smiled ruefully. "Sorry I had to run out on you at the market."

"It's okay." I gave what I hoped was a casual, unconcerned shrug. "Your business comes first. As a new bookshop proprietor, I totally understand."

He ran his forefinger around a wet circle left by a beer glass, his lips pushed out in almost a pout. "But I *wanted* to tour the market with you. And do some sightseeing. Maybe you'll give me a rain check?"

I'll give you more than that, was my cheeky thought. But I played it cool. "Sure. I'd like that." I picked up my glass and sipped. I thought of trying to arrange a time but refrained. Let him come to me.

Tim and Daisy returned to the table. "They said dinner will be right out," Tim informed us. He held Daisy's chair for her, a nice touch.

"I've offered to help Susie with the funeral meal," Daisy said. "I'm going to do my butterfly cakes. Myrtle loved them."

"They're scrumptious," I said. "I had one this morning when Ruth came by. She was also raving about them, you should know."

Daisy smiled, pleased. "Always good to hear."

"Ruth Orforo, the publisher?" Kieran asked. "She went to school with your aunt, right?"

I nodded. "Ruth was part of the gang, along with Myrtle, Persephone, and Fiona Fosdyke. They were all at the reading."

"I remember," Kieran said. "A distinguished group of women, for sure."

"My aunt was friends with them too," Daisy said. "But sadly she died while at college."

"I'm sorry to hear that," Tim said, his blue eyes sympathetic.

Kieran echoed his sentiments.

The kitchen door banged open and Susie emerged, holding two oval ceramic casserole dishes aloft. Steve was right behind her, holding two more.

"Careful, they're hot." Susie set the casseroles in front of Daisy and me, then stepped back for Steve to deliver his, along with a basket of bread he'd carried in the crook of his elbow. Susie rubbed her hands across her apron front. "Anything else I can get you?"

We looked at one another and shook our heads. "It's really nice of you to host a meal for Myrtle," I said, buttering a hot roll. "Let us know at the bookshop if we can do anything to help."

"I'll give it some thought," Susie said. "If that's all . . ." With a nod, she set off across the floor, intent on getting back into the kitchen.

Steve checked our beer glasses. "Give a shout when you want another," he said. But instead of leaving, he lingered, staring at the barstool where Myrtle last sat. "That old bird was a bit of a pain, you know? But now that she's gone, I kind of miss her."

Kieran fiddled with his fork. "We all do, mate. She was part of the community fabric." His lips twisted. "Even if she did indulge in the occasional spot of blackmail."

Steve reared back, his mouth falling open. Was he thinking about his covert visit to the betting shop? "I can't speak to that," he finally stuttered.

A cluster of people at the bar holding empty glasses looked his way, and he seized the opportunity to escape. "I'd better go serve the clamoring masses . . . enjoy your meal."

"You don't seem surprised," Tim said to me a moment later. "Kieran fill you in?"

"He did," I said. "It's shocking."

Daisy didn't seem fazed by the mention of Myrtle's shenanigans either, which meant she was also in the know. Both men were looking at us and not eating, and I realized they were waiting for us to begin. I picked up my fork and stabbed into a thick layer of cheesy, browned mashed potatoes. Savory steam rose toward my face and my mouth began to water.

For a few minutes, only the clinking of silverware and murmurs of appreciation were heard. Cottage pie was what we called shepherd's pie in the States, with ground beef, corn, and in this recipe, peas under the crust of potato. Here in England, I gathered, shepherd's pie was always made with ground lamb.

"Myrtle tried her little games with other people too," Tim

said, reaching for his beer. After a long swallow, he continued. "Clive Marlowe, for instance. I spotted him slipping her a wad of bills more than once."

"Maybe he felt sorry for her," Daisy said. "She used to come round the tea shop and ask for day-old baked goods."

I snorted, loud enough that they all looked at me. "Sorry," I said. "But Myrtle wasn't exactly hurting." Rather than tell them we'd searched her flat, I said, "George, her landlord, told us she owned all kinds of high-end electronics and art."

"Figures," Kieran said. "Her poor me act didn't exactly ring true. For one thing, her shoes were bespoke Italian leather."

I hadn't noticed that, but his observation only underscored that he came from a different world, one where people wore custom-made shoes.

"Speaking of Clive." Tim waved at Ollie, the darts player, who was making his way to the bar. "There's someone who has a tale to tell."

Interesting. I wondered how he and Clive were connected.

Ollie changed direction and came over to our table, grabbing an empty chair and turning it backward. "What's up, mate?" His brow lifted when his eyes met mine. "Vermont. Back again to trounce us, I see."

I flexed my fingers with a laugh. "Maybe. I don't always win, as you know." I gave Kieran a sly smile.

Ollie made a skeptical sound and turned to Tim, who said, "I wanted to ask you about Clive Marlowe and his dealings." Tim rubbed his forefingers against his thumb in the universal gesture for money.

"Oh yes, Clive. I have a friend who used to work for him."

His gaze returned to me. "But I don't want to speak out of turn. He's your relative, isn't he?"

"That's okay," I said. "He's trying to sell the bookshop to Best Books, so he's not exactly my favorite person. A team from there was in the shop checking it over the day Mum and I arrived."

My companions made shocked noises, exclaiming in horror. Kieran made a cross sign, as if warding off evil. "Please, no. That would be a travesty."

"Oh, we're doing our best to stop him," I said. "Aunt Violet owes him money, unfortunately, and he's trying to use that as leverage. Our plan is to pay him off quick as we can."

Daisy pointed her fork at me. "I'm going to promote the shop even more. You'll be bursting at the seams with customers."

"So will we," Tim said. "Right, Kieran?"

Kieran nodded, saying of course he would.

My heart warmed at this staunch show of support. "Thank you so much." I turned to Ollie and smiled. "So please spill."

Ollie leaned his chin on his arms, which were resting along the chair back in front of him. "Clive's quite the man-about-town. He's always got projects on the go, renovating flats here, doing shop retrofits there. But my friend—who used to run one of the building crews—said Clive is definitely dodgy." His forehead furrowed. "Bribes, favors, the whole bit." He put a finger to his lips. "But that's all I'm going to say."

Tim had seen Clive giving Myrtle money, which tied in with what Ollie told us. Had she caught on to Clive's schemes? Is that why he went to her flat the other night, to pay her off again? A more ominous thought crept into my mind. Or maybe it was to cover his tracks.

"I appreciate the info," I said to Ollie. "It certainly casts a new light on my cousin." Come to think of it, with relatives like Clive, who needed enemies? My stomach hollowed. Was that how Mum felt about her immediate family? Had they done something terrible to her? I set down my fork, unable to eat another bite.

"Is that it?" At Tim's nod, Ollie rose from the chair. "I'd best be getting on. See you in a bit." He shouldered his way to the bar, where he ordered a pint, laughing about something with Steve.

"I hope that helped," Kieran said to me. He must have seen something in my face because concern flashed in his eyes. "Are you all right? Did he say something to upset you?"

I waved my hand. "I'm fine. Just taking it all in, that's all." Pasting a smile on my face, I said, "Who's ready to get trounced, as Ollie said?"

But as it turned out, I had an off night at the dartboard. My mind was too preoccupied with thoughts of Myrtle's murder, the possible suspects, and the mystery of Mum's family. Far from the calm and alert state necessary to throw properly.

I was standing alone in a corner, sipping a fresh pint and watching the action, when Kieran came over. "Admit it," he said with a grin. "This is part of your strategy."

"What do you mean?" I couldn't help but return his smile. Being around Kieran had that effect on me. I immediately felt all bubbly.

He set his pint on the high-top table beside me. "You're letting us think you've lost your touch before you stage a comeback and wham, blow us out of the water."

A giggle burst out of my chest. "Yes, that's it. How did you guess?"

He moved closer, his shoulder almost touching mine. Little zings of attraction seemed to spark between us. Or was it one-sided, meaning all in my head?

"I meant what I said earlier." His voice was low, intimate. "I'll do whatever I can to help figure out who killed Myrtle. It's beyond ridiculous that anyone could think that your aunt is guilty." He sidled closer. "She saved my life when I first opened my shop, you know."

I turned to look at him, which brought my face only inches from his. Our eyes met. My throat thickened and I could barely speak. "She did?" Such eloquence.

He tore his gaze away, staring down at the table instead. "It was far from easy, setting up and getting started. I had a few bad moments when I almost gave up, almost tucked my tail and ran home. But she would make me a cup of tea and tell me to keep going. Then she'd send people over to rent bikes." He gave a little laugh. "Sometimes I got the feeling she'd practically forced them to."

Dear Aunt Violet. "I can see her doing that."

A shout over at the dartboard caught our attention. Tim and Ollie were in the last throes of a heated match, the on-lookers cheering and groaning by turns.

"Molly." Kieran's voice was tentative. "I've been wondering if you—I mean, if you might be—"

Before he could finish spitting it out, Tim sank three darts in the bull's-eye, causing Ollie to stamp his feet in mock dismay. "You're up, Kieran," he shouted, pretending to throw down his darts. "Maybe you can take the blighter out."

Kieran threw me a bemused, regretful smile. "There's my cue. Talk later?" He picked up his pint and strode toward his friends, calling out a riposte that made them roar with laughter.

Why did I have the distinct feeling that he had been about to ask me on a date? As I watched him square his shoulders for the first dart toss, I realized something else. Kieran Scott, son of nobility, had been *nervous*. I tossed my hair with a laugh. Well, well. *That* was interesting.

"How's it going?" Daisy sauntered over to my table, beer in hand. "You and Kieran looked pretty cozy over here." Her eyes twinkled with mischief.

I crooked a finger, inviting her to come closer. We leaned our elbows on the table and put our heads together. "Is it crazy to think he might like me?" As anyone who has been around the block knows, signals do get crossed. And people often play games. For all I knew, Kieran flirted with everyone in his orbit.

"You mean, does he fancy you?" Daisy nodded. "Uh-huh." She cut her gaze to Kieran and Tim over at the dartboard. "Totally. Head over heels."

Really? A warm rush doused me head to toe. "But why me? I mean, I'm okay-looking, I know that. But he's dated supermodels. And future princesses." I couldn't hold back a laugh at the absurdity of royals in this day and age. Although the weddings were spectacular.

Daisy eyed me over the rim of her glass. "Because his

parents made him. He's a regular bloke. Treat him like one and he'll be yours forever."

I hoped she was right, well except the "forever" part. So not ready for that. "How about for a date or two? Let's not get carried away."

Her expression was shrewd. "No, let's not." After a pause, she said, "In other news, Tim asked me out." She sighed with exaggeration. "Finally."

"Tell me all the details," I said, meaning it. It'd been a long time since I'd had a friend to confide in about relationships. I'd forgotten how much fun it was.

CHAPTER 11

"Good night," I called to my friends as we left the pub a while later. Daisy went toward the tea shop, Kieran to the bicycle shop, and Tim took off on his bicycle. He lived a few blocks away.

A little black shape came darting out of the bookshop's side alley, meeting me halfway across the street. "Puck. You are the cutest." I bent and picked him up, snuggling my face into his soft fur. Strolling slowly on cobblestones still warm from the day's heat, we watched as a crescent moon sailed above the chimney pots. Even at night, living on Magpie Lane was like dwelling inside a classic children's book. *Mary Poppins. The Secret Garden. The Wind in the Willows*, with Rat and Mole "messing about in boats." After seeing the punts on the Cam, I wanted to mess about in a boat too.

A rubbish bin crashed over in the alley, the lid rolling away and landing with a clatter. "Bloody 'ell," a male voice muttered.

Torn from my gentle fantasy world, I landed hard in a thriller. "Who's there?" I called. "Is that you, George?" He swore like George, that much was true.

No answer, but a dark shape detached itself from the shadows. Footsteps sounded, slow at first but then breaking into a trot.

Not again. And this time I wasn't having it. After hastily unlocking the shop and putting Puck inside, to keep him safe, I gave chase. "Stop," I yelled. "Stop, I say." I was already panting by the time I reached the mouth of the alley, where I almost tripped over the bin lid. Kicking it aside, I kept going.

The man was fast, like the person Kieran had chased the night of Myrtle's death. Was it the killer, returned to the scene again? Why didn't he stay away?

I reached the intersection with the back alley, pausing to see if he'd gone left or right. But then I heard the feet thudding ahead, continuing toward Ivy Close. One of George's tenants taking a shortcut home? But why didn't he say anything when I called out?

"You really need to stop," I yelled. "What a hero. Lurking about trying to scare women." My voice echoed off the canyon of buildings around me.

How quiet it was back here, I realized suddenly. How deserted.

My anger vanished, leaving me shivering. What was I doing out here all by myself? Chasing a possible killer?

Maybe he was hiding up ahead, waiting for me. A thrill

of sheer terror iced my spine and I took off again, this time toward home.

In my haste, I'd forgotten to lock the door again. How careless of me. Then, as I started to barge in, eager to reach safety, I noticed a note taped to the oval window. Without bothering to stop and read it, I pulled the paper off and carried it inside, then locked the door and checked it for good measure.

Puck wound around my ankles, mewing. "Hold on a sec. I'll get you a snack in a minute." I wanted to read the note first. In the shadowy half dark of the shop's night lighting, I read, *I'm sorry. C.* I flipped over the page, but that was it.

C? My thoughts went immediately to Clive. Had he had a change of heart regarding his underhanded attempt to sell the bookstore? Or was he confessing to Myrtle's murder?

Puck mewed again, his you'd-better-pay-attention squawk, so I hurried through to the kitchen, still holding the note. He ran ahead eagerly, racing me.

The note went on the table, and trying to be quiet, I put a few pebbles of kibble in his dish and filled a glass with water to take upstairs with me. Clarence was upstairs with Aunt Violet, but I gave his dish a few more as well.

"Molly. You're home." My mother stood in the kitchen doorway, wrapped in a bathrobe, her hair still damp from a shower.

"I hope I didn't make too much noise," I said before slurping a gulp of water. "I tried to be quiet." Well, except for the shouting outside. But the walls were thick in this very old house.

"No, I didn't hear a thing." Mum fluffed her hair as she

walked farther into the room. "Want a cup of cocoa? I'm going to make one before I climb into bed with a good book."

"Perfect. I'd love one." Cocoa was one of our favorite treats, and we made a game of trying new and creative additions to the hot drink. Peppermint and chocolate liqueur were two favorites. "It will be our first hot cocoa here in England." I'd seen a bottle of schnapps in the cupboard and I went to retrieve it.

"Sainsbury's had an organic fair-trade brand—what's this?" Mum was staring down at the note. "Where did this come from?"

Carrying the bottle, I joined her at the table. "It was taped to the front door. I thought maybe Clive left it."

Mum sat in a chair, or rather, collapsed as if boneless, the color draining out of her face. She picked up the note with shaking fingers.

"What is it, Mum?" I asked, alarmed. "What's wrong?"

She rested her head on her hand. "I wasn't ready for this."

I pulled out a chair and sat. "Please, tell me. You're scaring me."

Something in my voice must have penetrated her distress because she reached out and patted my arm. "I'm sorry, Molly. I've been working up my courage to tell you, but my brother beat me to it." She pointed at the note. "I'd know his handwriting anywhere. Plus he always signs as *C*, since he's always been teased about his name, Christopher Marlowe." Christopher Marlowe had been a playwright, one of Shakespeare's contemporaries.

"My brother." The implications took a second to sink in. "You mean I have an *uncle*?"

She pressed her lips together in a wan smile. "And an aunt. Janice. A cousin as well. Charlie is about your age. He works in the family thatching business with his dad. The Marlowes have been doing that almost as long as this bookshop."

"I have a cousin too?" My hands went up as I reared back in my seat. "Why did I never know about them?" Filled with angst that made it impossible to sit still, I got up and went to the cupboards, blindly opening and shutting doors as I searched for the cocoa. Mum had kept the existence of these relatives from me all my life. Well, except for a whisper here and there, an overheard conversation I didn't understand. I whirled around. "Dad knew, didn't he?"

Mum was studying the note, her finger tracing the letters. "Of course he did." Her face crumpled with pain. "He was the . . . um, 'inciting incident' as they say in novels." She rose from her chair. "Please, sit. I'll make cocoa and explain." Mum shared my habit of restlessness when facing difficult situations or conversations.

Unable to find the cocoa, which turned out to be sitting on the counter, I did as she said. Puck came over and crawled up into my lap, not seeming to mind when I began to pet him feverishly. My stomach knotted with anxiety as I waited for her explanation. Dad had been an only child, which meant I'd had no cousins or aunts and uncles growing up. And how I'd longed for a long holiday table surrounded by loving relatives, for the support of a tribe that always had your back.

"I don't know where to begin," Mum said with a dry laugh as she opened the fridge and pulled out a bottle of milk.

"I tried not to think about it—about them—for years." A drawer rattled as she jerked it open. "But maybe Chris's note is a good thing. Maybe he truly is sorry." She pulled out a measuring cup and filled it with milk.

"Did he do something to you?" I asked, pushing the words through my closed throat. My mind danced around the possibilities, as if dark shapes waited, jeering in the shadows.

Mum threw me a sharp glance. "No one laid a finger on me, if that's what you mean. But our family dynamic was far from healthy. Chris was the favorite, you see. I was the unwanted one."

Anguish tore at my heart. "No, Mum. That can't be true."

But she nodded, affirming that it was. "You know all those stories about changeling children? The ones the fairies bring and leave in the cot? My mother told me I was one of them, an imp sent to make her miserable."

Shocked, I sucked in a breath. "Mum, that's awful."

Mum shrugged. "I've come to realize that my mother was mentally ill. And I wasn't the easiest child—bright, inquisitive, unwilling to conform. But marrying your father and having you did a great deal to heal the wounds." Her skin pinked. "I know what love is. I'm very fortunate."

"So what's the deal with your brother? Did he think you were a changeling too?" My grandparents were both dead, but my resentment still had a target. Had Uncle Chris been the man lurking outside? So afraid to talk to his sister he'd resorted to leaving a note? A possible estrangement between my mother and grandparents must be what Persephone had been hinting about today at St. Hildegard's.

"Chris accepted the role of favorite, enjoyed it very much." Mum mixed spoonfuls of cocoa powder in a little milk. "And when he married Janice, well, the whole thing was written in stone. She's . . . not the nicest person, I'll just say that. So after I met your father and we went to the States, I basically cut them all off." She tapped her head. "It was vital for my mental health."

"I can see that." A new worry struck. "Being back here isn't upsetting you, is it?" Now I understood the magnitude of her sacrifice in moving to Cambridge. The risk that old wounds would be reopened.

"I'm fine." Mum measured sugar and added it to the pot. "I've been pondering whether or not I should get in touch with Chris. Now he's made the decision for me."

I stared at the note, tempted to crumple it up and toss it in the trash. "You don't have to do anything. Ignore it."

Mum selected a whisk from the crock and began to stir. "I might do that. I need to think a bit more."

"I wonder if Uncle Chris was the man I chased tonight." Puck mewed faintly as if annoyed by the mention of my rash action. If it had been him, what must he be thinking about his wild and crazy niece?

The whisk paused. "The man you chased? What are you talking about?"

I laughed. "That's why I asked if you heard me. There was a man lurking in the alley tonight. Like when we found Myrtle. I yelled at him and he took off. Stupidly, I chased him." I shook my head. What had I been thinking? "I found the note when I came to my senses and ran back to the shop."

Mum resumed stirring. "Sounds like it might have been Chris, then. But don't do that again. My nerves can't take it."

"Mine are pretty shot too." I thought back over the last couple of days and realized Mum and I hadn't really talked. We'd both been so busy, going in opposite directions most of the time. "Want to hear the latest about the murder case?"

Mum seized on the topic with interest, and as I hoped, it distracted her from her family woes. Over cocoa, I relayed what I'd learned so far, including Ollie's disclosures about Clive.

"As we thought," I concluded, "quite a few people had a motive to kill Myrtle. She tried and failed to blackmail Kieran. She tried to blackmail Ruth in the past, so maybe she made another attempt there. And there's some indication that she blackmailed Steve at the pub as well as Clive. Plus, I'd like to know more about her other friends, Persephone and Fiona. Persephone told me today that she hadn't known Myrtle very well. But we'll see. She might be lying." I bit my lip, holding back the poet's insinuations about our family. Mum didn't need to hear them.

"I doubt anyone is going to claim otherwise," Mum said. "Would you?"

"Honestly, no," I agreed with a laugh. "Anyway, we need to get back into Myrtle's flat and do a thorough search. Hopefully she kept some kind of record or other information about her targets."

"In addition to the family tree pointing to Aunt Violet, you mean?" Mum said with a rueful smile. "I sincerely hope

Inspector Ryan drops that line of inquiry." Her eyes flashed at the mention of the officer. "If he doesn't, I'll have to have a word."

"Go, Mum." As you can see, I come by my fiery temper honestly.

"Oh, by the way," Mum went on. "George came by tonight. We *can* get into her flat tomorrow. The police released it. Again."

"Good. I can't wait to go back inside." It had been frustrating to have our efforts stalled when we discovered the place had been ransacked. Hopefully the intruder hadn't removed the evidence we needed.

Mum sighed. "I'll be glad when the case is closed, as they say on television." She leaned forward. "On another topic, tell me about your night. I'm so glad you've found some young people to hang out with."

Over the rest of our cocoa, I gave her the highlights of my night and then, nice and relaxed and ready, we headed to bed. Before I went up, I grabbed Joan's journal, leaving the Wordsworth for Aunt Violet to appraise in the morning. As a favor to Daisy and her family, if they did want to sell, I planned to feature the book on social media.

Upstairs, I washed up and got into my nightgown, then climbed into bed with Puck and the leather-bound journal. The casement window was cracked enough for sweet evening air to filter in, and in the distance I could hear the murmur of traffic. Cambridge, like most cities, never really slept. But all was quiet in our little enclave.

I ran my fingers across the soft leather cover, strangely reluctant to begin reading. Inside were a young woman's private thoughts and dreams, written with the confidence that no one else would ever read them.

Only the fact that Joan's writings might shed light on Myrtle's murder convinced me to open the cover.

Joan Watson's journal

First day of term, St. Hildegard's, 1964

Alone. In my own room, sitting at a desk overlooking an incredible garden, the whole situation beyond my wildest dreams, and I can't write a blasted word. Not one.

It's so quiet here. Too quiet. I can't believe I'm saying this but I miss the thump of footsteps on the stairs and the twins shouting at each other. Mum hollering that dinner is on the table and get it while it's hot. Dad whistling to Sally, our sheepdog, before he goes out to check the flock before bed. Dear little Hazelhurst. I can't wait to visit you.

Maybe it's the weight of expectation that is stifling me. It's one thing to be in awe of and inspired by the greats who came before and another to have their superiority shoved in your face every instant. Theirs and that of the other students with their public school accents and smug smirks.

But a cat can look at a king, right? as my grandmother always said. And this little barn cat is going to do her best to shine. A lot of people have faith in me and I'm not going to let them down.

Someone is knocking at my door. I'd better answer.

•∤•

Later—The most incredible thing just happened. Persephone Brightwell, she of the illustrious literary lineage, invited me to a get-together. Oh, it was only six of us girls sitting around her room quaffing sherry, but it ended up being a hoot. Let me tell you about the cast of characters:

Persephone—already our Queen Bee, elegant, droll, lovely, a bit snobbish. Also a poet, and talk about a leg up—her father is famous.

Fiona—Old-school girl, the type who normally petrifies me with her hearty chip-chip-cheerio demeanor. But she's a big-eyed softie underneath all that.

Violet—Oh, sweet Violet. Bookish, kind—and extremely brilliant. Her family owns the legendary Thomas Marlowe bookshop. And judging by the cackles of the others, her brother is equally legendary.

Ruth—Steely ambition in a soft warm package, that's our Ruth. She's also quietly hilarious.

Myrtle—Ah. I hate to admit this, but I couldn't warm to Myrtle. She's the toadying type and I think P only invited her because she lives across the hall from me. And happened to be outside when we left. She also has a habit of watching everyone as though trying to catch them out in something. I don't trust her.

So Joan hadn't trusted Myrtle. And had thought Persephone was condescending, which she still was, judging by how she'd treated me today. How observant Joan had been. I loved her characterizations of the others, which made me *see* them, a group of bright young women on the brink of brilliant futures.

I closed the book and set it carefully on my nightstand, next to A. A. Milne. She'd given me enough to think about for tonight.

CHAPTER 12

We had unexpected visitors the next morning—Sir Jon and two police officers. I was in front of the AGA when they arrived, whipping up what Mum called my famous French toast. Thick slices of homemade white bread were dredged in beaten egg flavored with nutmeg and vanilla then fried in butter.

"Carry on, Molly," Aunt Violet said, her expression irked at the intrusion. But she politely asked the guests, "Tea? Or should I send Nina for coffee?"

Inspector Ryan placed his tablet and a manila folder on the table before shrugging out of his overcoat, which he hung on the back of a chair. "I'll take tea, thanks. How about you, Sergeant Adhikari?"

Sergeant Adhikari said, "Tea would be lovely, thank you." Trim in her uniform, she had inky hair and eyes and smooth bronze skin. She also carried a tablet.

"I can always drink another cup," Sir Jon said, rubbing his hands together. "It's a bit brisk this morning."

"Supposed to warm up later," Ryan said. He gave a slight shudder. "We can only hope."

When I pushed the full kettle onto the burner, I saw my hands were shaking. I clenched my fists to hopefully stop it. What were the police doing here so early? Were they going to arrest Aunt Violet? But if so, would they stop for tea first?

Maybe so, in England. Tea seemed to accompany every ritual.

I caught the French toast before it burned, flipping the slices over in haste. Aunt Violet came alongside me to retrieve the teapot and mugs from the cupboard. When I had a chance, I gave her a quick, covert hug. "It will be okay," I whispered, not sure of this in the slightest.

She nodded. "It will. Especially since my lawyer is here." She gave me a close-lipped smile. "Sir Jon is a barrister."

What couldn't the man do? In the United Kingdom, the legal system was slightly different than in the States. Barristers represented clients in court, while solicitors did everything but. How fortuitous that Sir Jon had stopped by this morning.

I slid the French toast onto a platter. Minding my manners, I asked the room at large, "Who would like French toast? We have real maple syrup." We'd brought a quart with us since it was very pricey here. England didn't have sugar maple trees, the way New England did.

Sergeant Adhikari looked interested and her face fell when Inspector Ryan said, "None for us, thank you. But please, go ahead with breakfast."

"I'll take a couple of pieces, Molly," Sir Jon said, his eyes twinkling. "You had me at maple syrup."

"If only I'd known it was that easy," Aunt Violet joked. She placed tea bags in the pot and added boiling water.

Her bustling movements pouring and serving tea occupied the next couple of minutes. I gave Sir Jon the first golden pieces, then dredged two more slices in the egg mixture and put them in the pan. Not that I was still hungry, but it gave me something to do.

Mum came down the stairs and popped into the kitchen. "Oh," she said. "I didn't know we had guests." She looked fresh and lovely in a slim linen skirt and sleeveless blouse, and Inspector Ryan definitely noticed. I didn't see a wedding band on his finger but that didn't mean he wasn't committed.

Oh, stop it Molly. He's probably here because he thinks your aunt is a killer.

"Please join us, Nina," Aunt Violet said, waving at an empty chair. "They haven't started the inquisition yet."

"All right." Mum sounded doubtful but she took a seat across from the officers. Sir Jon was at one end of the table, and Aunt Violet's seat was at the other.

I pointed at the pan and then Sir Jon's already decimated plate, raising my brows in question. Mum nodded and smiled. Good. She could have this batch.

"Thank you for the tea, Miss Marlowe," Inspector Ryan said, his voice oddly formal. "We do have a few more questions for you, so is there a place we can speak?"

"Right here is fine." Aunt Violet set her jaw. She picked up her mug with both hands and drank.

Inspector Ryan frowned. "I'm not sure—"

Aunt Violet set the mug down with a clank. "Sir Jon is representing me." Sir Jon's brows rose but he didn't object as he continued to shovel in French toast. "And Molly and Nina are my family. I have no secrets from them. So, unless you're arresting me . . ."

Ryan slid a glance at his companion. "Er, no. We are not." He shifted in his seat, uncomfortable. "We'll proceed then." After a moment to gather his thoughts, he went on. "About that family tree we discovered in Myrtle's flat."

Pushing aside her tea, the sergeant began to take notes on her tablet.

"What about it?" Aunt Violet sounded unconcerned but from behind, I saw her shoulders stiffen.

Inspector Ryan tapped a finger on the table. "According to the tree, her direct ancestor Thomas Marlowe was the oldest son in the family at that time. Why didn't the bookshop come down his—and eventually Myrtle's—line?"

"There was a will," Aunt Violet said. "And that document left the property to my direct ancestor, Samuel."

Sir Jon wiped his lips with a napkin then raised a hand. "If I may." After he had their attention, he said, "The 1540 statute of wills allowed property holders to designate heirs instead of entailing the property to the oldest male. A will would render Thomas's claim and that of any descendant null and void."

Ryan took that in. "Can we see a copy of the will?"

Aunt Violet, who had relaxed slightly, now sat up ramrod straight. "I'm sorry, but the will has been misplaced." She scoffed. "We're talking three hundred years ago or so about a three-hundred-year-old document, Inspector. Do you have family papers of that vintage kicking around?"

The inspector's smile was grim. "My ancestors were Irish peasants living in a leased cottage." Adhikari elbowed him. "But that's neither here nor there. Our concern is that the late Myrtle Marsh planned to challenge you for ownership of this property." Unspoken was the conclusion that Aunt Violet might have killed to prevent this.

Sir Jon opened his mouth as though to say something, but then his lips clamped shut. He took out his phone and began to search.

"But she didn't." Aunt Violet adjusted her glasses as if taking a closer look at what the inspector was proposing. "And she never even raised the subject with me. So isn't your theory merely speculative?"

Ryan frowned as he flipped open the folder. "She never emailed you?"

Aunt Violet shook her head. "No. At least I don't think so . . . maybe it went to spam." Aunt Violet wasn't a fan of computers. She only used her old, clunky computer for on-line bookshop transactions and communicating with customers and dealers.

The officer extracted a piece of paper and slid it across the table to Aunt Violet. "You never got this?" His tone was heavy with suspicion.

Her headshake was firm. "I did not. She picked up the page and read aloud, "'Dear Violet, I heard something very interesting the other day. Is it true that Best Books is buying the shop? We need to talk. I've stood by my whole life, watching while your branch of the family ran the place into the ground. You're not cutting out a legitimate heir this time. Myrtle.'" The page fluttered out of her fingers and onto the floor. I bent to scoop it up.

My aunt's complexion was chalky, almost bloodless. "I never got this. I swear to you."

"What an awful woman," Mum said. In contrast to Aunt Violet, Mum's cheeks were flushed with color, a sure sign that her temper was on the rise. "She was sending nasty notes while pretending to help us boost shop sales." She turned to Inspector Ryan. "Myrtle asked Persephone Brightwell to come do the reading. It was her idea."

I believed Aunt Violet, especially because she never would have accepted Myrtle's help, or allowed her into the house for that matter, if she'd received this not-so-veiled threat. Had the email gone to spam or . . . I studied the "to" address, which didn't look quite right. "Aunt Violet, what is your email address?" She recited it. "Well, there you go." I slapped the page down on the table in triumph. "Myrtle had the wrong address. This message never got to my aunt."

Aunt Violet grabbed the page again. "Molly is right. She spelled my email address wrong. The right one is on the shop website—if you don't believe me."

Sergeant Adhikari searched on her tablet, then showed Ryan the screen. "She's correct, Inspector. Miss Marsh made a mistake."

"I'd still like to check your computer," Inspector Ryan said. "We can get a warrant if necessary."

"Go ahead and look," Aunt Violet said airily. "I have no secrets." She rose from her chair. "Why don't we take a peek right now?"

Sir Jon jumped up. "Hold on, Violet. As your counselor, I want to be sure everything is handled correctly." To Inspector Ryan, he said, "I think you'd better get that warrant." His smile was wintry. "Although I'm not sure a judge will award it."

Inspector Ryan took the email back and tucked it into the folder. The tips of his ears were red but despite that telltale sign of stress, he appeared calm, resigned, even. "We'll be in touch," he said. "Ready, Sergeant?"

After they left, shown to the door by Mum, a calm descended on the kitchen, rather like that after a sudden and violet storm sweeps through. We were battered and disheveled but more or less intact.

When Mum returned, I served her a plate of French toast. "I can make more," I told Sir Jon who had demolished his.

"No, thanks, Molly. I'd better not." He examined his mug. "I wouldn't say no to a splash more tea though."

"Pass your mug," Aunt Violet said, feeling the side of the teapot under its cozy. "This is still hot."

Without being asked, I put the kettle back on, certain that more pots of tea were in the offing. My appetite had returned, so I dipped two more slices of bread into the egg mixture and placed them in the sizzling pan.

"There is something I need to bring up," Sir Jon said. "About the will. Do you think you can lay hands on it?"

"I don't know," Aunt Violet said. "Tom had it, last I knew. It's been years since I've seen it."

"Why do we need the will, Sir Jon?" Mum asked. "Surely after three hundred years there can be no question that Aunt Violet's branch of the family owns the shop."

He hesitated. "Until the new land registration act was passed in 2003, I'd say that was true. Before it went through, an owner had twelve years to dispute possession. After that, he was out of luck."

"We are way beyond twelve years." Aunt Violet gave a snort. "Plus, we were never *squatters*."

Although she was right, the mention of a change in the law alarmed me. "What does the new law say?" I asked.

Sir Jon exhaled, his expression troubled. "Basically that someone taking possession needs to petition the rightful owner, giving notice that registration of title will be transferring to the new resident should the owner not object. There have been many, many cases where someone moved onto land or into an abandoned house and, after the twelve years, was considered the rightful owner. The new law tried to close that loophole."

"But why would Violet petition anyone?" Mum argued. "As far as she knows, she has always been the rightful owner."

Sir Jon pursed his lips. "Therein lies the trap, I'm afraid. Violet would probably win a case due to the longevity of her family line owning and running the shop. However, Myrtle could have made life very, very difficult with a challenge."

"Not to mention the bad publicity," Mum said. "I can see the headlines now. 'Heirs battle over Cambridge's oldest bookshop. "We were cheated," Myrtle Marsh asserts.'"

"She probably wanted money to make it go away." I flipped the perfectly browned, eggy French toast over. "That was always her game, it seems." I thought of something else.

"Don't they record wills in a probate court here? They do in the States. Maybe we can get a copy that way."

Sir Jon, who seemed to know his inheritance law, explained. "Until 1858, wills were almost always recorded in church courts along with baptisms, marriages, and deaths. The problem is, there are many gaps in the parish records for all kinds of reasons. I'm guessing Myrtle already checked for the will before concocting this scheme."

"That sounds like her." The kettle had boiled, so Aunt Violet got up to make a fresh pot of tea. "She held a research position at the University, so she was pretty much an expert at digging into historical records."

And no doubt this skill had served her well in her blackmail schemes. If she had only used her abilities for good, we probably wouldn't be investigating her murder.

•◆•

Later that morning, George met the search team—Sir Jon, Mum, and me—at the door of his building. Aunt Violet had begged off, making the point that as the "lead suspect," as she put it, she'd better stay out of the victim's home.

"You're looking sharp, George," I said as I entered the foyer. He wore a crisp white shirt and tie with tweed trousers pressed to a knife-edge crease.

"I've been to the solicitor's this morning, haven't I?" He ushered us toward the stairs. "To my great surprise, he told me that Myrtle made me executor of her will." His headshake was bemused. "Not only did the old girl include provision to pay me any back rent, the rest of her estate will fund a scholarship at St. Hildegard's. For young women from Hazelhurst, specifically. Odd, really, since Myrtle came from King's Lynn."

Mum was from Hazelhurst. And so was Joan Watson, I remembered with a start. Why had Myrtle chosen that particular village? Grief . . . or guilt?

"How generous of her," Mum said, leading the way up the staircase, a tote holding our supplies slung over one arm. We were much better prepared this time, thanks to Sir Jon.

"I was a bit taken aback, I don't mind telling you." George pulled a key ring out of his pocket and unlocked Myrtle's door. "I had no idea about any of it." He pushed the door open. "Here we are."

I entered first, noticing a stack of flat boxes against one wall. Although the place was still a shambles, the spilled flour and sugar and broken glass had been swept up. "You've made some progress," I said to George.

He gave a grunt. "A little. Not only is it my job to pack everything up, I need to dispose of it. I might be renting a booth at the market." He laughed to show he was joking. Myrtle's artwork and furniture were far too valuable for that approach.

"When my parents died," Sir Jon said, "we used a firm to handle everything. They come in and appraise, then sell whatever you want them to handle. I can give you their contact information."

"I might take you up on that," George said. "This is all a bit overwhelming."

"We can help sort as we go," I said. "Put aside anything we think might be valuable, at least." I pointed at the shelves.

"She had some good books, I noticed last time." With Aunt Violet under suspicion, we wouldn't sell them, but maybe Sir Jon could.

"And I'll pack her clothes," Mum said, which was a really valiant offer. "Those will either be donated or tossed, I assume."

"Would you?" George's eyes lit up. "I really didn't want to go near her . . . her unmentionables." He folded a couple of boxes, sealing the seams with packing tape, and set them on the carpet. "Here you go, lass."

"Thanks," Mum said. "All right, Sir Jon. Point us in the right direction." She pulled pairs of disposable gloves out of the tote and passed them around. "I brought these, as you suggested."

Sir Jon had been strolling around the room, taking everything in. He pointed at the desk stacked with papers and folders, an empty rectangle revealing where Myrtle's computer had been. "Why don't you look through the desk, George? The police probably took her bank books and the like, but as executor, it makes sense for you to be the one searching that area."

"Absolutely," George said, moving in that direction. "Today's a good a time as any." He settled in the desk chair and put on a pair of gloves.

Sir Jon smoothed the fingers of his gloves. "These might be overkill, since the police have dusted twice. But I prefer not to muddy the waters, so to speak, with my paw prints."

"I don't think we left any last time," I said, chagrined we hadn't thought of gloves then. "We didn't get far, though. Not after seeing the family tree taped to the wall."

We all looked at the spot over the desk, where only a stray piece of tape remained.

"I wish I knew who got in here," George said. "Sleeping on the job, I was."

Mum tugged at her glove cuffs. "This is uncharted territory for all of us. Well, except you, Sir Jon."

George perked up. "Fast cars, pretty girls, and the like, I imagine."

Sir Jon laughed. "It wasn't *exactly* like a James Bond movie, I promise you." His gaze was thoughtful. "Although there was that one time in Paris when I found my contact dead." He shook himself. "But that's a story for another day. Let's get to work."

I flexed my fingers, eager to begin. "Any tips?"

The former secret agent pivoted on his heel, taking it all in. "Do you have your phone, Molly?"

"Of course." I extracted it from my jeans pocket. This was exciting. I felt like a real investigator.

"Take pictures of everything in this room before we begin." He followed me around as I photographed the bookshelves, the furniture, and the ornaments on the mantel. He checked the shots, making sure they were all clear. "Good. Now we have these for reference, should they be needed later."

He told George and Mum to do the same in their area before they started searching. "What I've found is key is to look for anomalies, whatever doesn't belong. And patterns. Habits. Trust your instincts." He gestured, encompassing the room. "This place looks like any flat owned by a harmless older woman, right? But she had secrets. Most of us do. We're in search of those secrets."

And evidence of her crimes.

My assignment was the bookcases. Thinking about what Sir Jon had said, I stood back and scanned the shelves. Books, books, and more books. A figurine or two. The box for the internet and wall-mounted television.

A dozen black videotape boxes lined up on the bottom shelf. *Wait a minute.* Myrtle didn't own a VHS player or even a DVD unit. So why would she keep movies in an out-dated format?

I practically ran to the shelves and pulled out a box at random. A handwritten page in the sleeve read "As Time Goes By." I remembered that show, a wonderful sitcom starring Judi Dench and Geoffrey Palmer as reunited lovers. Holding my breath, I pried the box open.

Banknotes fluttered onto the rug like a shower of money. Followed by a photograph of my aunt's friend Fiona Fosdyke locked in an embrace with Uncle Tom. It was dated two years ago.

"Look at this." Holding the photograph, I stood in the middle of the scattered money. Even at a glance, there looked to be thousands of pounds.

"Fiona and Tom," Sir Jon said. "Well, well, what do you know?" He waved the picture. "They were very much an item in the old days. Before Fiona married Gregory."

George took a look. "And she's still married to him, far as I know." He peered more closely at the picture. "That looks like Tom's house." He passed it along to Mum, who studied it with interest.

I crouched down and started picking up the banknotes. So Fiona and Tom had reconnected after decades apart—

like the characters in As Time Goes By. With Fiona's high-profile job and husband, that made her a perfect target for blackmail.

"You found this in a video case?" Sir Jon asked. "I wonder what's in the others?"

"Me too." I sat all the way down on the carpet and pulled out another box. "This one is labeled This Old House. Huh." I pried the case open and, lo and behold, it was also filled with money. This time I didn't spill the bundles but gently removed them and set the box on the carpet. Underneath the money was a photograph of Clive—talking to another middle-aged man in what appeared to be a building site.

"Can anyone figure this out?" I handed the picture to Sir Jon, who held it so George could also see.

"Oh ho," George said with a chortle. "I recognize that chap." He said the name. "He works for the city, in the enforcement department."

From my seat, I looked up at them. "Proof of bribes, like Kieran said?"

"Maybe so," Sir Jon mused. "I wouldn't want to be Clive when Inspector Ryan questions him."

"We now have motives for two solid suspects," I said. "It looks to me like Myrtle was blackmailing Clive and Fiona." Hopefully our discovery would turn Inspector Ryan's efforts away from Aunt Violet and George.

"Did Clive attend the reading?" Sir Jon asked abruptly.

Mum and I looked at each other. "I didn't see him," I said. There was no way I would have missed him. He was too loud and arrogant.

"I was in London that day, got back to Cambridge around

six." His expression was rueful. "That's why I was late to the reading. Went home, cleaned up, et cetera first. But anyway, I'm pretty sure I saw Clive at the train station, sitting in one of the pubs."

"So he might be guilty," I said. "If the timing works." Did Clive meet Myrtle before the reading—or even during—and kill her?

"It's a possibility," Sir Jon said. "I'll mention it to the police."

Mum helped me open the rest of the cases, most of which held only money, although a few included cryptic handwritten notes. But the case labeled Midsomer Murders contained something I certainly didn't expect to see. A yellowed newspaper clipping of Joan Watson's obituary.

Judging by Fiona and Clive's videotape cases, Myrtle's labels were sly jokes. What did this one mean? Had Joan Watson been murdered?

CHAPTER 13

❧

"Hey, everyone," I said, waving the clipping. "Myrtle thought Joan Watson was murdered. Or that there was something fishy about her death," I qualified. "But either way, someone paid her to keep quiet, looks like."

"Hold on," George said. "What are you talking about? Who is Joan Watson?"

Sir Jon stood with fists lightly clenched, a faraway look in his eyes. "Joan was at St. Hildegard's with Violet and the others. A lovely girl, I remember. Quiet but so bright. She committed suicide in her first year." He rubbed a hand over his face. "Or so the coroner ruled. Sedatives mixed with wine."

"She was Daisy's great-aunt," I said. "And she grew up in Hazelhurst. "Remember that scholarship, George? Maybe Myrtle created it in honor of Joan."

George nodded slowly, light dawning across his broad

face. "Oh, I see. Myrtle thought her friend was killed and that's why she wanted to start the scholarship. To rub it in their faces, like."

"But I don't understand why she didn't go to the police," Mum said. "I mean, I know she was a greedy old thing, but surely she wouldn't let a killer go free."

"Good point, Mum." My mind turned over the situation, trying to see it from Myrtle's viewpoint. "Maybe she couldn't quite prove who killed her. Maybe there wasn't enough evidence. And she held that over the person's head anyway."

"That could be," Mum said. "Even being accused can ruin someone's life."

There was a pause as we all considered Aunt Violet and George's situation.

"We need to know more about Joan's death," I said. "How did she die? Who discovered her? And so on."

Sir Jon had begun to pace, moving back and forth with his hands clasped behind his back. He halted in the middle of the rug. "I'll make a few calls, find out who worked the case. We might be able to get those questions answered."

"We could also talk to Daisy's family," I said. "See what they remember." I winced at the thought of intruding on their grief. "Although I hate to reopen old wounds if we don't have to."

"We'll play that by ear." Sir Jon swept his hand over the videotape cases, the money, and the newspaper clipping. "I'll show all this to Inspector Ryan, but otherwise, let's keep it to ourselves. Especially the case with Joan's obituary." His expression was grim. "If she was murdered, the last thing we want to do is tip off the killer."

A thought struck me. Was it possible that Myrtle's murder was connected to Joan's death? Maybe the killer had gotten tired of being blackmailed.

•◦•

"Are you sure you'll be all right?" Aunt Violet asked me for the third time. She and Mum were headed out for a spot of shopping and a late lunch, so I was going to be in charge of the bookshop while they were gone.

I waved away her concern. "I'll be fine." This was the first time I'd actually run the shop on my own and I was looking forward to it. Although I was rather weak when it came to book appraisals. I didn't know nearly enough to do that successfully yet. And I was totally incapable of driving a hard bargain as well. I prayed no one would try to negotiate today. So as long as customers came in and bought books for the listed price, I was all set.

"If it's slow," I continued, "I plan to start sorting through Uncle Tom's books." A couple of cardboard boxes sat behind the desk, ready for me to excavate.

Aunt Violet eyed the boxes with a sigh. "Thank you, Molly. I can't believe I put it off for so long. Maybe you'll find a treasure or two."

"That's what I'm hoping." But even if the books weren't especially valuable, I would enjoy leafing through old favorites.

Mum joined Aunt Violet at the desk, pretty in a sundress and fragrant with English lavender perfume. She thanked me as well. "I've been longing for a day off to browse through the shops. I haven't been to Marks and Spencer for ages."

"I hope you find lots of good stuff," I said. "Have fun."

"We'll bring you lunch," Mum promised as they left the shop. The door shut behind them with a jingle and I was alone. Well, except for two cats. Clarence was in his usual window and Puck was perched on top of a bookcase, looming over me like a gargoyle—a cute one, if there is such a thing.

Although work called me—adding books to the online inventory, updating social media, looking through Tom's boxes—I sat quietly for a few minutes just absorbing the shop's atmosphere. The ancient building settled around me, a tick here, a creak there. Outside the big windows, pigeons swooped down and strutted on the cobblestones.

I was cocooned by books, hemmed in by rows and stacks of volumes on bookshelves and tables. More than I could ever read in a lifetime. I could dip in and out of these books for a hundred years, sipping knowledge, imagination, beauty.

Oh, how I loved this place. I'd willingly spend the rest of my life here, puttering around with books.

Then my Puritan work ethic clicked in. *Time to get to work.* I flipped open my laptop and logged onto the internet, planning to check on the store pages and maybe create a new post for the shop. In the classic time-delaying tactic, I checked my social media first, following a couple of rabbit holes that presented themselves on friends' pages. After dragging myself away, I snapped pictures of Puck and Clarence and wrote posts about our adorable shop cats. Likes appeared almost immediately.

Tempted by a new idea, my fingers hovered over the search bar. Was my uncle on social media? I typed in his name and got a number of results, mostly from the United States. Not knowing the thatching company name, I typed in "thatching" and "Hazelhurst," and found a company called Shire Thatch with an address in Hazelhurst, but there were no pictures of my uncle on Shire's website, only a few generic shots of buff young men working on thatched roofs.

Hmm. How about Janice, his wife? A Janice Patterson Marlowe from Hazelhurst featured a profile picture of a Yorkshire terrier on her page. The rest of her page was locked down, no public information, pictures, or friends. *Darn.*

But there was more than one way to track someone down. Refusing to be denied, I typed her name and location in a search engine and watched as results loaded up.

Here we go. The local newspaper had an article about the annual meeting of the garden club at Hazelhurst House.

I clicked on the link, rewarded by a photograph of a dozen women sitting at a table under a vine-shaded pergola. The caption informed me that the dark-haired woman at the head of the table was Lady Asha Scott, the hostess. Kieran's mother, I realized with a burst of excitement. So the Scotts lived in Hazelhurst. I put a pin in that and studied the other faces, mostly middle-aged women. They weren't labeled, so I couldn't tell which one was my aunt. She was mentioned in the article as the new president of the club.

Studying the photo more closely, I decided my money was on the smug blonde cuddled up to Asha. That made sense, both due to her position in the club and how Mum had described her. Resentment began to burn in my chest. Did I really want to meet the people who had been so hateful to Mum? I was repelled—and curious, I had to admit. But no matter what, I wouldn't do anything that might hurt my mother.

The bells over the door jingled and Kieran walked in. My heart leaped, a reaction echoed by Puck, who chirped and thumped down from his perch before bolting to greet Kieran. Closing the laptop quickly, I stood up, relieved he hadn't caught me checking out his mother's garden club meeting. Even though it was my aunt I was interested in. "Hey," I said when he got closer to the desk. "What brings you here?"

His steps stuttered as if he wasn't sure himself. "Uh, I had a few minutes free so I thought I'd stop in to say hello." He glanced down to where Puck was winding around his jeans-clad legs. "What's up, Puck?" He scooped up the cat and began to rub his chin. "Who's the best cat-patter in the whole world, huh?"

I sincerely doubted he'd come to visit my cat but I waited patiently for their bromance to play out. Over in the window, Clarence grunted and turned his back on the proceedings. *I get it*, I told him telepathically.

Kieran finally released Puck and brushed at the cat hair on his T-shirt and jeans.

"The downside of a black cat," I said. "Even if he is short-haired."

He took a step closer, his eyes fastened on my face. After swallowing a couple of times, he asked, "I was wondering if

you'd like to go to dinner with me. Sometime. If you're free."
His expression became pained, probably because he heard
his voice shake a trifle. "The Holly and Ivy up the street is
quite good. Asian-French fusion."

"Oh, really?" How lame. I sucked in a breath, ordering my
heart to stop hammering. "I'd love to try Asian-French fusion." Whatever that was. "We didn't have much of that in
Vermont."

"I suppose not," he said. He pulled out his phone. "So
how about Saturday?" He winced. "I know that isn't much
notice."

Two days from now, so no, it wasn't. But I didn't care. I
pretended to check my calendar. "Let me see . . . yes, I can
do that. What time?"

"Um." He rolled in his lips, thinking. "Eight? I'll make a
reservation right now." His fingers flew over the screen. "All
set." He tucked his phone into his pocket.

I have a date with Kieran. I managed to stay cool. "I'm
looking forward to it."

Now that the ordeal was over, he appeared much more relaxed. "What else is new? Anything about Myrtle?"

"Come sit," I suggested, sitting again and patting the chair
next to me. "And I'll tell you."

He settled behind the desk, traitorous Puck immediately
seeking his lap.

"Well, I never." I pretended to be offended. "Did you
forget who took you in from the cold? Who feeds you?"
Puck's response was to stretch a paw out to my knee and
rest it there—while staying firmly on Kieran's lap. We both
laughed.

Kieran looked around, as if making sure we were alone. "So, what's the latest?"

Where to begin? Sir Jon had warned us to keep what we'd found confidential, but surely that didn't include Kieran or Daisy. They were on our team. But in the interest of keeping specific clues close to the vest, I decided to stay vague. The fewer people who knew everything, the better.

"Probably the biggest news is that we went over to Myrtle's flat this morning to take another look around," I said. "Oh, and get this. George is her executor, which made me feel much less guilty about snooping."

He listened intently as, without too many details, I told him we'd found evidence related to Myrtle's blackmail schemes. I didn't mention Joan's obituary since I wasn't quite sure how to broach that subject with Daisy, and she deserved to hear it first. And we needed to know more, to find out if it really was murder. After all, Myrtle could have been wrong, although the money she collected said otherwise.

"We called the police, of course," I went on. "But we did take pictures of everything for our own purposes first. Inspector Ryan wasn't very happy about us being there but what could he say? George has a right to look at everything Myrtle owned. But probably the main reason is that he's leaning toward Aunt Violet as a suspect—wrongly. He came over this morning to question her about Myrtle's Marlowe family tree."

"Myrtle had a Marlowe family tree?" Kieran asked. "What was that about?"

I explained that Myrtle was actually a distant cousin

since our families had been connected centuries ago and, if she'd had her way, the so-called rightful owner of the bookshop.

"You're kidding." Kieran's eyes were wide. "I mean, that's horrible. And why now?" Understanding dawned on his face. "Oh, I get it. With Clive going after Best Books, Myrtle thought there would be a big payday."

"Exactly. Or she would have pulled that trick before, right?" After hesitating, I decided to continue my confidences, this time with something even more personal. "Speaking of unknown relatives, I learned last night that I have an uncle. My mother's brother. And an aunt, his wife. I think she knows your mother. They're both in the Hazelhurst garden club."

Kieran put a hand to his head, playing up how amazed he was. "When I asked you what was going on, I didn't expect this barrage of news." He squinted in confusion. "Didn't I just see you last night?"

"A lot can happen in a day, I guess. Even in a quiet little bookshop." I opened my laptop and brought up the article about the garden club. Now that I'd raised the topic, I felt comfortable showing it to him. "I found this while searching for my aunt. There's your mother hosting the club."

Kieran bent close to study the picture. "That's our garden all right. I don't know which one is your aunt, though." He gave me a sly smile. "I always avoided Mum's club gatherings like the plague when I was growing up. All those twittering women. Plus they loved pinching my cheeks."

"I'll bet." I could imagine Kieran as a small boy, all big brown eyes and a mop of curls. "Anyway, hopefully I'll meet my uncle and the rest of the family soon. Although I don't have high hopes that we'll be close. They didn't treat Mum very well."

"I'm sorry to hear that." His mouth twisted with dismay. "Families. The best of times and the worst of times." Kieran was cleverly misquoting a famous Dickens novel, *A Tale of Two Cities*.

"We have a copy of that around here somewhere," I joked, glancing around with a laugh. The bells above the door jingled and a group of young women pushed inside. I sighed. "This has been nice but . . ."

Kieran gently moved Puck's paw and stood. "I should get back anyway." He smiled down at me. "See you later." He strode to the exit, earning glances of appreciation from the new customers. One even peered out the window until he was out of sight.

"You know who that was, don't you?" Although her friend was speaking behind her hand, her voice carried easily to my ears. The foursome clustered together and began to chat in low voices.

"Let me know if I can help," I called from the desk when they finished their confab. "Oh, and Kieran owns the bike shop next door if any of you are in the market."

"Maybe not for a bike," the cheekiest one said. They burst into laughter.

So this was how it would be dating Kieran Scott. I could handle it, I decided. I felt that thrill again. *He asked me out to dinner.* A new panic—what was I going to wear? But when one of the women asked me where to find Dodie Smith's *I*

Capture the Castle, I put that delicious subject aside until later.

An hour or so later, the shop quieted again. After making a reviving cup of tea—I had the habit now, no doubt—I went to work sorting the children's books.

Oh, what a trove of delights. In the first box, I found a complete set of L. Frank Baum's Oz series, which included fourteen books. Most people only knew about *The Wonderful Wizard of Oz*, since the classic was the basis for the iconic movie starring Judy Garland and her sparkly red shoes.

Wondering how much they were worth, I logged on and did a search. Not bad. They weren't in perfect condition but would fetch a respectable price. A full, perfect set generally sold for north of fifty thousand dollars.

If we could bear to part with these beauties, the proceeds would knock a big dent in Aunt Violet's debt to Clive. Rather than return them to the box, I unlocked the case holding especially valuable books and stored them in there.

The second box held a random assortment of older children's books, including *At the Back of the North Wind* by George MacDonald, a nicely illustrated *Alice in Wonderland*, and the very charming *The Brownies: Their Book*, by Palmer Cox.

The last volume in the box was much newer but no less wonderful. *The Strawberry Girls*, it was called, written and illustrated by Iona York. Calling to mind the *Flower Fairies* and *Brambly Hedge*, the pictures were magical. But the tale was long and intricate, leading the tiny sisters on a dangerous quest through a mysterious forest. Iona York lived in

Cambridgeshire, the biography said, and she had written the book for her daughters Poppy and Rose, the original, "Strawberry Girls."

How cool. I put that book aside to read more slowly later. It was a story to be savored.

The schoolhouse clock on the wall rang the hour. Three o'clock. Mum and Aunt Violet would probably be back soon. I stood up and walked around to stretch my legs, then stepped out of the shop into the lane.

As often happened in the afternoon, we were in a lull, although up on Trinity Street, foot traffic and bicycles passed in a constant stream. Since customers arrived in bunches, I was pretty sure we would be busy again soon.

My gaze fell on Joan's journal, which I'd brought downstairs, thinking I might have time to read between customers. Picking it up, I settled in an ancient leather armchair nestled in a nook but with a good view of the door.

Had Joan been murdered? I wondered as I opened the cover. If so, would I find clues within these pages?

Joan Watson's journal

An evening out.
Two in the wee hours has just struck on the quadrangle clock, and beyond my window, crickets chirp in the warm evening air.
I'm falling in love.
There. I've said it. Admitted the ridiculous truth.
But let me take a step back first. Persephone is responsible for it all, of course. She and Tom Marlowe

cooked up an excursion to the Cellar, a club located in an obscure little alley. But they both swore that the music was top notch and that we'd dance the night away.

After she let me borrow one of her new Mary Quant miniskirts, how could I say no? Feeling delightfully underdressed in my short skirt, especially with my long legs, I joined the other girls in Persephone's room for a drink before we went out. Fiona, Violet, Ruth, and Myrtle were there, along with Ruth's new friend, Catherine. What a lovely group we were, dressed to the nines, wearing far more makeup than usual and with our hair teased and curled.

After we were nicely tipsy, we put our coats on and went to meet Tom. He had two friends with him, Jon Parrish and Gregory Fosdyke. Tom and Jon were quite the live wires, keeping us entertained with quips, snatches of song, and even a skit or two as we walked through the streets to the club.

Fiona glued herself to Tom but everyone flirted with Jon. Except me. I ended up walking at the rear with Gregory. Although he was quieter than the others, he seemed solid and kind. Quite nice really. So different than the cloddish boys I grew up with in Hazelhurst.

That was my initial thought. A young man I could share my observations with. Could talk to about my classes and the poetry I was trying to write.

Not that Gregory is a writer too. No, he's much more serious, planning to study law and follow his father's footsteps into Parliament.

The club was a shabby hole in the wall, the kind of place mothers warn daughters never to go to. Whenever the door opened, snatches of catchy music escaped, and a poster announced a rhythm and blues band.

We girls exchanged excited looks. This was much different than sing-alongs at the pub or even the typical dance where we did the foxtrot and waltzed.

Inside, the club was dark and dingy and tightly packed. The music made me want to dance and after a pint (or two) I did. Mostly with Gregory, although a few numbers with Jon or Tom and then a random bloke or two.

My head was awhirl and my legs loose when we finally left, Gregory with his arm around my shoulder in a most proprietary way. Somehow we got separated from the others and ended up taking the long way home, through the quiet Cambridge streets, lingering on a bridge over the river, talking about all kinds of things. Laughing. Sharing confidences. He told me that his family was pushing Fiona on him, which sounded terribly feudal. The two families had long been allied. But he was resisting the match and so was she. That was obvious, judging by the way she clung to Tom.

At the gate, we said good night—and then he kissed me.

Sigh. There will be sweet dreams tonight.

CHAPTER 14

I was falling in love myself—with Joan Watson. Her journal took me back to 1960s Cambridge, to the unfolding of a blossoming young life.

One that had been cut far too short. So far, I had to admit, I didn't see any signs that Joan was depressed or suicidal. Yes, she was a little homesick, but who wasn't the first few weeks at college? I remember calling home one weekend early in my freshman year. The few people I knew were out doing something and I was alone in my dorm room. My parents were out too—rare for them—so I'd left a pretty forlorn message on voice mail. I still face-palmed myself at the cringe-worthy memory.

Mum and Aunt Violet entered the shop laden with bags and talking a mile a minute. Looking around, they spotted me in the chair. "There you are," Aunt Violet said as she dumped her bags behind the desk. "How did it go?"

I got up from the chair, eager to see their finds. "Great," I said, carrying the journal with me. "I made a few sales, but more exciting, I found a full set of Oz books in Tom's boxes. All firsts and in pretty good condition, so I put them in the locked case." I mentioned my off-the-cuff appraisal amount. "You'll have to fine-tune that, Aunt Violet."

She glanced up at the shelf where I'd put the collection. "That rascal. He told me he had some valuable books, but I honestly had no idea." She slid out of her light jacket and hung it over the back of a chair. "Be right back. I'm going to put the kettle on."

"What good news," Mum said to me after Aunt Violet bustled away toward the kitchen. "Selling those books will pay down a good chunk of Clive's loan."

"That's what I thought." I placed the journal next to my laptop. "And guess what, Mum? Kieran came by and asked me out to dinner." I couldn't restrain a giggle. "Of course I said yes."

"Maybe I should leave the shop more often," Mum said with a smile. "A lot happened while I was gone."

"I know. It's crazy." I hugged myself, thrilled that I had a real dinner date to look forward to. It had been far too long. Many men in Vermont thought watching sports and eating at the bar was a stellar night out. "I'm going to need something to wear."

"We can work on that." Mum indicated the bags. "I scoped out some really good shops."

I sat at the desk. "Show me."

While we waited for Aunt Violet to return with tea, Mum displayed her purchases. She'd bought a couple of lightweight pastel cardigans, a floral summer dress, and a slew of cosmetics and beauty products.

"These took me back," she said, unrolling a lipstick to show me the color. "Such a treat to go to Boots and buy a new lipstick."

"I've been wanting to go there but haven't had a chance. When we go shopping for my new outfit?" I suggested. "Kieran is taking me to the Holly and Ivy, which is apparently quite fancy."

Mum eyed me speculatively. "You need a little black dress. And I know just the boutique."

I loved the idea of me, a low-key librarian and wearer of much plaid flannel, rocking a little black dress. Kieran wouldn't know what hit him, which was the point, right?

Aunt Violet returned with a tray holding three mugs. "Here we are." As she passed them around, her gaze fell on the journal. "What's that, Molly?"

I picked up my mug and sipped. "It's Joan Watson's journal."

"The woman Myrtle thought was murdered?" Mum asked.

Aunt Violet sat down heavily. "What? How do you figure that, Nina?"

Apparently Mum hadn't given Aunt Violet the update during their shopping trip. "She had Joan's obituary clipping in a video box labeled Midsomer Murders," I said. "We kind of put two and two together." I explained our reasoning. Pointing at the journal, I added, "And I have to tell you, reading this, I don't see her committing suicide. She's having fun at college. And get this, she had a thing for Gregory Fosdyke."

Aunt Violet nodded. "I thought I noticed something

brewing between them. Meanwhile, Fiona was head over heels for Tom. That's why it surprised me when she married Gregory. Poor Tom was heartbroken."

I thought of the photograph we'd found at Myrtle's. "Fiona is still married to Gregory, right? A photograph we found— wait, let me show you." I brought it up on my phone. "This wasn't taken that long ago."

Aunt Violet sucked in a breath. "I had no idea . . . this must have been right before he died. See how frail he looks?" Her lips were set in a thin line. "And to answer your question, yes, she's still married to Gregory. They celebrated their fiftieth anniversary a few years ago."

The conclusion was obvious. "Fiona was one of Myrtle's blackmail victims." Certainty grew as I spoke. "Myrtle managed to get a photograph of her with Tom and held it over her head with threats to go to Gregory. Think of the implications. Think of the *scandal*. Gregory is in Parliament, right? It would be front-page news. Fiona might even lose her job at the college."

"Serious stuff," Mum said. "But why didn't Fiona come clean? Divorce isn't such a big deal nowadays."

"Gregory had his own health challenges recently," Aunt Violet said. "It was touch and go for a while, I understand. So while I certainly don't respect Fiona for keeping her relationship with Tom a secret, I can understand it, I suppose. Especially since he had a terminal illness. But poor Tom deserved far better."

As a staunch supporter of the great-uncle I never knew but wished I had, I agreed with her. "We need to talk to Fiona about this," I said. "I think she just moved to the number-one suspect spot. Well, right next to Clive and Steve Baker." I rolled my eyes. "A three-way tie."

Aunt Violet frowned. "Steve? He wasn't at the reading. And he works every evening at the pub."

"True," I said. "But remember the man Kieran and I saw lurking in the alley? Steve could have easily left the pub for a few minutes. Or it could have been Clive. Sir Jon thinks he saw him at the train station that evening."

Mum made a helpless gesture. "I keep thinking we're making progress, but it all seems more muddled than ever."

She had a point. "I suppose the truth will come out sooner or later," I said, crossing my fingers. "We need to keep moving ahead with what we know." I swiveled in the chair to face Aunt Violet. "Will you call Fiona? I'd love to go talk to her."

Aunt Violet reached for the phone. "Certainly. How does tea tomorrow sound?"

Fiona was agreeable to our visit, so Aunt Violet and I made a plan to visit her while Mum watched the store. That settled, we turned our attention to other tasks.

"If you have time, please price those Oz books today," I said to Aunt Violet. "I'll take pictures and post the listing online. I'm sure there will be lots of interest."

Mum raised her hand. "Can I help with the appraisal? I really want to understand how books are valued."

"Actually, I do too," I said. I thought of an idea. "What if you give us the guidelines and Mum and I try to value a couple? Then you can grade us."

Aunt Violet's lips twitched with pleasure. "I would love to teach you both. How about after dinner tonight?" As she spoke the bell jingled and a couple strolled in. Judging by how closely they were entwined, I guessed they were honeymooners from the Holly & Ivy. The inn sent us lots of customers.

Mum stood, ready to assist them. "Sounds like a plan. We'll need uninterrupted time."

A late afternoon rush began, resulting in very good sales for the day. Aunt Violet sold a rare copy of Lord Byron's poems to a local collector, thrilled that he mentioned the social media post as impetus to come in.

"I'd quite forgotten you were here," the collector admitted, clutching his new purchase. "I usually go up to London to buy books. Now I have you bookmarked."

Aunt Violet put a hand on my shoulder. "My niece is our new marketing genius. Thomas Marlowe is finally entering the twenty-first century."

"Without losing an ounce of charm." He accepted his credit card back from Mum and tucked it into his wallet. "Good day."

Mum ran a quick sales report after the door shut behind him. "Look at this, Aunt Violet. I think we can squeeze out another payment to Clive."

Aunt Violet bent over Mum's shoulder, studying the computer screen. "Good. I can't wait to get him off my back." Straightening, she turned to me. "Would you be willing to take him a check?" She glanced at the clock. "If you take my bicycle, you'll make it before his office closes." Mum was already printing the check for Aunt Violet's signature.

"Sure, I'll go." I glanced down at my sandals. "Let me change my shoes first. And grab a water bottle."

Aunt Violet's bicycle was, appropriately, a lavender seven-speed complete with basket and bell, and climbing aboard made me feel like an official Cambridge resident. I rode up the lane and onto Trinity Street, merging into the swarm wheeling along. Of course they all knew where they were going, often buzzing by me at top speed, so I had to stay alert and cautious. Especially since I wasn't wearing a helmet. Most of the riders were not, which surprised me. *I'll have to try this again*, I thought with a smile—after the bicycle rush hour.

Clive Marlowe's office was on a side street, in a charming pale green stucco building with large arched windows. A discreet sign by the front door read Marlowe Construction, and topiary bushes and flowerboxes made the entrance both elegant and cheerful. I locked the bicycle to a post and went inside.

A poster on an A-frame greeted me. Announcing Cherry Hinton Homes, an exclusive community, it read above a rendering of a charming bungalow.

"They're quite reasonable and going fast," a woman said from behind the reception counter. She was middle-aged and trim, with a chic haircut and tasteful make-up. She smiled. "Though you are a bit younger than most of our homeowners."

"Thanks, but I'm not here to buy a house," I said. "I'm Molly Kimball, from Thomas Marlowe, the bookshop. I have something for Clive."

Her perfectly painted mouth dropped open. "The American cousin? I've heard so much about you."

I'll bet. I continued moving toward her station, a thick and highly polished expanse of wood. A dense carpet cushioned my feet and antique prints depicting iconic Cambridge scenes hung on the walls. But despite the attractive décor, my gaze was caught and held by something very out of place on the countertop, next to a pencil holder and rack of business cards.

A pink knitting needle.

CHAPTER 15

"Where did that come from?" I asked, pointing at the needle. It looked exactly like the one that had killed Myrtle, theoretically from the pair that Aunt Violet had been using. The second one had disappeared too, pulled out of her knitting project.

"What are you talking about?" The receptionist stood, peering at the countertop. "Oh, you mean this knitting needle?" She picked it up, trying to hand it to me. "Is it yours?"

I backed away, my hands up. "No, it's not mine. But my aunt had a pair just like that." I was overreacting, right? There had to be dozens, if not hundreds of pairs of pink knitting needles in Cambridge alone. But the fact that one had turned up in the office of a murder suspect—well, he was a suspect in *my* mind—couldn't be a coincidence, could it?

The receptionist's brow cleared. "Did your auntie come

to the presentation? We had a number of pensioners attend."
She dimpled. "They all want one of those bungalows."

"No, my aunt didn't come to the presentation," I said between gritted teeth. "Where did that needle come from?"

"Let me think." She tapped the needle on the edge of
counter as she glanced around. Then she pointed with it. "In
Clive's office, on the carpet next to the wall. It caught my eye
right away, being pink and all."

As if hearing his name, the door to the office burst open
and Clive hurried out. "Claire, did you—" He broke off when
he saw me, practically screeching to a halt on the carpet.
"Molly. What are you doing here?"

"I came to give you a check." I opened my messenger bag
and pulled out the envelope. When he didn't move forward
to take it, I placed it on the countertop.

But his eyes were riveted on the needle in Claire's hand.
"Where did *that* come from?"

She shrugged. "I found it in your office." The dimples
flashed again. "Have you taken up knitting, Clive? I've heard
a lot of men knit nowadays."

He scowled. "No. What a ridiculous idea." He reached for
it. "Let me throw it away before someone gets hurt."

"No." The loudness of my voice startled even me. They
both stared. "We need to call the police. Inspector Ryan
needs to see that needle."

Claire's penciled brows shot up. "An inspector? But why?
It's only a *knitting needle*." She began to examine it. "Am I
missing something?"

I was watching Clive's face. Beyond the bluster, did I see

a hint of fear in those watery blue eyes? "Because one just like it was used to kill a woman."

My cousin's eyes bugged out. "Someone killed her with a knitting needle? The paper just said she was stabbed. I was in London that night, wasn't I, Claire?" He made a brusque gesture. "Pull up my calendar."

Claire gnawed at her bottom lip, her eyes darting back and forth between her boss and me. "Your calendar. Right." She set the needle down, which promptly rolled off the desk onto the floor, and started tapping on her keyboard.

Clive went for the needle, but I glared at him. "Leave it," I said. While they both hovered over the computer monitor, I stepped away a few paces, into the adjacent meeting area. Before I called Inspector Ryan and perhaps embarrassed myself beyond redemption, I needed to find something out.

Sir Jon answered right away. "Molly. How are you?"

"I'm fine," I whispered, turning my back. Over at the computer, Clive was reprimanding Claire for not moving fast enough. His barked orders seemed to cause her to fumble even more. "I have a quick question. Is there any way to know what the police took into custody from Aunt Violet's house?"

Thankfully he didn't ask any questions. "They always give a receipt, so normally you check that. But in this case, I was there when they searched the house. They were looking for a matching knitting needle, but they didn't find it."

I plopped down onto a folding chair, which was harder than it looked. *Ouch.* "I just did. I think." My only hope had been that the police had taken the needle before I checked the basket. If they hadn't, why didn't the killer leave it there, to frame Aunt Violet?

"Where are you?" Alarm was plain in Sir Jon's voice. "Are you in danger?"

Over at the computer, the pair was still squabbling. "I don't think so. I'm at Marlowe Construction. Clive is trying pretty frantically to prove he was out of town when Myrtle died."

"Hmm," Sir Jon said. "Like I told you, I'm pretty sure I saw him in Cambridge that evening."

"I think he's a big fat fibber," I whispered into the phone. Not only had he been in Cambridge the night of the reading, he'd acted surprised to hear Myrtle was dead. More evidence that he was up to no good at her flat?

"I'm calling Inspector Ryan right now," I told Sir Jon. "Talk to you later." Thankfully I had the inspector's number in my contacts, added from the card he gave Aunt Violet.

I braced myself for voice mail, but to my surprise, the inspector answered after a couple of rings. "Ryan here."

Now what? I gulped and said in a rush, "Hi, it's me, Molly Kimball. Violet Marlowe's niece."

"I remember," he said, his tone heavy with irony. How could he forget me, right? Not only had I discovered a murder victim, he'd seen me at the victim's home twice. "Did you find some more evidence?"

Thanks for the opening. "Actually, yes." I turned to look at the counter, where the pink needle once again sat on the ledge. Claire and Clive were still fussing over the computer. "I'm at Clive Marlowe's office and someone left a pink knitting needle here."

"A pink knitting needle, hmm." I distinctly heard laughter in his voice. "Those aren't exactly uncommon, you realize."

I jumped up and began to pace. "I know that. But you have to admit it's strange. Especially since Clive was in Cambridge around six p.m. the night Myrtle was killed. Claims to the contrary."

His tone sharpened. "How do you know that?"

My pacing had brought me near a podium, where a loose-leaf binder lay open. "Sir Jon told me. He saw Clive at a pub near the railway station." The top page was dated, and below it was a list of names. The Cherry Hinton presentation, maybe?

"Did he now." Ryan sighed. "Don't go anywhere. I'll be right over." He confirmed the address before hanging up.

I read over the list of names on the slight chance that Claire had been right and one of the attendees had left the knitting needle behind. None of the names were familiar, but I took a photograph anyway.

"Molly," Clive called. "Can you please come over here?" It sounded as though he was gritting his teeth.

"Sure." I sauntered over to the counter, not in any particular hurry. "Inspector Ryan is coming right over." I stabbed a finger at the needle. "He's very interested in seeing that."

Claire gasped theatrically. "He is? But why?" She turned the monitor to face me. "Clive was in London. See? This is his calendar."

More to humor her than anything, I took a good look at the calendar, which included his travel arrangements. He'd gone up in the morning—and had been scheduled to return the next day.

Clive stood with his arms folded across his chest, nodding in satisfaction. "This proves it. I was nowhere near the bookshop when Myrtle was killed."

His loyal assistant gasped again. "Who would ever think such a thing? Someone like you, a well-respected businessman, a community leader?"

"Good question." I stared at Clive until he met my eyes. "Especially someone who always operates on the up-and-up."

I knew he understood my insinuation when his beefy face reddened. "You need to look a little closer to home, miss." He wagged a finger at me. "Your aunt has made a right hash of things. Served her right that Myrtle was going to make a claim. She was all for the Best Books deal."

This was war. "I'll bet she was. Myrtle loved money. Why would she care if centuries of history were lost forever?" By the heat in my cheeks, I guessed my face was as flushed as his. "Too bad her claim was ill-founded. There was a will." If only we could find it. "Aunt Violet is the rightful owner."

Claire looked back and forth between us, puzzled and shocked by our animosity. "I'm going to put on the kettle. A nice cup of tea will help." She fled into the back room.

With an effort, I put aside the argument over Myrtle. That threat at least had been nullified. Locating the envelope, I waved it. "This is another payment on the loan. We're ahead of schedule now, Clive. And we're planning to keep it that way until you get every dime. Er, shilling."

We glared at each other in a standoff. Then movement at

the front door caught my eye. Inspector Ryan and Sergeant Adhikari had arrived.

Clive's ruddy complexion went white. "You really did call them."

I rested my hands on my hips. "Unlike some people, I say what I mean." I hesitated over my next words. Oh why not, we'd crossed the Rubicon and were now openly enemies. "You might want to rethink your story about London."

•|•

Naturally Inspector Ryan booted me off the premises before he started questioning Clive. I did have a chance to explain why I was at the office and how I had spotted the needle sitting there. And to mention the disappearance of the second needle the night Myrtle died.

Pedaling home, one of the inspector's comments rang in my mind. "I'll give you this, Miss Kimball, you are one of the most observant people I've ever met." He'd seemed almost reluctantly admiring.

I chalked up this ability to my native curiosity plus a splash of obstinacy, both of which were indispensable as a librarian. Roadblocks and leads that petered out only energized my determination to track down answers.

As I wheeled into the bookshop's back gate, I realized something surprising. My skills appeared to be quite transferable—to a murder investigation.

Mum and Aunt Violet were in the kitchen making dinner. Savory aromas from a roasting chicken greeted me along with the welcome sight of Mum whipping potatoes with a hand mixer. Mum's mashed potatoes were to die for, creamy with lots of butter and milk.

"What can I do to help?" I asked, slipping off my messenger bag.

"Set the table?" Aunt Violet asked. She inserted a thermometer into the golden brown chicken to see if it was done. Nodding in satisfaction, she shut off the oven.

I moved toward the dish cupboards. "Sure, I can do that." While I laid out dishes and silverware, I told them about my visit to Clive's office.

Aunt Violet stared at me, a gravy whisk suspended above the pot. "He had my knitting needle?"

"Or one that looked exactly like it." I placed napkins at each setting. "Claire really thought someone had left it by accident. Apparently, they had a lot of people attending a presentation about a new bungalow development recently."

Mum scooped the potatoes into a bowl. "That could be. Or one of them did it on purpose, knowing that it would implicate Clive."

I hadn't even thought of that. "You mean it was planted? That was kind of risky."

"Well, Molly," she said as she set the bowl on the table. Near my seat, I noticed. "We are dealing with a killer. And whoever it is, they must have nerves of steel. Myrtle was killed only yards away from quite a large gathering."

"Incredible, isn't it?" Aunt Violet poured gravy into a jug. "Can you come get this, Molly?"

I ferried the gravy to the table, followed by the platter of meat Aunt Violet had carved and Brussels sprouts for a green. Soon we were seated around the table digging in. I had Puck on one side and Clarence on the other, both hoping for samples of chicken. Puck was teaching an old cat new tricks, I realized with a smile. I may or may not have dropped a few morsels.

"So anyway," I said after the first few mouthfuls. "Besides the knitting needle showing up, remember how Sir Jon saw Clive near the railway station the night of Myrtle's death? I reminded Inspector Ryan about that little fact."

"And the inspector has Clive's blackmail picture from Myrtle's flat," Mum said. "It's all pretty incriminating."

"Poor Clive." I didn't mean it. "I'm sure he's not having a very good evening."

After dessert—apple pie with ice cream—we adjourned to the new meeting room, where Aunt Violet had set up a table. Here Mum and I would examine *The Wonderful Wizard of Oz* and *The Marvelous Land of Oz*, the first two entries in Baum's fourteen-book series. Aunt Violet carted in several reference books as I set up my laptop. Before proceeding, Mum and I washed our hands rather than don gloves, the latest thinking regarding rare books. Gloves could catch and tear fragile paper.

While lathering up in the loo, I thought about the night of Myrtle's death. I'd already theorized that someone might have used the loo's kitchen door to sneak out into the back garden and kill her. And they could have done the same to snag the second needle, after. Or come through in reverse, joining us at the reading.

Maybe it hadn't been someone attending the reading. The killer might have entered the house through one of the two back doors—kitchen and back hallway—to grab the needles. Clive had been to the shop many times and he no doubt knew that Aunt Violet was an avid knitter. I sighed. Too many doors, too many suspects, too many possibilities.

As I dried my hands, I could only hope that Clive would confess to Myrtle's murder. That would wrap everything up neatly. But I had a sinking feeling that answers wouldn't be so easily forthcoming.

"Are you ready?" Aunt Violet asked once we were seated at the table, the beautiful old books waiting in front of us.

Mum and I exchanged looks and giggles. "I feel like I'm back in school," Mum said.

Aunt Violet gave us a mock frown. "That's because you are. Listen up, ladies." Playing along, we cleared our throats and sat up straight. "The important factors to keep in mind while valuing books are these: edition, condition, and scarcity. Let's begin with identifying the edition. The Oz books were extremely popular and published by more than one company."

As instructed, we turned to the copyright page of the first book. Here, after consulting the handy Oz value guide, we determined that this particular *Wonderful Wizard of Oz* was a first edition with a "C" binding, published by Geo. M. Hill, Co. *The Marvelous Land of Oz* was a 1904 first edition from Reilly and Britton, who published the series from the second book on. Also taken under consideration was the so-called state of the book, which accounted for corrections mid-printing of an edition and other changes. Ours were both second state, which meant lower values but, in this series, still extremely valuable.

Working together, we came up with suggested values and our rationale for Aunt Violet's confirmation. "Good work," she said with approval, agreeing with our value range. "Tomorrow you can do the other twelve books."

Mum and I looked at each other and groaned, mostly for Aunt Violet's benefit. We'd both had a great time examining the gorgeous classics.

"Don't worry," Aunt Violet went on. "The first pass gets easier and faster, almost second nature. But you absolutely need to verify the details. When your conclusions are challenged—and they will be—you need to be able to defend them."

Verify details and defend conclusions. I could see some similarities between valuing books and solving mysteries. But when it came to murder, the stakes were of course much, much higher.

⁘

That night, after I got into bed, I opened Joan's journal to the next entry. Her voice had been in the back of my mind all day, snippets of what she'd written floating through my thoughts. With a purring Puck curled up next to me, I began reading.

The next few entries focused on the lectures and tutorials Joan attended and, more interesting to me, her dates with Gregory. They went to a pub for dinner and darts, and to a movie, and they punted on the river.

Joan Watson's journal

Sigh. What could be more romantic? Gregory and I went punting on Sunday, only the two of us and a picnic basket. He was quite good at it, really, only almost falling in once. After punting along the Backs, we found a private spot under weeping willows and feasted on roast beef sandwiches and bottled beer.

Then we snuggled and talked about all kinds of things. Life. College. Our friends. He kissed me several times but remained a gentleman. Unlike the fumbling we spotted in other punts. Some people have no shame. That's all I'll say about that.

But Gregory . . . he's perfect. And maybe I'm getting ahead of myself, but I can't help but wonder, what will Mummy think?

I also wondered what her mother would think. From what I knew of England sixty years ago, class was often a dividing line. Archaic as it seemed, Gregory's world was quite a stretch for a farmer's daughter. Opposition would probably come from both families.

The next journal entry mentioned Persephone.

One of my secret hopes has come true and I can scarcely believe it. I've been invited to a very small writer's group here at St. Hildegard's. As Persephone Brightwell put it, it's a place to share, be inspired, and grow. She hopes that we can co-publish a volume of short stories and poetry in the second term. Ruth Orforo, who hopes to work in publishing, has offered to edit and print. It's a dream come true. Only now I have to write something print-worthy.

That *was* exciting, and I wondered what had become of the group, if they ever had published. Maybe Persephone could tell me. Turning the page, I spotted Myrtle's name. So far, she'd been a minor player in the group, mentioned at outings but not a central figure in the action.

What a dreary night. Cold and rainy, with a creeping wind that whispers winter. After dinner, I holed up in my room to do some reading. Not easy when I keep seeing Gregory's face instead of the words on the page.

The knock on the door came as a welcome interruption. Myrtle, who lives next door, holding a mug. "Can I trouble you for a tea bag? I hate to go out in this weather." We all had electric kettles and kept a supply of cocoa powder, tea bags, and instant coffee in our rooms.

Glad for an excuse to stop studying, I suggested that she join me for a cup. After we made our tea, I sat in my chair and she took the bed.

"This is so nice," Myrtle said, blowing on her hot tea. "When-ever I thought about going to college, I always imagined chummy nights in with friends."

She sounded wistful, and I immediately felt bad about not inviting her over more often. But I'd been so busy and, quite frankly, there was something about her that put me off. Maybe I'd misjudged her.

"Yes, there's nothing like a natter with a good friend," I said.

"Especially about boys, am I right?" She smiled at me. "You and Gregory seem to be getting on quite well."

*I ducked my head, trying to hide a foolish grin. "We are,"
I said lightly. "He's a good sort." Putting it mildly.*

*She was silent for a moment, her finger tracing the design
on the bedspread. "No skeletons in the closet, then?" She
laughed. "All those families have them, don't they?"*

*My hackles stood up. What was she getting at? Gregory's
family was wealthy, yes, but did that mean they had more
secrets than say, my family?*

*"I don't know what you mean," I finally said. "He's pretty
straightforward about things." He'd even told me about his
parents pushing Fiona as a match.*

*Myrtle eyed me and I noticed the calculation in her gaze.
"That's good," she said. "I hope . . . well, anyway." She
laughed.*

*"So what is it your father does?" she asked after an un-
comfortable silence. "You're from Hazelhurst, right?"*

*"He's a dairy farmer." I muttered the words, not liking
being questioned about my family. Too many of my fellow
students pigeonholed people by their backgrounds. Dairy
farming, as you might guess, came fairly low in the pecking
order.*

*"Interesting," she said, gazing around my room. "He
must do well. The school fees here are quite high. My parents, well thankfully, I had a little money from my Gram. But
I'm living on birdseed." Her mouth twisted.*

*"Tell me about it," I said, gritting my teeth. "I'm a schol-
arship student." How soon could I get rid of this nosy
woman?*

*"Ah," she said. "Good for you." A pause, then, "What
do you think about Ruth and her friend? Catherine, is it?"*

The abrupt change of subject startled me. "I don't think anything. Why?"

Now it was her turn to duck her head. But I still saw the sly expression on her face. "No reason." She traced her finger over the pattern. "I think they're . . . odd, that's all" She gave a nasty little laugh. "Always together. Inseparable, almost."

I was only half done with my tea but I stood, now desperate to get rid of her. "I'm sorry, Myrtle, this has been nice, but I really need to get back to work. I'm so behind."

She grumbled a bit but finally left, another of my tea bags in her hand. I would have given her the whole tin if I'd had to. I didn't know what Myrtle's game was, but I certainly wasn't going to play.

Here was Myrtle in action, and to be honest, it chilled me, especially after hearing Ruth's story. Her motivation was laid bare as well, an attempt to keep up with the better-heeled students she probably envied.

The question was, did Myrtle's schemes have anything to do with Joan's death, or were there more secrets to unfold?

CHAPTER 16

"Looking for pictures of Kieran?" Daisy asked me with a teasing grin. Her hands never stopped moving as she poured tea and coffee and set pastries on plates.

Still holding the morning paper, I moved closer to the counter and lowered my voice. "I'm actually looking to see if someone got arrested."

Her eyes widened. "Oh, do tell. Give me a moment. I want to hear." She passed cups and plates to a group speaking French, and after they settled at two tables, she began dispensing my usual coffee order.

While she worked, I told her about our discoveries at Myrtle's flat—minus Joan's obituary—and my visit to Clive's office, making sure no one sitting nearby could hear me. I rattled the newspaper before folding it and tucking it under my arm. "But there's nothing in here. So maybe Ryan didn't arrest him."

"Or not yet, anyway." Daisy set my tall, steaming coffee on the counter. Her smile was sly. "I wonder what the inspector thinks about you scooping him again."

I thought back to Inspector Ryan's attitude. He had remained very professional, but I had the distinct feeling I annoyed him. "He doesn't like it. But what can he do? I had legitimate reasons to be in both places." Meaning Myrtle's flat and Clive's office. "I can't help it if I'm naturally talented." I batted my lashes with a smirk, showing Daisy I was joking.

"You certainly are," Daisy agreed. She gestured toward the bakery case. "Can I interest you in something to eat? I've got cream scones with lemon curd."

Despite the horrible name, lemon curd was delicious. "I'll take three. Mum and Aunt Violet will want one too." I remembered my other news, even more exciting than Clive's possible arrest. "Guess what? Kieran asked me out to dinner."

Daisy clapped her gloved hands. "Hurray. I'm so happy. You two are perfect for each other."

That was nice to hear, even if a little hard to believe. "Really? You think so?" Insecurity began to gnaw. "He's literally from a different world."

She blew out air. "Oh, so what. I think he's the lucky one in this match. And you can tell him I said so." She tucked the lid of a pastry box into place and set it on the counter, then rang up my order. "Now on to the important part. What are you going to wear?"

"I don't know," I wailed. "I have *nothing*. But Mum and I are going shopping. Want to come along?"

"I'd love to," Daisy said, accepting my money. "I need some new togs myself." Her face grew more serious. "Have you started reading my aunt's journal, by chance? No biggie if you haven't gotten to it." Her anxious eyes belied that last remark, and judging by her hunched shoulders, she was bracing herself against what I might say.

"I've read a few entries so far and she's wonderful, Daisy. Truly." How was I ever going be able to tell her that Joan might have been murdered?

Her shoulders relaxed. "So I've heard. Maybe I'll be ready to read the journal myself sometime soon." More customers were entering the shop, and in response, she gently pushed the bakery box toward me. "Talk to you later, Molly. Have a good day."

Taking the hint, I picked up the box in one hand, coffee in the other. "You too, Daisy."

Over scones, Aunt Violet and I discussed our tea date with Fiona Fosdyke that afternoon. "I suppose we could walk," Aunt Violet said. "But it's a bit far. I'll have George pull the car out of the garage."

I hadn't been in an automobile or any form of motorized transit since arriving and I hated to break my streak. "What about cycling over? I can rent a bike next door." Which gave me a perfect excuse to see Kieran.

"We can. Plus I need the exercise," Aunt Violet said with a laugh. "How do you suppose I stay so trim? Cycling is the answer."

"Especially with all these luscious baked goods around," I said, taking a bite of scone. It melted in my mouth, the lemon curd providing a pop of flavor.

"I have an even better idea," Mum declared. She had an adorable dab of curd above her lip. At my gesture, she wiped her mouth. "Molly and I both need bicycles. Let's go buy a couple."

"Really, Mum?" I had left my old ten-speed in Vermont. Not that I'd ridden it all that much. Between struggling with steep hills, frequent snow and ice, and narrow roads edged with deep ditches, bicycling had never been my sport. But here in Cambridge, a bicycle was pretty much indispensable and much safer, since many streets downtown were closed to vehicle traffic.

"I saw some lovely ones in the rack," Mum said. "And they're on sale."

Aunt Violet took the shop's helm while Mum and I walked next door. She was right, there was a charming array of women's bicycles in the For Purchase rack. Like Aunt Violet's, they came equipped with baskets and bells.

Kieran emerged from the shop, smiling ear to ear. "Lovely morning, Molly, Nina. Can I help you?"

Mum placed her hand on a pink bicycle. "I want to buy this one."

"And this is my choice." The bicycle was painted a lovely turquoise that made my heart lift. The cheerful color would definitely stand out in a sea of black bicycles, making identifying my ride easier in the bike racks.

"We'll get you set up straight away, then." Kieran unlocked Mum's bicycle from the rack. "Hop aboard and we'll do the adjustments."

Half an hour later, we were the proud owners of two beautiful bicycles and matching helmets. "Want to go for a spin?" Mum asked. She patted her handlebars. "Put Beatrice through her paces?"

"Oh, you named yours?" I studied my bicycle, thinking about what to call it. "Belinda. Yes, Belinda would love to go for a ride."

After letting Aunt Violet know our plans and grabbing snacks and waters to go, we set off along the cobblestone streets.

Mum led the way and I followed, enjoying the cool air rushing against my face as we wound through the University and over the river. We took a cycle path Mum found, a route leading through water meadows and past grazing sheep and cows. In places, trees and bushes arched over the narrow route, creating tunnels. It was hard to believe we were still in the city.

"Where are we going, Mum?" I called, guessing she had a destination in mind.

"You'll see," she called back. "How are you doing?"

"Great," I said. "Lead on." The cycling was wonderful, flat and easy, and I felt like I could do it forever. Then I spotted the cows blocking our way.

Cool as could be, Mum veered onto the grass around the herd and kept going. I followed, legs pumping fast, praying all the while that one wouldn't move in front of me.

We soon entered civilization again in the form of a small village. Mum pedaled along the business district for a few blocks before veering onto a side road. Straight ahead at a curve in the lane was a quaint cottage with scaffolding around it. Two men were working on the partly thatched roof, and a van in the drive was lettered Shire Thatch.

I braked hard, almost falling over. Wasn't Shire Thatch my uncle's company? How had Mum known they would be here? She was off her bicycle now, kickstand engaged, and staring up at the men, hands on hips. I parked mine nearby, making sure the stand would hold before letting go.

Finally noticing us, the men paused in their task of fastening straw bundles to a framework, and after a moment, the older man waved. With a shock, I recognized him as the man I'd seen at the newsstand and later that morning, on the bridge. Had he been trailing me after all? My uncle, because it had to be him, hurried across the scaffolding and down a ladder, the other man following more slowly.

"Nina. Is it really you?" He halted several feet away, his eyes locked on her face.

"It's me, Chris," Mum said with a laugh, running a hand through her hair. "How have you been?"

Uncle Chris took another step forward, hands lifted as though he wanted to embrace Mum. Then they dropped and his expression became wary. "I'm all right." He tipped his chin toward the cottage. "Busy as ever, as you can see."

Mum took my arm and drew me forward. "Chris, this is my daughter, Molly."

"Nice to meet you, lass," he said with a tentative smile.

"Nice to meet you too." *Now that I know you exist.* Maybe Uncle Chris was all right. It was his wife who was the real problem, according to Mum.

Uncle Chris backed toward the van. "Would you like a cuppa? It's about that time."

"Sure. I could use a cup," Mum said. She threw a glance at me, lifting her brows as though to ask if I was okay. I nodded.

"Hello," the younger man said to Mum. "I'm Charlie Marlowe."

She shook his hand. "And I'm Nina, your aunt from America."

Charlie looked a lot like his father and by extension, Mum. Dark hair and eyes, attractive features, and a nice smile. His palm was dry and calloused when he shook my hand. "Welcome to England, Molly."

"Thanks," I said, marveling at the fact that I had a cousin. My *only* cousin. Maybe we would even become friends.

His father had pulled out a tartan bag and was filling disposable cups with strong tea. Charlie passed around a packet of McVitie's.

"My favorite," I said, taking one.

Charlie's brown eyes twinkled. "Mine too." He took two before passing the packet to Mum. "We work up quite an appetite, going up and down ladders all day."

"I'll bet." What a contrast between work environments. His outside on roofs, mine inside with books. Although thatching was a beautiful and historic craft. Both branches of the family dealt in the past, I realized. Interesting.

Standing in a circle, we sipped tea, making innocuous comments about the weather, the bookshop, and the thatching job. Uncle Chris answered my questions and offered to do a personal demonstration of techniques when I had time. Mum didn't mention my uncle's note and neither did he, and all of us stayed away from the topic of Myrtle's murder. By the time we finished our tea, the ice was broken and we'd even shared a laugh or two.

"We'd best get on," Uncle Chris said, collecting the empty cups.

"Us too," Mum said. "Aunt Violet is expecting us back."

"Good to see you, Molly," Charlie said. "Maybe we can grab a pint some time."

"I'd like that," I said, lifting the kickstand on my bike. "How about at the Magpie? It's right across the street from us."

"The Magpie?" Uncle Chris said. He turned to his son. "Isn't that the bloke who got in trouble a while back?"

"I have no idea." Charlie said with a laugh and a shrug. "Don't mind Dad. He never forgets a good piece of gossip."

Uncle Chris rested his chin on his hand, thinking. "Is his name Steve Baker?"

Adrenaline shot through my veins when he mentioned Steve. I'd been planning to talk to Steve about Myrtle, but in more of a check-off-the-list way. I hadn't considered him a prime suspect. What had Steve done? It must be serious or Uncle Chris probably wouldn't bother mentioning it.

"Steve and Susie Baker own the place," Mum said. "They're both quite nice."

My uncle nodded. "Yeah, I'm sure he is. I don't know Susie. She must be his second wife. But he's got a bit of a gambling problem. Or did. About fifteen years ago, he was caught up in a sweep when they shut down an illegal ring."

And Steve was still betting. Legally, it appeared, but covertly. The question was, did Myrtle's threats to expose him drive him to murder?

🐾

In concession to the tradition, Aunt Violet and I dressed up to take tea with Fiona, despite the fact we were riding our bicycles. I had on a full-skirted white cotton dress with a poppy print, and white flats, and Aunt Violet wore a vintage lavender dress with a matching bolero. The velvet flowers on her hat bobbed cheerfully as she pedaled ahead of me.

Belinda was getting quite a workout for the first day of ownership, I thought as we peddled through Jesus Green, a huge park and former grazing area. Now, instead of cows and sheep wandering about, there were tall trees filtering the afternoon sunlight and people strolling or relaxing on benches.

Mum had been quite happy to stay at the shop, helping customers while continuing to price the Oz set. She seemed relieved that the visit with her brother had gone well, and I thought her strategy had been perfect. For one thing, she knew that Aunt Janice wouldn't be at the thatching job, and for another, the setting was quite public so as to discourage heavy topics. Time would tell if my cousin and I would actually hang out together. I'd probably let him make the first move.

Reaching the river, which edged the green, we bumped over a bridge and arrived in Chesterton—yet another village that had gradually become part of Cambridge proper as the city grew.

Aunt Violet halted her bicycle on the side of the path. "How are you doing, Molly?" Despite the pace she'd been setting, she wasn't at all winded.

"I'm great," I said. "This is really fun." On a bicycle, I

got to enjoy the sights while covering far more ground than walking.

"We're almost there." Aunt Violet put her feet on the pedals. "Only a little farther."

She led me through a maze of side streets until we reached a lane ending at a tall wooden gate. A natural brick wall was to the left, and to the right stood the end wall of the house, also brick but painted light green.

"Fiona has quite the enclave here," Aunt Violet said. Hopping off her bicycle, she wheeled it through the gate. Inside, we left our bicycles next to the gray Mercedes sedan parked under a tall tree, far enough away that an accidental oops wouldn't scratch the paint.

Then we turned to face the house. The main section was Georgian, flat-fronted cream brick with a central entry framed by two windows on each side and five above. Tiny dormers pierced the roof.

"Wow," I said, immediately falling in love. "What a gorgeous place."

Aunt Violet took my arm and gently turned me to face the grounds. A long lawn edged with flowerbeds stretched to the Cam. Punts drifted lazily by and a pair of swans circled. I wanted to run down that lawn screaming in joy, it was that inviting.

"Hello," called a feminine voice. "I see you made it." Fiona stood in the open front door waving at us. Today a double-breasted skirt suit restrained her formidable bosom while revealing admirable legs, and her hair was freshly curled.

"It's so good to see you, Fiona, dear," Aunt Violet said

warmly. For a moment it seemed the two women might embrace, but they settled for a warm handclasp.

"Please, do come in," Fiona said, drawing Aunt Violet into the house. "How nice of you to visit, Molly." She stood back until both of us were in the entrance hall, where an elegant stair led up. Through doorways to the left and right I glimpsed a formal living room and dining room, both furnished in period style. I gawked around at everything while she ushered us into the drawing room, where French doors stood open to a lush side garden. A pair of hideous porcelain pugs regarded us from the mantelpiece.

"Please have a seat," Fiona said, indicating a seating area of green silk upholstered sofa and wingback chairs. "I'll be right back," she said before hurrying out another door.

Aunt Violet elbowed me, nodding toward the dogs. "Chinese, eighteenth century," she whispered. "Worth a pretty penny."

I was no antiques expert but glancing around I picked out other valuables—Ming vases, a curio cabinet full of porcelain figurines, paintings in gilded frames. Thinking of the contrast between this mansion and Myrtle's admittedly modest flat, I wondered if envy had driven her as well as greed.

Fiona returned, carrying a large silver tray. She set it carefully on a low marble-topped table, the bone china teacups shivering gently.

"Here we are," she said, plumping down on an armchair and picking up the teapot, which matched the floral-print teacups. She deftly filled three cups. "Lemon, sugar, or milk, whatever is your fancy."

Aunt Violet gave a little laugh. "I was just thinking how different this is from tea in our rooms at St. Hildegard's. Thick old stained mugs and sometimes even recycled tea bags when we were hard up. Remember?"

Fiona set down the pot and handed me a teacup. "I certainly do. Persephone 'borrowed' a few of those mugs from the buttery." In England, colleges often called their dining halls butteries.

I added a splash of milk to my tea, watching the clear liquid cloud up. There was quite a contrast from happy-go-lucky Fiona in a miniskirt flirting with Tom to this stately matron, queen of all she surveyed. Which Fiona did she prefer, I wonder?

Fiona dropped a lump of sugar in her cup, and I took one as well, for the novelty. Tilting her head, she studied me. Her blue eyes were still clear and lovely, and I could see the girl she had once been. "How are you settling in, Molly? Enjoying Cambridge, are you?" Her smile faltered. "Well, most of it has been enjoyable, I imagine."

Neat sidestep around the elephant named Myrtle. "I love everything about Cambridge," I declared, my enthusiasm ringing out in that muted, tasteful room. "Books have always been my life and now I know I come by that passion honestly." Well, unless we did cheat Myrtle's branch, which I highly doubted. "Mum and I have great plans for the bookshop"—besides solving murders on the premises—"all with Aunt Violet's blessing, plus I've made new friends already."

"Kieran Scott asked her out," Aunt Violet said, setting her cup down with a genteel rattle.

Fiona's mouth pursed in admiring surprise. "Oh, he's a lovely boy. Good family, too."

An understatement on both counts. I squirmed in my seat, feeling as if I were back in high school, having my latest crush scrutinized. Judging by the fond smiles aimed my way, I guessed they approved.

I waved a hand, aiming for casual and hoping the subject would be dropped. "We're going out to dinner at the Holly and Ivy. Ruth said she is staying there. Oh, and by the way, is Persephone still in town?" Hopefully a deft enough maneuver to bring the conversation back on track and away from my love life.

"She's still here with me, for another week or so, at least." Fiona picked up a plate and pushed it my way. "Biscuit?"

No McVitie's on offer, so I took a gingersnap and bit it, almost breaking a molar. Yikes. Then I noticed that Aunt Violet was dipping one in her tea first, to soften it. Gotcha.

"I've so loved having Molly and Nina here," Aunt Violet said. "Besides helping in the shop and setting up a social media campaign, Molly's been sorting through Tom's children's books. I've been putting that off for years."

At the mention of Aunt Violet's brother, Fiona dropped her biscuit onto the carpet. "Oh, sorry. Clumsy clot." Blushing, she bent to pick it up.

She still cared about Tom. Cruelly taking advantage of her feelings for the greater good of our mission, I said, "I wish I'd had a chance to know him. He seemed like a wonderful man. And going by pictures when he was young? Wow. Hot, as my friends would say."

Under the face powder, her cheeks flushed bright pink.

"Yes. Yes, he was. We all thought a great deal of Tom, didn't we, Vi?"

I'd wondered what strategy Aunt Violet would use to advance our cause, but to my surprise, she went right for the jugular. "You loved him, Fiona, didn't you? Not only way back when but at the end of his life as well." She paused when Fiona began to stutter, but then spoke right over her. "We saw the pictures. The ones Myrtle had."

"That witch blackmailed you, didn't she?" I said, surprising even myself with my bluntness. "I'm glad you loved my uncle. He deserved love." The circumstances were messy, yes, but who was I to judge?

Fiona's eyes went wide with shock, but then her face crumpled into lines of sorrow and regret. "You're right. I did love him." With her shoulders hunched, her fingers began to fret at her napkin. "He was the love of my life. I was such a little fool," she ground out, "marrying Gregory instead of following my heart."

"And then you found out Tom had cancer." Aunt Violet leaned across the table, her voice gentle.

Her friend nodded. "Yes. We ran into each other—" Her mouth opened. "Myrtle. She's the one who told me. I was with her when we saw Tom. At Tea and Crumpets." Daisy's shop, right across from the bookshop. So of course Tom frequented the place.

"Do you think she set you up?" I asked. In hindsight, this seemed obvious.

Fiona still appeared astounded. "You know, I think she might have. In fact, right after he came in and said hello to us, she made an excuse and left. So Tom and I . . ." Her cheeks flushed deeper. "We sat and talked. Oh, how we talked." She laughed. "I think Daisy had to kick us out when she closed." Obviously lost in her memories, she continued to shred that poor napkin.

After a moment, Aunt Violet said, "So you began seeing each other."

Fiona tore her eye away from her lap. "Yes, that's right. We only had . . . what? Less than a year, anyway. But I think I brought him some comfort."

"When did Myrtle start blackmailing you?" I asked.

Putting a hand to her forehead, she closed her eyes. "Right after the funeral. He was barely in the ground before I got the first call. Oh, she had me good, she did. Earlier, and I could have chosen to be with Tom, let the chips fall where they may. And I might have. Yes, I would have. Probably. But I didn't have him anymore . . . plus Gregory was having health challenges of his own. And the children . . . they never would have forgiven me if I'd left their father now." She gave a little headshake. "He almost didn't make it, this past winter."

Game, set, and match to Myrtle. She had Fiona completely boxed in.

I glanced at Aunt Violet. Did we dare to go ahead and plainly ask Fiona if she had killed Myrtle? She certainly had motive—to get this evil blackmailer off her back. As long as Myrtle was alive, there was a risk that she would reveal the affair to Gregory or Fiona's children.

Voices outside the open French door startled us. We all stiffened as Persephone strolled into the room, braid swinging, a huge smile on her face. "Lovely. Company for tea." She turned to look at the man behind her, who was tall and lean, with iron gray hair and handsome if weathered features. "Gregory. It's Violet Marlowe and her niece, from the bookshop." Her eyes glittered. "You know, Tom's sister."

CHAPTER 17

I really didn't like Persephone, I decided, despite her being a so-called national treasure. Poor Fiona's face, already flushed, was now the color of the poppies on my dress. Our hostess did her best to hide her distress by jumping up. "Persephone. Gregory. Would you like tea? I can fetch more cups."

"Don't flutter about so, dear." Gregory's tone was both fond and lofty. "Relax. I don't need tea." He was dignified, stuffy, even a trifle condescending, but I couldn't help but think about how Joan had seen him—kind, funny, even charming in his quiet way. Had Gregory, like Fiona, been smothered by family expectations and propriety?

Fiona had barely settled herself again when Persephone said, "I'd love a cup." So Fiona bounced up again and excused herself, while the poet gracefully lowered herself into an armchair, smiling in victory. I wondered if she'd kept Fiona hopping the whole time she'd been staying here. Probably. According to Joan's diary, Persephone had been the queen bee in their circle of friends. If anything, the passing years seemed to have only strengthened her position.

"Hello, Violet." Gregory held a hand out to me. "I don't believe I've had the pleasure."

"Molly Kimball," I said. "Nice to meet you." His grip was firm, his eye contact intense as he took my measure. I was thankful that this incisive man couldn't read my mind and somehow discover that I knew his secrets.

"Likewise." He released my hand with a nod. "Now if you'll excuse me, ladies, I'm going to retire to my study. Duty calls."

After he strode away, Persephone said, "What a lovely day. Too bad Gregory and I were holed up doing paperwork. But it needed doing. Taxes." She wrinkled her nose.

We made noises in answer because there really wasn't a comment to make. Fiona soon came back, carrying a fresh teacup for Persephone. "Where did Gregory go?" she asked.

"His study," Aunt Violet said. "Isn't it interesting how none of us are retired? He's in Parliament and still practicing law, correct? And you're working at St. Hildegard's, Fiona, and Persephone, you're penning new poetry."

"Trying to, anyway." Persephone accepted the teacup with thanks. "By the way, my advance reader copies have arrived. Ruth had a few shipped here. Would you like to see them?" Advance reader copies were sent out as part of a publicity campaign, to hopefully build interest and garner reviews.

Aunt Violet clapped once. "I certainly would. Will you sign it for me? For us?"

"I'd be delighted." Persephone sipped her tea then set her cup on the table. "Fiona, love," she said as she got up. "Do you want to see a copy?"

Fiona startled. She'd been staring out into the garden, her gaze distant. "What? Sorry. I drifted off for a moment."

"My advance copies are here," Persephone said. "I'll bring you one." Her voice was bright, but she rolled her eyes behind her friend's back as she left the room.

"Are you all right?" Aunt Violet asked Fiona, speaking under her breath.

Fiona didn't meet her gaze, instead focused on the teapot as she refilled our cups. "I'm fine. I've got to focus on Gregory's health, that's the important thing." Meaning she would tuck away her grief for her lost love and go on.

Could I ever be that brave? Of course, I hoped if and when I got married, it would be to someone I truly loved. It didn't seem worth it otherwise. But these women from an earlier generation had faced pressures I didn't, I supposed.

Persephone came sashaying back into the room, a book nestled in each elbow. "Wait until you see it. It's gorgeous." With a flourish, she presented copies to Aunt Violet and Fiona.

"It really is," Aunt Violet said. "Congratulations."

The book was beautiful, with a cover inspired by a vintage botanical print of apples. The title, *Words of Knowledge: Poetry by Persephone Brightwell,* was printed in scrolling, gilded script. The endpapers featured the same apple design, but in faded sepia.

"Don't you love it?" the author asked. "Such a clever title. And the apple theme reminds one of Isaac Newton, and therefore Cambridge, where it all started."

She accepted Aunt Violet's copy back and, after sending Fiona for a pen, wrote a dedication in black, slanting, arrogant handwriting. *To the lovely ladies of the best bookshop ever, Thomas Marlowe,* I read after Aunt Violet passed the book to me.

Curious, I leafed through, noticing that the book was divided into eras, the first being St. Hildegard's. It would be interesting to see how her talent, style, and subject choice changed over the years.

"There you are, my charming hostess." Persephone passed Fiona her signed book.

"I have an idea," I said. "Why don't I take a picture of you with your new book, Persephone? On that bench by the river would be perfect."

"Ooh, yes. What a grand idea." Her hand fluttered to her hair then down to her skirt, a plain navy cotton A-line.

"We're not in a hurry, if you want to change," I said, guessing her concern.

Persephone stood. "I think I will. Be right back."

Once her footsteps on the stairs died away, Aunt Violet said, "Fiona, I desperately need your help."

Fiona put a hand to her neck, where she fiddled with a necklace. "You do?"

Aunt Violet inched to the edge of the cushion. "I don't know if you realize it, but the police suspect *me* of killing Myrtle." She was taking the indirect route in questioning

Fiona, I noticed. Probably much wiser than asking her if she was the killer.

Fiona gasped, her fingers covering her mouth. "They do? Why that's absurd, Violet. When I read she was stabbed, I thought she had been mugged. Oh, do you need a barrister? Criminal law isn't really Gregory's forte but he—"

"No, I'm all set there," Aunt Violet said. "Sir Jon is representing me." She waited a beat, then said, "You're not Myrtle's only blackmail victim, Fiona. We've uncovered several others, haven't we, Molly?"

"We have," I said. "She had quite a sideline going."

"You think her death was related to *blackmail*?" Fiona whispered this last.

"If there's another reason, we haven't found it," Aunt Violet said. "She wasn't blackmailing *me*, but the killer chose to frame me anyway." Her fists clenched. "I'd tell you more details about that, but Sir Jon wouldn't like it. My defense, you know."

"They framed you? Oh my, that is horrible." Fiona rose and began to pace. "Anyone would think I had the perfect motive, wouldn't they?" She gestured around the lovely room. "If Gregory knew . . . my marriage would be destroyed. The children would hate me." She stopped dead and stared at us. "Did you think I—"

Possibly yes. But Aunt Violet prevaricated. "We thought you might know something that would help. Maybe you saw or heard something. That night or another time. The police aren't really digging, you see. They don't once they have a viable suspect." Her mouth turned down. "And right now, that's me."

Fiona remained rooted to the carpet. "I'll give it some thought, Violet."

Light footsteps tapped on the stairs. "I'm back," Persephone caroled out as she swanned into the living room. Her hair was loose and flowing, and she'd changed into a full floral skirt and a white peasant blouse. Very appropriate poet attire. "Ready, Molly?"

◀▶

"Fish and chips at the pub tonight?" Mum asked when Aunt Violet and I returned to the shop. "I can't believe I haven't had them since coming home." Cambridge had become home, I noticed, displacing Vermont.

"Sounds good to me," Aunt Violet said. She set Persephone's book on the counter. "Look what we were blessed with today."

Mum picked up the book and began to leaf through. "Oh, this is beautiful." She glanced at us. "How did it go?"

"Okay, I think." After giving both cats a quick pat hello, I opened my phone photo gallery. "Persephone showed up, unfortunately, which kind of cut our discussion short. But I did get some new photos of her for the web." I held up the phone so Mum could see.

"We did talk to Fiona about Tom and the blackmail," Aunt Violet said, pulling on a cardigan. It was much cooler in the shop than outside. "But she didn't confess to killing Myrtle."

"She knows something, though." My intuition told me this was true as soon as I uttered the words. "Remember how she zoned out a couple of times?" I brought up a social media account and started writing a post about Persephone's new book. I tagged Ruth, to make sure she saw it.

"I hope someone knows something," Aunt Violet said with a sigh. "Who have we got for suspects?"

"Fiona, still," I said. "Ruth, a long shot. Steve. We need to talk to him. Clive, definitely. Other people we don't know about. Maybe she had something on Persephone. Who knows?"

A voice came from the doorway. "Add me to the list." George wandered in, his normally cheerful face downcast. "I just had a nice visit from the police." He turned to Aunt Violet. "And yes, I would love a cup of tea." He bent to pat Puck. "How you doing, little man? They feeding you all right?"

"So what's this, George?" Aunt Violet asked briskly once we were settled around the kitchen table. I'd had too much tea already but accepted a cup from Aunt Violet anyway. It was about the ritual as much as the liquid, I'd come to realize. "I know Myrtle owed you back rent, but that was settled with the will, wasn't it?"

"It was." George remained gloomy despite a speedy infusion of his favorite biscuits. "But they were questioning me up one side and down the other. Did I know about the will? No, I did not. Then it was, how much did I resent her for not paying me? Was I hard up and in need of her money? They even asked me about a presentation I went to. I've been thinking about buying a home and renting out my own flat. So what?"

Uh-oh. Talk about a backfire. "Um, George, that's my fault." Sort of. I quickly told him about my visit to Clive and the discovery of the knitting needle. "They must have found your name on the sign-in list," I said. Remembering that I'd taken a picture, I brought it up on my phone. Yes, there he was, third from the bottom.

"Don't blame yourself, Molly," George said. "They obviously don't have a strong case so they're digging hard." His brow creased. "But if this keeps up, I'll give Sir Jon a call. See if he'll take me on."

"I'm sure he would," Aunt Violet said. "If he can represent both of us, that is."

"How about this?" A glint of humor lit George's eyes. "Whoever gets arrested first can have him."

"Deal," Aunt Violet said. "Let's hope it doesn't come to that." She held up both hands with fingers crossed.

I studied the list of potential bungalow buyers but didn't see any other names I recognized. That I could decipher, that is. "George, did you see anyone else you knew at Clive's presentation? Maybe they left the knitting needle." Clive must have convinced the police that he wasn't anywhere near the bookshop the night of Myrtle's murder. So where had the needle come from?

George thought for a moment, then shrugged. "I didn't see anyone familiar. A bunch of ladies, mostly. A few couples."

Of course he hadn't seen our killer. That would have been too easy.

A text flashed onto my phone from Daisy. *What are you doing later?*

Fish and chips at pub with Mum and Aunt Vi. Join us?
Love to. We need to talk about shopping.

Yes, we did. My date with Kieran was tomorrow night. Oh
boy. One good thing about investigating a murder, it certainly
overshadowed first-date jitters.

⁂

The pub was packed for fish-and-chips night, which apparently was a local favorite. After seeing that all the tables
were full, the four of us sat at the bar. I was in Myrtle's old
spot, I realized with a touch of uneasiness—and sadness.
Maybe she'd been a difficult and conniving woman, but she
didn't deserve to be murdered.

"What can I get you?" Steve asked as he placed napkin-
rolled utensils in front of us. All of us ordered the special,
Daisy and I had ale, and Mum and Aunt Violet ordered white
wine. As I watched the pub owner shuttle back and forth
serving customers, I wondered if we would have a chance to
chat tonight. It didn't look good.

Uncle Chris's revelation about Steve's involvement with
the gambling ring drifted through my mind. Had the threat
of Myrtle revealing his past misdeeds tipped him over the
edge? Maybe her demands had escalated, since to all appear-
ances, the pub was doing well. But it must have been difficult to siphon off money without alerting his wife. In the
bookshop, for example, all three of us were very aware of
how much money was coming in and going out.

"So, shopping tomorrow," Daisy said, dragging my

thoughts away from these ruminations. "I close at noon. Does the afternoon work for you?"

"Perfect." I sipped my ale, then wiped creamy foam off my lips. "I can't believe our date is *tomorrow*." I laughed. "It kind of snuck up on me and now I'm out of time."

"Has it been a busy week?" Daisy asked. She lowered her voice. "Any progress?"

I knew what she was referring to. So speaking quietly under the hubbub around us, I gave her the latest updates, the last tidbit being George's interview with the police. Mum and Aunt Violet were busy talking to another couple at the bar.

"Crikey." Daisy rolled her eyes. "George is a suspect? What about me, am I next?"

"Was she blackmailing you too?" I asked, joking. Who wasn't being blackmailed by Myrtle was probably the question.

Just then Susie burst through the kitchen doors holding four platters of fish and chips aloft, and to my joy, she headed straight for us. We'd watched with watering mouths as previous orders had sailed by.

"Here you are, ladies," she said, serving Mum and Aunt Violet first, then moving along to Daisy and me. The platters held piles of golden chips and good-sized pieces of battered fish. It all smelled incredible.

"Busy night," I said, unrolling my utensils. "I'm glad we managed to squeeze in."

Susie laughed as she nudged a bottle of vinegar our way. Daisy picked it up and began to sprinkle the condiment on her food. "We love it but it's all getting to be a bit much. Maybe I can talk Steve into retiring and buying that bungalow after all."

"Bungalow?" I asked, thinking immediately about Clive's project. It must be coincidence, but I went ahead away. "Are you talking about Cherry Hinton Homes? My cousin Clive is building those."

She nodded. "Yes, that's it. I went to a presentation the other day. Very tempting, it was. Good terms." She gestured at the pub. "And as much as I love this old place, I'm ready for something new." She spoke behind her hand. "Modern plumbing especially." With another smile, she whisked away, off to serve someone else.

Daisy handed me the vinegar. As I dispensed a generous amount over my chips and fish, I pondered the meaning of what we had just learned. Had Susie left the knitting needle at Clive's office? Maybe we'd gotten it all wrong. Maybe Susie, seeing that her husband couldn't—or wouldn't—stop Myrtle's extortion, had taken matters into her own hands.

In between forkfuls, I studied the list of names from the presentation. One scrawl looked promising, since the first-name *S* was clear. I pushed the phone over to Daisy and pointed to the line. "What's that name?"

She picked up the phone and squinted at the handwriting. "I don't know." She scrolled up and down the list. "I see George's name. But you can't read most of them. And half didn't leave phone numbers or emails. Don't blame them. Who wants to be hounded?"

"I wouldn't, either." I stuffed a big forkful of fish into my mouth. Oh, yum. Fresh and light yet savory. Next I bit into a hot, flavorful chip. Yum again. No wonder England was famous for fish and chips.

"What's this?" Daisy sounded shocked. She thrust the phone back toward me. "Look. Someone named Joan Watson went to the presentation."

CHAPTER 18

Daisy was right. Someone had signed in as Joan Watson. My heart thudded. Would someone really use that particular name as an alias? And why?

I picked up my ale and sipped to ease my suddenly dry throat. "Maybe it's another Joan. There have got to be dozens of them in England and maybe even a couple in Cambridge."

She had her own phone out now. "Yeah, there are over a hundred Joan Watsons in the UK. So you must be right. It gave me a shock, that's all."

"I can understand that." I put down my fork, unable to eat right now. Snippets of what I'd read in the journal floated into my mind, a familiar conflict churning in my chest. I wanted to share what I'd learned about her lovely aunt with Daisy but I was hesitant to open the wounds of loss.

Thankfully she solved my dilemma for me. "Have you

learned anything interesting in her journal? I realized that I've been such a coward. I want to read it as soon as you are done."

"Well, I won't spoil it for you," I said. "But I will tell you this. Your aunt was a delightful person. I wish I'd had a chance to know her."

"Me too," Daisy said wistfully. "You're so lucky to have your Aunt Violet still with you."

Yes, I am. "I know, especially since I didn't meet her until we moved here." I didn't add that I hadn't even known of her existence. That was Mum's business, the fact that she'd been estranged for so long. In fact, I hadn't even told Daisy about the encounter with my uncle and cousin. If all continued to go well with them, they could gradually become part of our lives.

And now that my thoughts about Daisy's aunt were out in the open, my appetite returned. The Magpie Pub's fish and chips deserved my full attention and enjoyment.

⁂

Later that night, overstuffed from the high-calorie meal, I lumbered up into bed with Puck and picked up Joan's journal. I'd been reading it slowly so I could really absorb each entry, plus I was reluctant to reach the end. Once I did, there would be nothing more of Joan's, ever. That made me sad.

I wondered about her poems, where they were. Although she mentioned her writing output, saying she'd had good days and bad, I hadn't seen any poems in the other notebooks. Maybe her parents had kept them.

Puck gave a little chirp as he turned over, all four paws in the air. "I know what you want," I said, laughing. He loved it when I rubbed his soft belly. When he'd had enough, he rolled again, onto his side.

"I get the hint," I said, pulling my hand away. I opened the journal and began.

Joan Watson's journal

Saturday started as a very good day. But oh, how quickly things can go downhill! No wonder my joy is always tethered, like a balloon with a very short string.

Our little poetry society met right after breakfast in the garden. It was a beautiful morning, a warm and golden late October day. Except for the bright leaves carpeting the grass, there was no sign that bleak November was right around the corner.

The six or seven of us sat on the grass, on plaid blankets someone had thoughtfully contributed. Persephone provided a huge hamper of tea, biscuits, and fruit as usual. Our ritual was for each of us to read aloud and then everyone else commented.

They were all kind, but my heart thumped and my palms went damp every time it was my turn. I really don't like reading aloud. But as Persephone says, we need to get used to it, practice for when we are famous.

Ha. But, to my relief, they liked my poem, which had an All Hallows' Eve theme, appropriate to this time of year. "You're so imaginative," one girl commented. "Where do you get your ideas?"

Since she wrote the sweet treacle you might read in women's magazines, I wanted to ask why she didn't have any. But I held my tongue. Am I the only one who feels the weight of history here, who can sense the ghosts around us? There are places in this city where the veil between past and present is wavering and thin, where one feels as if it's possible to step through . . .

I'll have to explore that later—Anyway, after we all read, we discussed our upcoming publication. We're each submitting two or three of our best poems, with the aim of producing an issue in the spring. Exciting stuff.

So, I was in good spirits when I returned to my room. Gregory had called and invited me to lunch at the Holly & Ivy. I knew where that was, of course, since my older brother and his wife run a tearoom down the lane from the hotel. The Holly & Ivy is small, but very exclusive, a definite cut above the usual pub fare we gorge on.

Since it was such a fancy place, I wore my fine wool plaid dress, new stockings, and my court shoes with the buckle. My best tweed overcoat looked nice, as did my gloves and hat. I almost felt chic.

Gregory came to St. Hildegard's to meet me. "You look lovely, Joan," he said, kissing me right in front of the porter. Didn't I tell you it was a good day?

Then he stepped back and looked at me, his expression nervous. "I got a call a little bit ago. From my parents. They're in town."

I stared at him, puzzled. "Does this mean you

need to cancel?" Why hadn't he simply called and left me a message? I could be working on my poems instead.

He shook his head. *"I've invited them to join us. But if you'd rather not . . . I'll beg off. I can see them for dinner."*

"What do you want to do?" I asked, sliding my hand through his arm. *"I'm happy to meet your parents. Or not."*

Patting my hand, he stared down into my eyes. *"Thank you for understanding, Joan. Let's go have lunch."*

We took a cab to the hotel, an indulgence I certainly never allowed myself. As we disembarked in front, I wondered if I would happen to see my brother or sister-in-law. They'd get a kick out of seeing me all dressed up for a meal, I was sure.

The Holly & Ivy was historic, quaint, tiny, and immaculate, like a dollhouse. We stood in the lobby while the clerk rang Mr. and Mrs. Fosdyke's room.

"They're staying here?" I whispered, shocked. Had this all been planned without me knowing?

He ran a finger around inside his collar. *"They are. I only booked us for lunch because I've been here before a bunch of times. Honest, Joan. I had no idea they were coming this weekend."*

But did they know about his lunch with me *was* the question. I remembered that they wanted Fiona for Gregory. I was an interloper.

The overdramatic thought made me smile, and I

squared my shoulders. At least I was a good-looking interloper.

A moment later, Mr. and Mrs. Fosdyke came down the stairs, heads held high, smiles chilly. "How nice to meet you," Mrs. Fosdyke said. "Percy and I so wanted to meet the young woman Gregory has been raving about."

And it went downhill from there. I won't give a blow-by-blow account. Suffice it to say that I can't even remember what we ate. It was the most miserable meal I ever had.

Poor Gregory was mortified. "I'll make it up to you, Joan," he said later. "We'll go up to London, just the two of us, and see the sights."

"They don't like me," I said sadly. "It was very obvious." I didn't come from the right background. No wealth, connections, or pedigree.

"It's not you, Joan." He was livid. "It's their outdated, ridiculous notions of what they want my life to be, as their son. Who they want me to marry. But I'm of age. I'll do what I want, not what they want."

Does Gregory have the mettle to stand up against his parents and the centuries-old traditions of the Fosdyke family? I'm not sure.

I should probably end it now.

When I read that last sentence, I actually jumped. Puck raised his head and glared. "It's okay," I told him, smoothing his fur. "Something surprised me, that's all."

After I got over the initial shock, caused by what I knew about Joan's death, I calmed down. She was talking about ending her relationship with Gregory because she wanted to avoid the uphill battle of forming a serious relationship without his parents' blessing. This was over fifty years ago, I reminded myself. Parental approval meant more then, especially for someone like Gregory, poised to follow his father into politics. I'd heard about the often brutal class system in England, how much pressure there was to marry someone of the same status.

So why had Joan killed herself, as everyone had believed? So far I had seen absolutely no sign that she was depressed or hopeless.

I leafed ahead in the journal, eager to find out if anything had changed. The next few entries focused on school and her poetry, which she said was going well. A couple more dates with Gregory were mentioned, so she hadn't pulled the plug yet.

The journal abruptly ended. But when I studied the book closer, I saw that several pages had been removed. Not ripped out, but *sliced* close to the gutter—the space where pages met the binding. The pages after the excision were blank.

Someone had removed Joan's last words. But who? And why? Was Joan murdered, the way Myrtle had implied with the Midsomer Murders label?

◆◗

The next morning, Mum and I finished pricing out the Oz books, coming up with a total that made my eyes water. If we found other treasures of this caliber in Tom's collection, the bookshop's income would soar. We'd easily pay Clive off and start building a nest egg.

"This is the draft listing," I said to Aunt Violet, showing her the computer screen. "Please check it out to make sure I got everything right." We were posting the books for sale on the bookseller sites Aunt Violet used as well as on the shop website. I also planned to do social media posts, although I wasn't sure if serious collectors used them. But I was positive the beautiful and quirky Oz books would get lots of attention. The illustrations were amazing. Plus most people didn't know there were other installments beyond the first book, *The Wonderful Wizard of Oz*. I looked forward to delighting them with the news.

Aunt Violet peered through her glasses at the listing, then made a couple of tweaks. "Very good, Molly." She rose from her chair. "You can go ahead and post."

My fingers trembled slightly as I uploaded the listing. It was such a responsibility to get this right. Our claims about the books' condition and value had to be completely accurate. Thomas Marlowe's reputation depended upon it.

Mum and George were rearranging the position of a bookcase in the back, and hearing his familiar cry of "Bloody" something or other, I remembered what Susie had said the previous night.

"I'll put the books back, George," Mum said. "Thanks for your help."

George appeared around the corner. "Too early for tea, love?" he asked Aunt Violet, who was sealing a package for the mail.

"Never," she said, placing the book onto the stack going out. "Have a seat."

He sat next to me behind the counter, watching as I wrote a social media post. "Nice pictures."

"Thanks. I really enjoy doing this." My fingers flew as I added hashtags. "Oh, I wanted to ask you something." Finished with the post, I swiveled my chair to face him. "Did you see Susie Baker at Clive's bungalow presentation? She told us last night that she went to one."

George rubbed his chin, thinking. "Yes, I did, come to think of it. She was up front so I didn't talk to her. Left as soon as I could after, before that Claire woman could buttonhole me."

So Susie had attended that particular presentation. Had she left the knitting needle behind? It would have been pretty easy if she had waited until the place thinned out. Otherwise someone helpful might have pointed it out.

"Is there any particular reason you're asking?" George's expression creased with suspicion. "You think *Susie* left that knitting needle behind?"

"Not really," I said, feeling like a rat for suspecting such a nice person. Especially in light of the fact that she and her husband were hosting a meal for Myrtle Sunday afternoon, after the memorial. We'd gotten the word earlier that the event was a go.

"But I think someone left it, maybe to frame Clive," I went on. Should I share this new information about Susie with Inspector Ryan? Probably, if it meant turning police suspicions away from Aunt Violet and George.

"What motive would Susie have to kill Myrtle?" he pressed. "Myrtle wasn't blackmailing the Bakers, was she?"

She had been, but I didn't want to tell George what I knew about Steve's gambling problems. While I trusted the old gent, the information might slip out anyway and I didn't want to hurt the pub's reputation.

"I didn't see any proof implicating them among Myrtle's things," I said honestly. "But I do know that Steve gave her free meals."

"Free meals?" George's tone was incredulous. "He did that for all the pensioners in the neighborhood."

Probably so, since Steve was a generous sort. But I was also sure that Myrtle pushed the envelope.

Aunt Violet returned, carrying a mug of tea for George. "I made a fresh pot if you want one, Molly."

Here was my excuse. "I think I will grab a cup," I said, pushing back my chair. "Be right back." Grabbing my phone, I slipped out of the bookshop and into the kitchen. Then, worried that someone would overhear, I went outside.

Inspector Ryan wasn't available, so I left a message. "Hello, Inspector," I said, trying to sound confident and unlike someone implicating innocent people to get her friends and relatives off the hook. "I learned something interesting last night. Susie Baker, owner of the Magpie Pub, attended the same meeting at Clive Marlowe's office as George. The one where the pink knitting needle was left behind, we think, unless Clive was lying." Clive wasn't on my relatives-I-want-to clear list, sad to say. "So do with that what you will."

I gritted my teeth in frustration. With the addition of Susie, the suspect list was getting longer, not shorter. Would we ever figure out who killed Myrtle?

CHAPTER 19

"Look at that dress," Daisy said, touching my arm. "It's you."

Mom, Daisy, and I were strolling along quaint Rose Crescent, which was lined with shops like Jo Malone and Crabtree & Evelyn. Daisy had halted in front of a cute little boutique called Pomegranate.

"I love the style," I said. The dress was black, with a V-neck, fitted bodice, and knee-length full skirt. The sleeves were three-quarter. The other "little black dresses" I'd seen today were too skimpy for my taste—short party dresses with no sleeves and plunging décolleté.

Daisy reached for the door latch. "Let's go in."

"Um, I hope I can afford it." With its tasteful, minimal display, Pomegranate looked like the kind of place I generally avoided—upscale and eye-wateringly expensive. I'm more down-to-earth and thrifty, as my outfit of well-worn jeans, faded tee with plaid flannel shirt, and running shoes attested. My last dressy outfit came from a consignment shop.

"My treat," Mum said, almost pushing me through the door. "You only live once."

"Plus you're going on a date with Kieran Scott," Daisy said loudly enough for the shop assistant and a couple of browsing customers to overhear. They stared at us with curiosity. "You never know. There might be photographers."

"I sure hope not," I said in dismay, my sneakers stumbling on the thick carpet. "I hate having my picture taken."

"Don't worry," Daisy tossed over her shoulder. "You'll be camera-ready by the time I'm done with you." She halted in front of the counter. "Good afternoon. My friend wants to try on the black dress in the window."

"Of course." With a shake of her silky auburn hair, the assistant put her phone aside and eyed me up and down in an expert manner. "The changing rooms are in the back. Through the red curtains."

We went in that direction and were soon joined by the clerk, who brought over two dresses in different sizes and hung them in a changing cubicle. "One of these should fit," she said. "Let me know if you need anything else."

"In you go," Daisy said, ushering me into the tiny closet. "We'll be right here." She and Mum sat in little chairs to wait, Daisy dispensing water with lemon from an urn for them to sip.

Behind the curtains, I took off my jeans and T-shirt then slipped one of the dresses over my head. The garment fit perfectly, flattering my top half and skimming over my hips. The length was good, just above the knee.

"Come out when you're ready," Daisy called.

Before I obeyed her order, I took another look at myself in the mirror. Even without makeup and my hair hanging loose and somewhat tangled, I looked good. My pulse leaped. Good enough to impress Kieran? Yes, quite possibly.

I pushed the curtains open in a dramatic gesture. "Ta-da!"

Mum and Daisy gazed at me with identical expressions of amazement.

"You look incredible," Daisy cried. "I knew that dress was perfect for you."

I stepped out, smoothing the skirt and twirling in front of the three-way mirror. "You were right. Not only does it look good, it feels comfortable." I hated uncomfortable clothing, one reason I rarely dressed up.

"You should wear black boots with that," Daisy said. "Do you have a pair?"

"Sure do." A tall leather pair with modest heels that might be okay for navigating cobblestones. We didn't have far to walk tonight, thankfully, only up the lane to the Holly & Ivy.

The clerk was looking on with approval. "That looks great on you," she said. "Good choice."

I glanced at Mum, who nodded. "I'll take it."

While the clerk rang up the sale, I browsed through a rack of earrings next to the counter. "What do you think of these?" I asked Mum and Daisy, holding up a pair of chandeliers with tiny jet beads.

"Love them," Mum said, taking them from me. "Add these to the bill."

"No problem," the clerk said. "I hope you don't mind me

asking, but where are you from?" she asked me. "Such fun to see all the visitors."

"Oh, I'm not visiting," I said with pride. "I moved here recently from the United States. Vermont, to be exact. Mum and I work at Thomas Marlowe. The bookshop on Magpie Lane."

"That's a lovely store," she said. "Welcome to Cambridge." She handed me a pink bag with handles, my dress and earrings safely tucked inside with tissue paper. "Enjoy."

The door jingled shut behind us. One hurdle down. I'd found the perfect dress for my date. "Any ideas what to do with my hair?" I asked Daisy, smoothing my ruffled locks with my free hand.

She was thumbing through her phone as we walked. "On it. Looking for styles."

"Break time," Mum said, heading for a table and some chairs outside a bakery. She pulled out a chair and sat.

"My treat," I said, setting my precious bag on a chair. "What would you like?"

"The double chocolate brownies are really good here," Daisy said. "Believe me, I've sampled every bakery and tea shop in town. In the interests of research, naturally." She dimpled.

"Ah. That's one word for it," Mum said. "I'd like to research a brownie too, Molly."

A few minutes later, I returned with a tray holding coffees, brownies, and glasses of ice water. Mum and Daisy were staring at something on Daisy's phone.

"I can't believe that went viral already," Mum said.

"It must have been one of the customers," Daisy said. "The store would fire her for doing that."

I set down the tray. "What's going on?"

Daisy glanced up at me, her expression apologetic. "Me and my big mouth. Someone posted a picture of you on social media, Molly."

"Me?" I plunked down in a chair. "Why? I'm nobody."

"You're somebody now." Daisy handed me the phone.

The shot showed me looking at earrings in the boutique. *Kieran Scott's new girl, rumor has it,* the caption read. *American lovely caught browsing on Rose Crescent, Cambridge. Has our fav KS gone country?* But I certainly looked less than lovely with my hair askew from the changing room, dressed in an outfit suited to rambling in the woods.

I cringed. What was Kieran going to think when he saw this? I hoped he wouldn't assume that I'd sought out the publicity. That was the last thing I wanted.

"Try the brownie," Mum urged. "It will make you feel better." She'd already gobbled half of hers.

I picked up the thick, fudgy square and took a nibble. The chocolate and sugar went right to my bloodstream. She was right. I did feel marginally better. One good thing about my new dress was the full skirt. It would hide a multitude of sins—or sweet-eating sessions.

●●●

"What do you think, Aunt Violet?" I stood in the middle of the bookshop and twirled so she could view my dress, boots, and hairstyle. Daisy had pulled my hair back in front and curled the rest with an iron before coaxing it into long, rippling waves.

She clapped her hands together. "You look lovely, my dear. Just stunning."

Daisy, who stood nearby beaming proudly, said, "She does clean up nice, doesn't she? You're going to knock Kieran's eyes out."

"So is that terrible picture of me." I cringed in memory.

"What picture?" Aunt Violet asked.

Mum entered the shop, carrying a tray with four glasses of wine. "I told her it's nothing, but she doesn't believe me." Resting the tray on the counter, she passed the wine around. Lifting her own glass, she said, "To another good week at Thomas Marlowe."

We joined Mum in the salute, although it was only Friday and we were open tomorrow for a half day. But we'd all agreed earlier that instituting a Friday happy hour was a good idea.

"I want to see this *nothing*," Aunt Violet said, not letting the subject go.

Daisy pulled out her phone and opened the page. "Some nasty piece of work took this while we were shopping." She showed the phone to Aunt Violet.

"I think you look cute, Molly," Aunt Violet said. "But it is rather disturbing that they posted this online. And made those comments about Kieran."

"Well, a tabloid did, to be absolutely correct." I took a sip of the soft, fruity wine. "But I'm sure that person got paid for the photo."

Aunt Violet looked speculative. "Well, if they're paying for snaps of you, then maybe I should get in on that." When we all stared at her, mouths hanging open, she laughed. "I'm joking. But even if I wasn't I'd at least make sure your hair was combed."

"Thanks, Aunt Violet." I rolled my eyes. The one time I hadn't was apparently recorded for posterity.

The shop door opened with a jingle. "Oh darn. I thought I locked that," Mum said. Then her expression hardened. "No. You've got to be kidding me." She set her wine down and squared her shoulders, fists lightly clenched as though for battle.

A middle-aged blonde woman was making her way through the store, nose lifted as she stared around. Her hair was styled in an immaculate pageboy and she wore a neat mauve wool skirt suit and sleek leather pumps.

As she drew closer to where we stood—or in the case of Aunt Violet, sat—a frosty smile slid over her face, her blue eyes boring into Mum. "Hello, Nina. How nice to see you." Her tone said clearly that it was anything but.

Mum's return smile was equally frosty but her tone was chipper. "Hello, Janice. What brings you to town?"

Aunt Janice laughed, triggering my memory of the garden club tea photograph. She was the woman seated next to Kieran's mother. And maybe I shouldn't prejudge people, but I could tell already that she was an awful person. Snobbish, rude, unkind. Why hadn't she stayed away?

"Seeing you of course, silly. Chris told me you were back, so I came quick as I could. I'm so, so busy these days." Aunt Janice turned to me, raking her gaze up and down my body, which the curl of her lip said she found wanting. "This must be Molly. Oh, pet, you look just like your father." The head-shake clearly adding, *poor thing*.

I tossed back my wine, not caring if it meant she accused me of having a drinking problem. When I caught her staring, I asked, "Would you like a glass, Auntie? It's very good."

"No, thanks," she said with a shudder. "I can't stay long."

Daisy had finished her wine and was making motions that indicated she was leaving. I hurried over to her, and together we walked to the door. "Thanks again, Daisy," I said, kissing her cheek. "I so appreciate your help with everything."

"No problem," she said, grinning. "You can return the favor, all right?" She peeked behind me at Aunt Janice. "And good luck. She's a right cow."

"Perfect description. I'll talk to you tomorrow."

Her smile was roguish. "You'd better. I want to hear *all* about it." Meaning my dinner date.

My innards lurched at the thought of Kieran, which seemed to happen with annoying regularity. The thoughts and the lurching both. "And you shall."

Daisy gave me a final once-over. "I'm pretty proud of myself. You look amazing." She headed off toward the tea shop with a wave.

As I shut the door behind her, I glanced up the lane toward the bike shop. No sign of Kieran yet, but he was supposed to be here any minute. *Eek*. When I returned to the others, the conversation had turned to Myrtle's murder.

"I couldn't believe my eyes when I saw the paper," Aunt

Janice was saying. "You get here, Nina, and next thing you know, there's a mysterious death in the back garden."

Mum's head went back. "That had absolutely nothing to do with me. Or Molly."

"Or Aunt Violet," I said hotly. "Myrtle had many, many enemies. For all we know, you're one of them. Take a number and get in line." I hadn't considered Aunt Janice a suspect, but at that moment I felt it would be a pleasure to uncover proof of her guilt.

Aunt Janice backed away, a hand to her neck. "I . . . I don't know . . . what . . ."

My great-aunt was on her feet now. "Janice. I know you're family, but I can't allow you to make insinuations like that in my home. Either apologize to Nina or leave."

Aunt Janice darted a glance at Mum. "I'm sorry, Nina," she said, her expression unrepentant. "I was merely making an observation." She cupped an elbow, fingers tapping on her lips. "For the record, Violet, I don't believe you did it, either. But I do have to say this: someone *really* doesn't like you."

As if she'd been deflated, Aunt Violet sank into her chair, her features tight with anguish. The fact someone had killed Myrtle in our back garden—with Aunt Violet's knitting needle—already pointed to this fact, but the way Aunt Janice said it had sent a knife into my heart as well.

"It's been nice to see you but—" I began, planning to make Aunt Janice leave, forcibly if necessary. But the doorbell jingled, announcing Kieran's entrance.

Everything faded away—malicious Aunt Janice, my worries about Aunt Violet, Puck trying to claw my leather boot—and I saw only Kieran, framed in light. From the big windows behind him, but still.

He stared at me and I stared at him. He looked "scrumptious", as Daisy might say, dressed in slim black jeans, a blue button-down, and a tailored tweed jacket. His curls had been tamed but his chin still had a hint of scruff. *Yum.*

"You look lovely, Molly," he said, advancing across the room.

I dipped my chin. "Thank you. So do you." I tossed my hair, feeling flirty. "I'm looking forward to dinner."

Aunt Janice was quite frankly gaping. "Kieran Scott?" Her mouth flapped. "I know your mother." Her incredulous glance at me plainly revealed what she was thinking. How did her pathetic niece end up with someone like Kieran?

"You do?" Kieran asked politely. "What's the connection?"

"Your mum and I are in the garden club together," Janice said in a furious rush. "I'm Janice Marlowe, Molly's aunt. We live in Hazelhurst. Right in the village, the enormous thatched cottage. It's listed, one of the oldest buildings in town. Right up there with the manor house—"

"Nice to meet you," Kieran said, cutting off the flood. He turned to me. "Are you ready to go?" He sent a smile around the room at large. "Hate to rush off but we've got a reservation."

"I'm ready," I said. "See you all later." I picked up my bag then slipped my hand through his arm. As we ambled toward the door, Janice called after us, "Give my best to your mother, Kieran."

Once safely out in the street, I burst into giggles. "Thank

you for rescuing me," I said. "I was about ready to throw Aunt Janice out on her ear. She's a piece of work."

"So I gathered," Kieran said. My arm was still in his and we moved smoothly in rhythm, my heels clopping on the cobblestones. "Unfortunately you can't pick your relatives."

Leaning closer, I said in a low voice, "But you can pick your friends." The last thing I wanted was to spoil our evening with complaints about my aunt.

He flashed a grin. "Am I your friend, Molly?" He squeezed my arm with his.

Gazing up into those dark eyes so intent upon mine, I could barely breathe. Then I grinned back, lightening the mood. "Yeah, I guess so."

He feigned hurt. "You guess so? She guesses so," he told a couple walking by who stared before hurrying away.

I rolled my eyes with a mock sigh. "All right, I admit it. We're friends. After all, you sold me the best bicycle ever."

"And are you enjoying the best bicycle ever?" he asked. The topic of Belinda occupied us the rest of the short walk to the inn. The dining room entrance was at the rear and we had the choice of inside or out. Outside was a patio hemmed in with ivy-covered trellises strung with lights.

"Let's sit outside," I said to Kieran. "It's such a nice evening."

A slim, stylish woman with choppy streaked hair stood behind the podium. "Good evening, Kieran," she said in a French accent. "How are you tonight?"

"I'm great, Monique," he said. "This is Molly, Violet Marlowe's niece." To me, he said, "Monique and her husband Michael own the inn."

"He cooks and I clean," Monique said with a smile. "How nice to meet you."

"Same here," I said. "You have a lovely place. I'm looking forward to our meal."

"We'd like to sit outside," Kieran said.

"Good choice on a night like this." Monique picked up two menus. "Right this way."

She placed us at a table in the corner at the back. From here we could see the rest of the outdoor enclosure and view a glimpse of the lane. Soft music played over hidden speakers, something French with accordions. A candle flickered on our table, next to one perfect pink peony in a vase.

I scanned the menu, curious to see what Asian-French fusion looked like. *Eclectic yet delicious* was the answer.

"Do you want an appetizer to share?" Kieran asked. "Your pick."

"Hmm," I said. "Should it be the quinoa and lotus-stem tikki or the calamari with coconut?" In the end we ordered the calamari, along with duck confit with kumquat sauce for me and lamb with truffle sauce for Kieran. He also ordered a bottle of Pinot Noir, which he said paired with both meals.

"You'll never guess what happened today." I dipped a crispy encrusted piece of calamari in a sweet and spicy sauce. "A photo of me went viral."

Kieran's lips pursed and his brows went up. "Oh. Page three?"

"No." I drew out the word. "Nothing as exciting as that." He was referring to the now defunct British tabloid tradition of daily topless photos. Using a clean finger, I brought up the picture of me at the store, then slid the phone over the tablecloth. "Believe me, if you weren't mentioned, I'd never show this to you."

He wiped his hands on his napkin and picked up my phone. After studying the post closely, he gave me a level look. "I'm sorry, Molly. The last thing I want is for you to be dragged into my problems." He slid my phone back to me. "For what it's worth, I think you look great. As you always do."

"Thanks." I shrugged one shoulder. "I'm not too worried about your *problems*. I mean, we spend most of our time on this quiet little lane running our businesses. Not exactly tabloid fodder."

Right then, our server arrived with our piping-hot dinner plates and I put thoughts of gossip columns and unflattering photographs aside as we dug in. Every single bite was delicious. During our meal, we kept the conversation to light topics—sharing favorite books and television shows, travel adventures, that kind of thing. We were both slumped back, groaning over a post-dinner cup of coffee when I spotted Ruth Orforo strolling onto the patio.

When I waved, she detoured over to our table, telling the couple she was with to go ahead and sit. "Hello, Molly. Kieran." Glancing over the remains of our meal, she smiled. "They feed you well here, don't they?"

"I'll say," I said. "This is the first time I've been, and I loved it." Then I remembered what I wanted to tell her. "Persephone gave me an advance copy of the book. It's gorgeous."

Ruth inclined her head in thanks. "I'm quite proud of it. It was especially fun going through the older work. Brought back many fond memories of St. Hildegard's, when I first met Persephone, as you know."

"You have a copy of the retrospective already?" Kieran asked me. "I know Mum has been chomping on the bit to get a hold of it."

"I'll send her a copy," Ruth said. "Shoot me a note, okay?"

I wondered about Joan, what Ruth had thought of her work. "Did you know Joan Watson? I've been reading her college journal. Her great-niece, Daisy, runs Tea and Crumpets down the street. She had some of Joan's things in her attic."

"Joan?" Ruth sank down into a nearby chair. "Of course I knew Joan. We were very good friends. And she was incredibly talented." She seemed lost in thought for a moment. "We were all stunned by her death. I always wondered if there was anything I could have done."

"A suicide, was it?" Kieran put in. "I remember hearing about that from Daisy. So sad."

"I haven't read any of her poetry," I said. "But reading the journal makes me wish I could. Her personality really shines through."

"Her work was marvelous," Ruth said. "And she was so prolific." Her brow creased. "Daisy didn't find any of her poems?"

"Not that I know of." I thought back to the contents of the box. "We only found study notes. And that journal."

Ruth glanced over her shoulder at her waiting friends, then rose to her feet. "I wonder where they went. I always wanted to publish Joan's work. And if you do come across anything, please let me know." She smiled. "Nice to see you both. Have a good evening."

Lost in thought, I murmured a response. Where were Joan's poems? Did her parents have them? It would be wonderful to share her work with the world, even if posthumously. *If I can, I will.* Joan deserved no less.

CHAPTER 20

"Smile for the camera," Kelsey Cook said with a grin as Kieran and I exited the restaurant. She readied her camera and stepped closer.

Kieran scowled. "What are you doing here?" He moved slightly ahead of me, as if to shield me from the photographer's view.

Kelsey grinned again as she lowered her camera. "Little bird told me." She put a finger to her lips. "And no, I'm not going to say who." Her mischievous eyes darted to me. "Hello, Molly. Welcome to the world of rumor and innuendo."

I couldn't hold back a smile. Who could resist this photographer's ironic honesty about her profession? Kieran couldn't either, because he relented. "All right, take a couple. But make sure Molly's hair looks good." He winked at me.

"No problem, milord," she muttered, lifting her camera. "She's a beauty."

I tried to smile naturally, thankful this wasn't a regular occurrence in my life. For his part, Kieran put his arm through mine and pulled me close, looking as if he was happy to be out with me.

Kelsey checked the pictures. "Not bad, not bad at all. Thanks for being a good sport, KS. Molly." She glanced up at me. "You work in the bookshop, right?" At my nod, she said, "You know that poet, did a reading for you the other night?"

"You mean Persephone Brightwell?" I asked. "Yes, we're acquainted." Sort of.

"I'd love to get a few pics of her. Now that she's winning awards and all that." Kelsey was still playing with her camera. "But I saw her the other night and she actually shouted at me to get lost. Not that I haven't heard that before."

My pulse leaped a little. "Really? She's a publicity hog if I've ever seen one."

Kelsey made a face as she backed away. "Didn't like the cut of my jib, I guess. I've got to dash. Ta." She turned and strode up the lane toward Trinity Street.

"I'm not quite ready to call it a night," Kieran said as Kelsey's footsteps died away. "How about you?"

My pulse leaped again, this time with excitement. "Me neither. Why don't we take a walk?" I liked evening walks, especially after a large meal.

"Sure," Kieran said, starting up the lane. "That sounds good. We can stop somewhere for a drink if you like."

I put a hand to my midriff. "Once I can fit something in. You were right about this place. The food is fantastic."

Popular, too. Vacated tables had filled again almost immediately.

"Isn't it great? I tell everyone about it," Kieran said. "I like
promoting another business on Magpie Lane."

His comment gave me a warm feeling. We Marlowes were
part of a community on our sweet little side street. People
were going in and out of the pub, making me think about
Steve and Susie. I really hoped neither one had anything to
do with Myrtle's death. Losing them would be a blow to the
neighborhood for sure.

We strolled down Trinity Street to King's College, crossed
the bridge, then wandered along the river walk. Lots of other
people were out enjoying the evening, students in groups and
older couples, the occasional runner or cyclist getting some
exercise.

"Want to sit here?" Kieran asked, indicating a bench di-
rectly across from King's Chapel. The last rays of golden
sun gilded the majestic buildings reflected in the river at our
feet. Ducks quacked and swam and punts glided by, trailing
laughter and chatter in their wake. "This is one of my favorite spots."

"I can see why," I said, checking the bench for any stray
dirt or debris before smoothing my dress and sitting. "My list
of favorite Cambridge places is growing by the minute."

"It's a very special city. I've loved it since my first visits
as a child." Kieran rested his right am along the back, close
enough for me to feel his warmth but not intruding on my
space. This was good. All night I'd sensed us growing closer
as we got to know each other, but Kieran was setting a nice,
slow pace. Not only was I reluctant to jump into anything,

there was the real potential for heartbreak here. I really liked him.

A runner huffed along the path, arms swinging. "He's got a lot more energy right now than I do," Kieran commented.

"Seriously," I said with a laugh. The man was dressed in neon shorts and a T-shirt, sneakers with reflective tape flashing as he trod along. As he drew closer, his features came into focus. "It's Sir Jon." In his seventies and still a runner. I was very impressed.

I must have said his name louder than I intended because his head whipped around and he slowed with a wave.

"Hello," he said between puffs. He halted, bending over with his hands on his thighs, using the hem of his shirt to wipe his face. "Nice evening, isn't it?"

"It certainly is," I said. "Kieran and I ate at the Holly and Ivy tonight. It was excellent."

His smile was roguish as he glanced back and forth between us, but he didn't comment on our obvious date. Instead he said, "I'm sorry I've been out of touch. I had to dash up to London again on business. But Violet's been keeping me posted."

I thought back to when I'd last spoken to Sir Jon. While I was at Clive's office, I realized. "So much has happened over the last couple of days. George is the executor of Myrtle's will, so he's been questioned. He was at the presentation at Clive's, where I found the knitting needle right before I called you last. And oh, get this. So was Susie Baker."

"Susie not Steve?" Sir Jon asked. He eased himself down into a crouch and bounced up and down slightly. "Interesting. I wonder if she knows about his gambling?"

"So do I," I said. "And my uncle—yes I finally met Mum's brother—said Steve was in big trouble a few years back. Illegal gambling ring."

Sir Jon nodded. "I'll have to look that up." He rose to his feet in one lithe move. "The police are hot after Clive now, by the way." His smile was somber. "Something about bribing officials? No arrest yet but they're building a case, my sources tell me."

"It couldn't happen to a nicer guy." Then I realized poor Kieran was being forced to listen while we caught up. "I'm sorry. This case can be all consuming."

"I get it," Kieran said. "I want to find out who killed Myrtle as well." He pointed a finger. "What about that man we saw in the alley, Molly? Has anyone ever identified him?" He told Sir Jon how he'd given chase but had been unsuccessful.

"Actually, a witness was found during the door-to-door interviews," Sir Jon said. "I got the update only an hour ago. This person also saw a man in the alley around the time Myrtle died, a time estimated from the physical evidence." He paused a beat. "They saw a male, burly and of medium height. But they didn't see his face clearly. And the witness couldn't identify him from photographs either." Meaning the police had probably shown the witness pictures of Clive and George, maybe even Steve, if Inspector Ryan had taken my call seriously.

My spirits sank. Every time we moved forward, we stopped just short of the mark. Nothing was conclusive yet.

"This is driving me crazy," I blurted. "Nothing is fitting together."

Sir Jon regarded me with sympathy. "Been there, Molly. All we can do is keep pressing forward. The truth will eventually come out."

"I hope it's soon," I said. "This is taking a toll on poor Aunt Violet." *Someone really doesn't like you.* Aunt Janice's cutting words jeered in my mind. "And George too."

Sir Jon's chiseled features rarely betrayed much emotion, but he appeared troubled now. "I don't like it either. I'll call Ryan tonight and put a bug in his ear regarding the other suspects." His smile was ironic. "Of which there are several." He began to stretch, preparing to start running again. "And I'll be by tomorrow to see Violet."

After he set off with a jaunty wave, Kieran said, "I hope I'm half that fit when I'm his age. If I live that long."

"Me too." The romantic mood had been broken and I was restless now. But not quite ready to say good night. "Shall we go have that drink?"

We wandered arm in arm back over the bridge and, after a little discussion, popped into our local, the Magpie Pub. How I loved the idea that this was our place. That people knew my name—and my favorite beer.

Dinner service was over but the place was jammed with people enjoying a carefree Friday night. Kieran and I found a cozy table near the fireplace. "I'll go order," he said. "Your usual?"

"Yes, please. A half-pint, though." I was still more than full from dinner.

Kieran made his way to the bar, where Susie was dispensing drinks. A large table beside me cleared out, a boisterous group of students, and as they went out the door, another party pressed in. Steve brought a tray over to the table and began to clear.

"Busy tonight," I said.

He glanced over his shoulder at the waiting patrons. "You got that right. Been like this all evening."

"Were you in the alley the night Myrtle died?" My hand flew up to my mouth. Had I really asked that now, in the middle of a crowded pub?

He stopped shoveling dirty glasses into the tray and stared at me. "No, I was not. What's this about, Molly?"

I backtracked a little. "Someone, a man, was out there, according to a witness." *And Kieran and me,* but I didn't say that. "I thought he might have seen something important. Poor Aunt Violet is suffering something fierce over the death of her friend." This was laying it on a bit thick but basically true.

His expression softened. "Look. Why don't you and your young man go into the snug? I'll pop in there in a few and we can chat."

"The snug?" Was Kieran my "young man"? Too bad the barkeep couldn't answer *that* question.

Steve pointed to a doorway I hadn't noticed. "Private room. Kieran's been in there a time or two."

I intercepted Kieran as he was returning from the bar, glasses in hand. "Let's go sit in the snug." His eyes lit up. "Steve wants to talk to us."

The light dimmed slightly. "All right. Lead on." He followed me around the bar.

The snug was a tiny room holding only a leather banquette, a round table, and a couple of chairs. Capacity: four persons at most. Stained-glass windows provided privacy from prying gazes in the main room.

"I see why they call it a snug," I said, sitting on the banquette. Steve's remark floated into my mind. Who had Kieran sat in here with? That was a question I'd never ask.

Kieran placed the glasses on the table and sat beside me. "Cheers," he said, lifting his glass. We clinked. "What's this about, then?" he asked before taking a sip.

"My big mouth," I said. "I asked him if he was in the alley that night."

He didn't need to ask which night. He took his phone out of his pocket and placed it on the table. "Molly. That was a risky move."

I sipped bitter ale, my eyes on his face. "Do you really think Steve is guilty? I thought he might have seen something."

Kieran shifted on the leather seat. "True. But that begs the question: why would he be hanging around in the alley?"

Honestly, there wasn't a good reason I could think of at the moment. "You're right. Sorry." I squeezed my eyes shut. "I'm too impulsive sometimes."

He put his hand gently on mine. "For what it's worth, I like that about you. In fact, I like—"

Steve whisked into the room, shutting the door behind him. "We're in a bit of a lull. But I only have a few."

Kieran withdrew his hand as Steve pulled a chair over and perched. "So what's this about a man in the alley?" Steve asked.

"We heard tonight that someone saw a man lurking," I said. "Either the killer or a potential witness."

Steve's expression became wary. "Are they looking at a man for it, then?"

Kieran's hand went to his phone, but he pretended to be casually toying with it.

"I don't think it's conclusive one way or the other," I said. Women were suspects too, in addition to Aunt Violet. Susie, for one. And Fiona. Could the person have been wrong? Maybe they only thought the lurker was a man. Fiona was tall and solid, Susie less so.

Steve made a disgruntled sound. "They are fiddling about, aren't they? Get on with it, I say."

Would a guilty person say that? Now that I had the opportunity to question him, I had no idea where to begin. What should I ask him? How should I approach the topic of Myrtle's blackmail?

Maybe I should just go ahead and rattle his cage. He wouldn't do anything here in the middle of a crowded pub, would he? Plus I had Kieran as a witness. "I know what Myrtle did to you," I said. "You weren't alone."

His eyes flared as he lurched back in his seat, almost sending the chair over. "How on earth—"

"Easy," Kieran said in a warning tone. "No one is accusing you of anything."

Steve ran a hand over his cropped hair. "Sorry. It's just that . . ." He glanced over his shoulder before lowering his voice. "I can't have Susie finding out. She'll give me the boot." His tone was pleading.

I thought of Susie's attendance at Clive's presentation and the knitting needle left behind. Maybe she already knew.

"You're gambling again," I said in a sympathetic tone.

"I saw you go into a betting shop the other day, Steve. But it's not up to me to tell anyone." Besides the police, of course.

Slumping back, he crossed beefy arms over his chest. "Yeah. I need to get a grip on that. Call my sponsor."

"Back to Myrtle," I said. "She was blackmailing you, wasn't she?"

His mouth twitched as he thought about what to say. "Yeah, she was," he finally admitted. "She knew about some . . . trouble . . . I'd had in the past. So I gave her free meals and the odd spot of cash to keep her off my back. But I didn't kill her." Recovering his confidence, he slapped a hand on the table. "And I have an alibi. I was here the entire night." He jumped to his feet, pushing in the chair. "I'd better get back. So if there isn't anything else, Miss Marple?" Referring to Agatha Christie's fictional detective.

I accepted the jibe with good grace. After all, I was sitting in the man's business premises, lucky he hadn't banned me.

"I'm sorry, Steve," I said. "I keep hoping someone will be able to prove that Aunt Violet is innocent." Identifying the real killer would be a bonus.

Again, his face softened at the mention of her name. "Vi's a good old gal, she is. If I hear anything that will help, I'll let you know, all right?"

Once he was gone, Kieran regarded me with bemusement. "I don't think I've ever been on a date quite like this before."

"Me neither." I spun my glass in circles on the table. "I'm sorry, Kieran."

He put an arm around my shoulders. "I didn't say it was a bad thing." After a moment, he whispered, "Do you think Susie has an alibi?"

I laughed. "I tell you what, trying to clear loved ones aside, this investigating thing is like a rabbit hole. Once you fall in, you can't extricate yourself."

✦

After we finished our beer, Kieran walked me home. "Thanks for a wonderful evening," I said, unlocking the shop door. "I had a great time."

He moved closer. "So did I, Molly. Truly." We looked at each other for a moment, the light over the door casting a spotlight on us. Then he swooped in and kissed me, a light, sweet touch of our lips. "I'll see you soon."

I watched him stride away, whistling, my fingers to my lips. Then I laughed at myself for acting so sappy and went inside.

Puck immediately glued himself to me while I was locking the door. "Want a bedtime snack?" I asked. He took off, bolting across the shop toward the kitchen door. I detoured by the desk on the way, remembering Persephone's new book. That would be my bedtime reading tonight since I was finished with Joan's journal.

Oh, Joan, I thought as I dispensed a little kibble into the cat dishes. *Will we ever know the truth about your death?* What a loss to us all. I filled a glass with water, then headed upstairs with Persephone's book and my cat.

The poetry collection was arranged chronologically, and

although I was often a dipper, I started from the beginning, curious to read her college poems.

The first few selections featured common motifs of life in Cambridge. The clannish colleges, punts on the river, the changing seasons. Quite clearly she was getting her legs under her, trying different approaches to developing a unique voice.

One more poem, I decided, my eyelids already drooping. This one was about winter. A line struck. *A creeping wind 'round the stair, a whisper of winter in the air.*

Hmm. *A whisper of winter.* That turn of phrase sounded familiar. I picked up Joan's journal and leafed through, scanning the pages.

Joan's line was *a creeping wind that whispers winter.* Not a direct quote but the same words used a different way.

I wouldn't be happy if I were Joan. Had Persephone read Joan's journal? No, that seemed far-fetched. But maybe some of Joan's inspired phrases had been included in her poems.

Which were missing. Was I overthinking this? I read them both again.

No, I was on to something. I knew it and so did my nervous system, judging by the speed of my heartbeat and my damp palms. This was huge. Persephone Brightwell was considered Britain's greatest living poet.

Had she stolen her friend's work to get there?

CHAPTER 21

Sunday afternoon, mournful organ music droned as funeral goers drifted into the Round Church for Myrtle's service. Aunt Violet, Mum, and I had snagged seats a couple of rows back from the front, close enough to show involvement, but certainly not claiming a close relationship.

No, that honor appeared to belong to George, her executor, who sat alone in the front, dressed in his best tweeds, ever-present cap in his lap for once.

I stared up at the stained-glass window over the altar, admiring its glowing colors and intricate design. This historic church, built almost a thousand years ago, was a wonder of stone arches, ancient carvings, and enormous round pillars. We were in a newer part off the original structure, the famous circular nave that gave the church its name.

Aunt Violet's friends entered in a bevy that stirred the air, people turning to watch as they rustled down the aisle, heels clicking. An attractive woman with hair cut in a stern beige bob walked beside Ruth. Catherine, I guessed.

They settled in the row right in front of us, shoulders bumping as they whispered. More latecomers drifted in: Susie and Steve—who sat across the aisle with Daisy and Tim—and Clive, who chose our row, forcing us to shift over a seat. I suppose he thought we Marlowes should stick together. For the funeral, at least.

I nodded in greeting as Clive settled next to me, his heavy cologne tickling my throat. I quickly put a tissue to my nose, praying I wouldn't cough.

He grunted a reply, staring straight ahead as though deep in thought. Why had he come to the service? I doubted that he genuinely mourned Myrtle's passing, in light of her blackmailing him. But honestly, if you used sorrow as a measure, most of us probably shouldn't be here.

How sad. I hoped that when I passed away—with any luck many years from now—people would miss me. Not merely show up, as these folks had, to make sure that I was truly gone. Conveniently, here were all the suspects, dressed to the nines and appearing appropriately somber: Susie, Steve, and Clive. Fiona and Ruth. What about Persephone, though? The potential plagiarism I'd discovered last night bothered me. And I'd never considered Catherine, mainly because she'd been in London the whole time. Or so I thought. Was one of them the killer, hiding glee—or guilt—under a mask of grief?

Quick footsteps sounded on the tile floor and I turned to

see Kieran striding down the aisle. Seeing that our row was full, Kieran slid in beside Aunt Violet's friends, who broke into huge smiles of welcome as they made room.

Right after he sat down, the organ music changed tempo to something majestic with deep, sonorous notes, and everyone rose for the vicar's entrance. The service had begun.

Thankfully the funeral was short, featuring only a few words from the vicar, a prayer read by George, and a sung hymn or two. It was obvious from the vicar's eulogy that he barely knew Myrtle, although he praised her volunteer efforts and regular attendance.

She'd also left a small bequest to the church, he said, although when I saw George's ears redden, I guessed he'd made it on her behalf. But it gave the attendees something to talk about when we burst out of the church into the warm May air, relieved to have done our duty.

Kieran came up beside me, handsome in his suit jacket and white shirt. "Heading to the pub?" he asked while taking off his tie. We fell into step with the well-dressed throng making its way to the street.

"You bet," I said. "Want to buy me a pint?"

"Sure." He grinned. "I heard the first one is on the house, so definitely."

"Big spender," I joked back. Susie and Steve were not only putting on a spread, they were hosting a short open bar. How generous, especially considering their rocky relationship with the deceased.

Inspector Ryan and Sergeant Adhikari were standing to one side, watching everyone leave the church. Of course they were here. Didn't killers often attend the funerals of their victims? Or so I'd heard.

I caught the inspector's eye, so instead of slinking past, I had to speak. "Hello there," I said. "Joining us at the pub?"

The sergeant's brows went up but the inspector shook his head. "Good day, Miss Kimball." His keen gaze went beyond me to others walking by.

Dismissed, I turned back to Kieran with a shrug. He hadn't even thanked me for my work.

We meandered down Trinity Street to Magpie Lane, still in company with the funeral attendees. The easel sign outside the pub door read Closed for Private Party, but since that was us, we joined the crowd pressing through the door.

"The old girl would be pleased," George said, coming up behind us. "Quite a good turnout." Perhaps it was the offering of a free meal, but we seemed to have gained a few bodies since the church.

A rush of affection swept over me as I stared into George's broad, kind face. "She was lucky to have a friend like you." I took his warm, callused hand and squeezed his thick fingers. This reliable old gent was one of my favorite people, I decided.

George blushed and stammered. "It's nothing really. We've all got to look out for each other, haven't we?"

Kieran clapped him on the back. "That's right, we do. Let me buy you a drink." He winked at us before wading through the throng toward the bar.

"Price is right, I understand," George called after him. He craned his neck, studying the crowd, then excused himself to follow Kieran.

I kept moving, knowing that Kieran would find me. Daisy was in the back room, where a long table had been set up. She and Susie were putting the finishing touches on a buffet that included hot chafing dishes, finger sandwiches, and salads. Daisy's butterfly cakes and other desserts were on a smaller side table, along with coffee and hot-water urns.

"This looks amazing," I said, thinking about what I should eat. After a late breakfast, I hadn't had lunch, so I was starving.

Susie pulled off a metal lid to reveal bubbling lasagna, and the aroma made my mouth water. "I guess we're doing all right by the wicked old thing. Should give us a couple of points with the Man Upstairs." She settled the lid back in place and turned down the Sterno flame.

"Susie." Daisy put a hand to her mouth, stifling a startled laugh. "You don't mean that."

A strange light shone in the pub owner's eyes. "I could tell you tales . . . but I won't. Let just say we're lucky lightning didn't strike the church." With that remark, she nodded at the buffet, swiped her hands across her apron, and marched off.

"Whoa," I said, fanning my face. "That was intense."

Daisy sidled close. "I agree. Something certainly got her knickers in a twist."

Now that's a funny saying, I thought with a giggle. But on a more serious note, Susie definitely held a grudge against Myrtle. Enough of one to kill Myrtle and try to frame Clive?

People began lining up for food, so I moved out of the way. Kieran showed up with my beer and we stood at one of the high tables to drink them.

Kieran leaned his elbows on the table. "I had such a good

time last night," he said in a low, warm voice, his eyes smiling into mine.

Was it corny to say my heart skipped a beat? Well, it did. "Me too," I said, raising my pint glass. "Cheers."

He clinked his glass with mine. "Cheers." After a long swallow, he said, "Let's do it again." His brows rose. "How about next Saturday?"

"That might work," I said, holding back a little. Before he could respond, someone passing by stopped to say hello. That broke the spell, and after that, we drank beer and watched the crowd mill around.

Aunt Violet and her friends were still together, along with Mum, and I watched as they filled plates of food then found a table. Somebody, namely Persephone, had already been hitting the wine, judging by her pealing laugh and exaggerated gestures.

Kieran shook his head at her antics. "Someone better shut her off."

"You're telling me." The other ladies were laughing along, except for Fiona, who sat a little apart, concentrating on her meal. Maybe she'd had enough of the poet—and I didn't blame her. Persephone's condescension toward her hostess had been obvious and rude.

The line thinned at last, so Kieran and I loaded plates, then returned to our corner table, where Daisy and Tim joined us. I chose a slab of the lasagna and a serving of chopped salad mixed with creamy dressing, plus a big slice of hot homemade baguette.

"Some of us are going to stay and play darts tonight," Tim said to the table at large. "Are you in?"

"Maybe," I said. "After this boatload of carbs, I might be too lazy."

"I'll hang out and watch," Daisy said with a sigh. "I want to take it easy for a bit."

"Me too," I said. So much had happened lately, I felt like I couldn't catch my breath. I scooped up a forkful of lasagna. "I'd better pace myself. I want one of those butterfly cakes, Daisy."

"They seem to be a favorite," she said, eyeing the depleted platter on the dessert table.

"Everything you do is my favorite," Tim blurted. Then he blushed furiously.

Kieran and I hooted, but Daisy sidled closer to Tim. "You're not so bad yourself," she murmured. A blonde curl fell over one eye, giving my pretty friend the allure of a classic film starlet. Tim was entranced.

I glanced at Kieran, who grinned. Watching Daisy and Tim's relationship unfold was sweet.

"Want another?" Kieran asked, tipping his chin toward my empty pint.

"In a few." I dabbed my mouth with a napkin. "Please excuse me for a minute." The first pint had just caught up with me.

Seated at the end of the bar, Clive was swilling down lager with the intensity of a man on a mission. He set the heavy mug down with a thump as I edged past. "Molly."

"Clive. You made it." I hadn't seen him since the church service.

"No thanks to you." His small blue eyes were hot with

rage. "What were you playing at, calling the police on me?" The veneer of civility he'd worn earlier had vanished. This was Clive the street fighter.

I took a step back, bumping into someone. "Sorry," I threw over my shoulder to whomever. "I didn't call them on *you*. I called about the pink knitting needle." And if it implicated my cousin, so be it.

Steve, whose nose must be finely tuned to trouble, appeared behind the bar. My savior. "Clive. Want another?" He slid a glance at me, giving me the signal to escape.

I took the opportunity to scamper away, almost running down the hall to the restroom. Persephone pushed through the swinging door as I approached. "Molly." She came right up to me and gusted wine breath into my face. "How are you, dear?"

"Fine, thanks." Again I found myself stepping back, this time threatened with an overabundance of affection instead of anger.

She moved closer. "Her bones are put to rest, but specters still roam the night."

"What? What does that even mean?" Trust a poet to say something cryptic.

Persephone's wine-heavy eyes brightened. "That wasn't bad, was it? I must go jot it down."

Shaking my head, I pushed the door open and entered the ladies' room. Catherine stood at the sink, combing her glossy bob.

"Hello," I said. "I'm Molly Kimball, Violet's niece. You must be Catherine."

"I am," she agreed, her eyes watching me in the mirror. "Lovely to meet you. Violet is a dear." Her voice was soft, almost timid.

As sometimes happened, meeting a quiet person made me babble, to fill the uneasy air, I suppose. I went on about moving here, the bookshop, meeting Ruth—

"You're the one who found her. Myrtle." Still staring at me, she tucked the comb into her bag and picked up a mini-can of hair spray. "I always knew her crimes would catch up with her." She sprayed her hair like someone trying to poison bugs.

"I heard what she did to you. Or tried to. It was despicable." We're told not to speak ill of the dead, but I found myself saying, "It's no wonder that someone finally snapped." Not that it made murder right, merely understandable.

Catherine's mouth dropped open. "How dare you! Ruth didn't do it." She popped the can into her bag.

I threw up my hands. "Wait, I wasn't implying—"

But it was too late. She whirled around, her immaculate hair set in place like concrete. "They said you were snooping around, trying to pin the murder on someone. Well, it won't be Ruth."

Out the door she went, and I stood rooted to the floor, in shock. First, because she'd jumped to such a wrong conclusion, and second, because someone was telling people about my investigation. I guess I hadn't been as covert as I'd thought.

The crowd began to thin once the funeral meal was over and the pub opened for regular business. I stayed in the back room with my friends, watching as they played darts. But I was content to sit and relax, chatting with Daisy about this and that.

"I suppose I should call it a night," I said around nine. It felt like midnight.

"I'll be right behind you," Daisy said. "Those scones don't bake themselves." She got up around dawn to bake, so customers could enjoy fresh treats.

Kieran and Tim were still playing, so I said goodbye with a promise to see them in the morning. Kieran and I still hadn't set another dinner date but for once I was pretty chill about the whole thing. I just *knew* we were getting closer, destined for something good.

Outside, the air was fresh and cool, the sky a deep navy blue. Lights shone golden in windows up and down the lane. As I started across the lane, a dark shape darted toward me. "Puck." I gathered his warm body into my arms. "What are you doing outside?" He could be so sneaky sometimes. Now that he was mine, I preferred him to stay inside at night, where it was safer.

At the bottom of the lane, headlights flashed on, too bright and blinding me. Probably some idiot who didn't know about the driving ban in this area.

Then an engine roared, and as I stood frozen in horror, clutching my cat, the automobile raced toward us.

CHAPTER 22

At the last minute, I jumped, using muscle memory honed by living in Vermont, where I'd leaped mud puddles, ditches, rushing streams.

Puck clung to me with his claws as we fell to the cobblestones. I landed hard on my hip. *Ouch!* Before I closed my eyes with a shriek of pain, I glimpsed the car as it rushed past, the wheels inches from my prone body.

Aunt Violet's Cortina. Or a car that looked exactly like it.

Tires squealed as the car turned onto Trinity Street. The pub door flew open and Mum ran over, her heels clattering. "Molly. Molly, are you all right?"

"I'm *alive*," I said with a laugh. Puck was now sitting on my chest, staring down at me. Ordering me to get up. I wasn't sure I could. "We almost got run over."

"I saw that, on my way out of the pub." Mum brushed my

hair back, frowning as she studied my scalp. "Did you hit your head?"

"Shall I call an ambulance?" Inspector Ryan appeared, looming over us. Where had he come from?

"My head is fine," I said. "I landed on my hip, only because I'm clumsy and tripped. The car didn't touch me."

"Help me get her inside, Sean," Mum said.

Sean? The surprise of hearing her call the inspector by his first name helped boost me to my feet. My hip ached but I could walk. That was the good thing. "Give me an ice pack and a belt of whiskey and I'll be fine," I said as I hobbled between them to the shop door, Puck still cradled in one arm.

"Did you see who was driving?" Inspector Ryan asked, supporting me while Mum unlocked the door. "Or notice any details about the car?"

"I didn't have time to see the driver," I said, "but funny thing, it looked exactly like Aunt Violet's car. But I'm sure they made more than one."

Mum and Inspector Ryan exchanged glances. "Where does she park her car?" he practically barked.

"In the garage down there," Mum said, pointing. "You don't think . . ."

"Can you handle her from here?" he asked. "I'll be right back." He took off at a trot down the lane.

"Someone stole Aunt Violet's car?" I asked. "But how? And who?"

"Good question." Mum's voice was grim. "How about sitting in this armchair? I'll go get the ice and whiskey."

I'd sort of been joking about the whiskey but I didn't

bother to object. Leaning back in the chair, I patted my poor traumatized cat and pondered the situation.

Had someone just tried to kill me? Oddly, I was able to consider this in a fairly detached manner, which meant I was probably in shock.

Mum was tucking an ice pack next to my hip when Inspector Ryan returned. "The car is gone." He fumbled for his cell phone. "I'm calling it in. Do you remember the plate number?"

"No, I'm afraid not," Mum said. "It's registered to Aunt Violet, though."

Footsteps thumped over our head. "I think she's awake, Mum."

"Good." Mum handed me a mug containing an inch of whiskey. "I'll go fetch her."

I worked on sipping the whiskey while the inspector barked orders into his cell phone. I really hoped they would get Aunt Violet's nice old car back in one piece. Didn't thieves sometimes chop up cars for parts?

Mum and Aunt Violet hurried into the room, my aunt wearing a fluffy dressing gown over her nightie. As soon as Inspector Ryan hung up, she said, "Inspector, my spare keys are missing. Car and garage. They're on a silver St. Hildegard's College key ring."

His expressive brows drew together. "Missing? Since when?"

Aunt Violet's headshake was rueful. "I honestly don't know. George and I each have a set, and we never use the spares. They're usually hanging in the kitchen. Come, I'll show you." They hurried away.

I stayed where I was, allowing the cold pack to numb my hip and the hot trace of whiskey to burn away my fear.

Someone had deliberately taken those keys. Had they also planned to run me down?

◆◆

"Molly," Daisy cried when I hobbled through the tea shop door the next morning, still bruised and aching. She ran around the end of the counter to hug me. "How are you doing, you poor thing?" Only a couple of other customers were in the place, sipping hot beverages with heavy-lidded eyes as they tapped at laptops.

I gave her a crooked grin. "I'm okay. A little sore, but still in one piece." The over-the-counter painkillers were finally kicking in.

"Thank heavens." She gave me a last squeeze and returned to her station, where she began making me a coffee. "I couldn't believe it when I heard the news." Her mouth turned down. "The whole pub was abuzz."

"I bet." I lowered myself into a chair, deciding I'd sit here and drink my coffee. "Kieran texted me about ten times." He'd wanted to come see me but I'd already gone to bed.

"They found the car, right?" Daisy dispensed steaming java into a mug, then brought it over to me along with a pitcher of milk. No one needed her assistance right now, so she joined me at the table.

I poured milk into my mug and stirred. "Yes. Late last night. Parked down an alley, driver's-side door open." I took the first wonderful sip. "No leads on who was behind the wheel, although we believe they stole the spare key from our kitchen."

Daisy shivered. "How scary." After glancing around, she leaned across the table. "Any idea who?"

"Oh, I have an idea." I swallowed more coffee, enjoying its comforting warmth. "Someone who was trying to shut me up." We hadn't had a chance to really catch up, so now I told her about my encounters at the pub with Clive and Catherine. "And Persephone was being weird last night," I added.

"When is she not?" Daisy laughed. "I swear that woman is in her own world."

"Yeah, on planet Persephone," I joked. Needing a break from the subject and my ever-churning thoughts, I grabbed a newspaper sitting on the table.

Ah, there it was. "Kelsey Cook took a picture of us. See?" I held up the paper.

"Ooo, you do look nice," Daisy said. "How was your date? I never even asked."

"It was great," I said. "He wants to go out again soon."

"Fab. Maybe we can do another double date soon."

"I'd like that." Thinking about Persephone had reminded me of Joan and the request I had for my friend. "Actually, Daisy, I have a favor to ask." I inhaled, knowing that every time I mentioned her late aunt, it opened a wound. "Can I look through the rest of Joan's notebooks?" At her puzzled look, I added, "I'd rather not go into it now, but I'm piecing something together. To do with her poetry."

She pointed toward the ceiling. "Go ahead up. You know where everything is." Then she made a growling sound.

"Oh, what a fool I am. You can't climb the attic stairs right now."

"I'd rather not," I admitted. Climbing up one flight to my bedroom had been difficult enough with my bruised hip. "I'll wait a day or two."

"No, no." She looked around the shop. "Why don't I nip up and grab them? If anyone comes in, tell them I'll be right back."

"That I can do," I said. "One more thing. Do your aunt and uncle have any of Joan's poems? According to the journal and her old friends, she was very prolific. But there aren't any poems in the journal, and I didn't see any the first time we looked through her papers." Once again I was working purely on instinct, but the excitement nestled in my gut was spurring me on, telling me I was on the right track. Of exactly what, I wasn't yet sure.

"I don't think so. She's never said anything if so. Why don't I ask her?"

"If you don't mind." She hurried out and I chose another newspaper to glance through while I waited. Maybe our picture had made it into more than one. I wouldn't want to have to constantly watch out for photographers, but I had to admit it was a little exciting. And far less stressful than thinking about last night's close call.

◆◆◆

Back at the bookshop kitchen, Aunt Violet was putting on the kettle, dressed in an apron that read "Kiss me. I love books." "You're up and about early, Molly," she said as I came through the garden door.

"I know." I dumped the bag of notebooks on the kitchen table. "I'm on the trail of something so I couldn't sleep." I omitted mention of my aches and pains, not wanting to become a whiner.

She eyed the spiral-bound notebooks spilling out of the bag with curiosity. "Where did those come from?"

I sat in a chair and began to stack them neatly. "They belonged to Joan Watson." I wanted to say more but was wary of bandying about accusations before I had proof.

Aunt Violet fed both cats, who were weaving and whining around her ankles. "Looking for clues regarding who killed her?" She rolled up the cat food bag with a crinkle. "I'm still stunned that Myrtle thought she was murdered."

"Something like that," I said, getting up from the table. I stole a piece of paper from Aunt Violet's shopping notebook and grabbed a pen. My plan was to write down scraps of verse or interesting phrases, then match them against Persephone's poems. "I didn't find anything in the journal, but someone cut out the last few pages."

"That's strange," Aunt Violet said. "I wonder if the killer did that."

"Or Joan." I settled back at the table. "She might have regretted something she wrote." Although in that case, I'd expect the removal to have been rough from ripping out the pages, not neatly sliced.

"No sign of any of her poetry so far?" Aunt Violet asked. She placed several tea bags in a pot, draping the strings over the rim. "I did remember something the other day. Tom was going to read some of her work, give her some feedback."

I looked up from the notebook. "Tom? Really? Why was that?"

"He was reading poetry at Cambridge." Aunt Violet poured steaming water into the teapot. Here in England, they called majoring in a subject "reading" it. "Quite the expert, he was. I suppose she wanted his opinion on the quality of her work."

Lucky Tom. "Daisy is asking Joan's brother if he found her poems among her belongings from college." I slapped the stack of books. "These are all notes from Joan's lectures and assigned reading."

Aunt Violet was pulling mugs out of the cupboard. "Do you want tea?"

"Yes, please." I squinted at tiny writing and a drawing along one margin of a page. I used to doodle and write myself notes during classes too, especially when they were boring.

Joan had sketched bare trees arched over a cobblestone street. *Haunted Cambridge* captioned the picture. Then a few words about *cobbled streets echoing with footsteps from the past*.

The hair stood up on the back of my neck. "'Oh, haunted Cambridge,'" I muttered, pushing back my chair. Although I knew I was right, I wanted confirmation.

"Quoting poetry this morning?" Aunt Violet asked with a smile.

"You could say that." Getting up, I headed for the hall

door. Puck chased me, thinking we were playing a new game. "The question is, whose?"

By the time I got back to the kitchen, four more people were seated around the table—Mum, George, Sir Jon, and my uncle Chris Marlowe. I braked sharply, my sneakers squeaking on the tile. "Where did you all come from?"

"It was the sausages," George said. "They lured us in."

"Sir Jon, so good of you to bring these. They're lovely." Aunt Violet was now unwrapping butcher's paper to reveal plump, juicy sausages. On the AGA, a large stainless steel frying pan awaited.

"What do you have there?" Sir Jon asked me, cup of tea in hand.

"Persephone's new book." I put it down on the dresser holding a display of antique dishes, then gathered up the note-books. With Uncle Chris here, I wasn't going to discuss my discovery that Persephone Brightwell had plagiarized Joan Watson's work. After I finished moving the notebooks, I asked Aunt Violet what I could do to help.

"How about beating some eggs?" she suggested. "We'll do scrambled today."

I grabbed a dozen from the refrigerator and began break-ing them into a ceramic bowl.

George and Uncle Chris were talking about thatching. "I did that for a while," George said. "There's quite a trick to it."

"Dying art, it is," my uncle said. He sipped his tea. "But still plenty of work for us."

"I enjoyed visiting your job," I said. "I hope I can see a demonstration soon."

Uncle Chris turned in his seat to face me. "A call just came in. I'll be doing a cottage in Hazelhurst next month. Iona York's place. Maybe you can visit us while we're there. It's a total strip and re-thatch."

Iona York. Where had I heard that name?

"The children's book author?" Sir Jon said. "She wrote *The Strawberry Girls.* I recently read in the trades that they're publishing an anniversary edition this summer."

"I just found a first edition of that book," I said. "In Tom's boxes." I pulled out an eggbeater and began to spin the handle, watching as individual eggs turned into a frothy mass.

"Her daughter is getting married in June," Aunt Violet said, swirling melting butter in a pan for the eggs. "At the same time as the Strawberry Fair, naturally. One of Cambridge's most popular events."

"I remember the Strawberry Fair," Mum said. "It's fun. Lots of music and art."

An idea struck. "Do you think we could host a reading with Iona, if she has time? I'm sure lots of people would love to hear her read from *The Strawberry Girls.*"

"That sounds like an excellent idea," Aunt Violet said. "I'll send her a note this week."

After we'd finished eating, Uncle Chris placed his fork carefully on his plate and said, "I want to come clean about something, Violet." Everyone quieted, except for Clarence, crunching kibble.

"What's that, Chris?" Aunt Violet asked, checking the teapot.

Uncle Chris's eyes were on Sir Jon. "I understand the police are looking for a man seen in the area the night Myrtle

Marsh was killed." His throat worked as he swallowed. "I think it's me they're looking for."

We all stared at him as he raised both hands. "Oh, I didn't touch the old bird. I didn't even see her. I was on my way over here, but after seeing all the commotion, I thought better of it. So I popped off to a pub for dinner. When I came later, I saw the panda cars." Meaning the police. "I was in the alley when a young bloke shouted at me and chased me off."

"That was Kieran," I said, my voice heavy with disappointment. Another dead end. But at least we knew who the lurker was.

"You didn't see anyone in the alley?" Sir Jon asked. "Or hear anything?"

"There were a few people on Ivy Close," Uncle Chris said. "That's the way I came in." His eyes widened. "I did see one person in the back alley, headed toward Trinity Street. An older lady. On the short side, wearing a hat and a big coat." He glanced around. "She resembled that poster in the bookshop. Saw it on my way in here this morning and thought, I've seen her somewhere. Finally worked it out."

The only poster we had in the shop was the one announcing Persephone's reading. "Hold on," I said. "I'll go get it."

The poster was still standing on the easel. I gripped it by the edges and carried it back into the kitchen.

"That's her," Uncle Chris said. "I can't forget that face, can I?"

I knew what he meant. Persephone had a force of personality that shone through, despite her small stature. Her gaze was intense, like a laser beam.

"What time was it when you saw her?" Sir Jon asked.

Aunt Violet gasped. "You surely don't think Persephone—"

"I'm not thinking anything, Vi," Sir Jon said. "Maybe she was taking a shortcut to the bookshop. A lot of people do that, I gather."

"Like Paddington Station at times back there," George said.

Uncle Chris rubbed his chin. "I'd say it was around six or so when I saw her. As I said, after noticing something was going on at the shop, I popped over to Bene't Street for some dinner. Then I came back after, hoping to see you all then."

The police could confirm his meal easily enough. "I think you should call Inspector Ryan right away," I said. "Maybe Persephone saw something." Or . . . maybe she had a reason to resent Myrtle. Uncle Chris mentioning Persephone to the police would lead them to talk to her again, which couldn't hurt.

My uncle slapped his knees and rose to his feet. "I'll do it. Right now." He pulled a mobile phone out of his pants pocket as he walked toward the garden door.

The rest of us looked at one another. "At least one mystery is solved," I said. "We know who was lurking in the alley."

A few minutes later, Uncle Chris returned. "I'm going

down to the station now." He pulled a cap off a wall hook and settled it on his head. "Wish me luck. And thanks again for breakfast." He hesitated, his eyes darting to Sir Jon and George. He cleared his throat. "But before I go, Nina and Molly, can I have a word with you?"

The three of us stepped out into the bookshop. Obviously uncomfortable, Uncle Chris snatched his hat back off and turned it around in his hands. "I want to apologize. My wife . . . well, she can be bit of a pain sometimes. I understand she came over here last night."

"She sure did," Mum said, her lips tight. "And to be honest, Chris, she was in her usual form. She managed to insult all of us within minutes." She made a helpless gesture. "I really don't know what the point was. She can just stay away."

Uncle Chris's eyes flared with surprise at Mum's vehement statement, but then he said, "Don't blame you a bit. In fact, you might as well hear it now. We're more or less on the rocks."

"Oh, I'm sorry," Mum said, sounding sincere. "Although Janice and I never got along, I hate to hear about a marriage breaking up."

He clapped his hat back on. "It's been a long time coming. Anyway. Thanks for your support. I hope I'm welcome here at the old bookshop."

"Anytime, Chris. You know that." Mum walked my uncle to the door.

"See you soon," I called. As I'd thought before, I wouldn't mind spending some time with my uncle and cousin. "Let me know a good time to visit a thatching job."

He acknowledged that with a wave and reply and soon was gone.

"Whew," Mum said. "I didn't see that coming." She held up two crossed fingers. "I thought Chris and Janice were welded together."

"Maybe she started picking on *him*." I tucked my laptop in the crook of my arm. My next task was to type up a side-by-side comparison of Joan's and Persephone's writing. "And she was probably lining us up as her next set of victims." I'd encountered serial bullies before, and this was how they operated.

"That could be," Mum said. "She'd better stay away from here. I'm too old to play those games."

George had left too, so only Sir Jon and Violet were in the kitchen. Dressed in an apron and rubber gloves, Sir Jon was loading the dishwasher while Aunt Violet cleaned the pans by hand. They made a very cute couple.

"Now there's a social media opportunity," I said as I set my laptop on the table. I reached for my phone with a teasing gesture. "Secret agent, barrister, man-about-town helping with the dishes."

"Don't you dare." Sir Jon wagged a glove at me in mock anger. "I can't have my softer side becoming common knowledge."

I gave a huge mock sigh. "Your secret is safe with me." I put my phone down and flipped open the laptop, then retrieved Persephone's book and Joan's notebooks from the dresser. Mum poured a cup of tea and wandered into the bookshop to get ready to open. Speaking of couples, I hadn't even asked her how she'd gotten on a first-name basis with

Inspector Ryan. It wasn't something I wanted to hit her with cold, so I'd have to wait for the perfect moment.

While half listening to Aunt Violet and Sir Jon's chatter, I opened a new document and created two columns. If only I could find some of Joan's actual poetry. Unpublished poetry, since Persephone wouldn't have borrowed words others had seen.

The kitchen wall extension rang, startling me. "I'll get it," Aunt Violet said, wiping her wet hands across her apron.

"Fiona," Aunt Violet said, glancing at us. "How nice to hear from you. . . . What's that? You want me to come over? Right now?" She put a hand over the receiver.

"I can give you a lift," Sir Jon said. "The Aston Martin is parked a couple of blocks away." Of course Sir Jon drove the vehicle favored by James Bond.

"Would you?" Aunt Violet took off her apron. "She sounds very upset."

"Can I go?" I didn't want to miss this new adventure. Meaning a ride in the Aston Martin as well visiting Fiona.

Leaving Mum in charge of the bookshop, we were soon racing along in Sir Jon's silver convertible, Aunt Violet in front, me crammed into the tiny rear. Although the roads were too congested to really put the powerful little car through its paces, many admiring glances came our way. Aunt Violet had tied a silk scarf around her hair and donned a pair of tortoiseshell cat's-eye sunglasses, while Sir Jon was dashing in a pair of aviator specs. I was their decidedly less glamorous companion squashed in back.

With shouted directions from Aunt Violet, we were soon pulling down the narrow lane to Fiona's gate.

Sir Jon parked along the side of the street. "I haven't been here for ages," he said, assisting Aunt Violet out of the passenger seat then gently tugging my arm to help me disembark. "Right after their wedding, I think."

As we moved toward the gate, I said, "I've been reading Joan Watson's journal. I got the impression that she and Gregory were falling in love."

Sir Jon opened the gate and ushered us through. "They were. He was very, very torn up after her death. But a year or two later, he and Fiona tied the knot. A lot of family pressure, I've always thought. On both sides."

No one answered the door when we knocked. Or rang the bell. "How odd," Aunt Violet said. She pulled out her phone and called. "No one is answering," she said, frowning. "It rang and rang." Still frowning, she charged down the front steps and trotted along the path. "I'm going to try the side door."

"I hope Fiona isn't sick or something," I said, trailing behind. Sir Jon followed, scoping out the house and property as if looking for signs of trouble.

"At our age, you never know," Aunt Violet said. "She sounded so upset on the phone."

French doors to the garden stood open to the morning air, the room beyond dim and quiet, one long curtain swaying in the breeze. Bees buzzed around a newly blooming rosebush and birds hopped and chirped around the flowerbeds.

"Fiona?" Aunt Violet called. The curtain flapped. She stepped closer, one foot on the threshold. "Are you in there?"

I pressed close behind my aunt, eager to find out what was going on. I don't know who saw it first because we both gasped loudly then tried to get through the door at the same time.

Fiona Fosdyke lay stretched out upon the thick antique carpet, the pool of blood around her head soaking into the fibers.

CHAPTER 23

Realizing we were obstructing each other, I fell back and let Aunt Violet enter first. "Sir Jon," I called over my shoulder. "Fiona is hurt." I already had my phone out, ready to call for help.

Aunt Violet was on her knees beside her friend, feeling for a pulse. "She's alive." Her face twisted in distress. "Who did this to you, Fi? If only we'd gotten here sooner."

Maybe we could have prevented the attack. Or witnessed it and caught the culprit.

Sir Jon pointed. "That's what hit her." A gold sculling trophy lay on the carpet nearby. "I wonder who did it. And why."

"Look at that." A silver St. Hildegard's key chain sat next to a teacup on the coffee table, a couple of keys attached. Aunt Violet's missing car keys? "I bet the same person who tried to run me over hit Fiona just now," I said, my fingers fumbling on my phone screen. "Fiona must have figured it out." The dial screen finally lit up and I hit the right digits, remembering that it was 999 in England, not 911.

"Persephone Brightwell is down by the river," Sir Jon said. He was standing by the front windows, which faced the long garden to the river. "She's hailed a punt."

I hurried to join him, phone to my ear. Persephone was stepping into a punt, one of those for-hire boats, I guessed.

"Let's go." I thrust the ringing phone at Aunt Violet. "Talk to the police. Tell them what's going on and get an ambulance here." I prayed that Fiona would be all right.

Sir Jon and I burst outside and raced down the lawn in long-legged strides. I was dimly aware of my bruised hip protesting, but sheer adrenaline pushed me onward.

"There's another punt coming," he said, pointing. A young man dressed in a trademark striped shirt and boater hat was trolling along, looking for passengers.

We waved frantically and shouted until he saw us and steered over to the bank, pulling up to the house dock.

"Where to?" he asked, glancing between Sir Jon and me. I could almost see what he was thinking since Sir Jon was more than double my age. *But he's fitter than you*, I wanted to tell him. *Plus, this isn't a romantic excursion.*

"Follow that punt," Sir Jon said, throwing some banknotes at him before he could quote rates. "And hurry." We flung ourselves inside, barely rocking the stable craft, and our punter dug in his pole.

"Which one?" he asked, a valid question since the river was busy this morning.

I scanned the other punts on the river, finally focusing in on one holding a lone female passenger. Her gray hair shone in the sun. "That one. With the older woman."

"I'll try to catch up," he said, grunting as he pushed the pole into the river bottom. "He's moving really fast for some reason."

She had probably paid him a hefty fee, I guessed. Her punt was skimming along with speed, easily overtaking others.

Sir Jon was on his phone. "Yes, Inspector. We're heading west along the river. The perp is in a punt. So are we."

"Did he say perp?" our chauffeur asked me. Punt operators were called chauffeurs instead of punters, which has negative connotations in British slang.

"He did," I said. "That woman is a criminal." I didn't go into details. He'd read about our caper in the newspaper soon enough, I was sure.

Sir Jon finished his call. "They'll be waiting up ahead. The problem is, she can get out at any point and go anywhere. Unless we catch up."

"I'm trying," the chauffeur said, grunting with effort. "Honest."

I half expected Sir Jon to take over, but instead he directed the chauffeur to pull over to the side. Was he going to run up ahead and try to intercept Persephone when she got out? But what if she went on for miles before doing that? He'd be exhausted.

"Call the inspector with the address," Sir Jon said as he clambered from the boat. "Side street or bridge. Soon as I reach her."

Gliding along in our punt again, we watched as he went over to a group of bicyclists. More banknotes went flying and soon Sir Jon was whizzing down the path, dodging pedestrians and baby carriages.

"Who is he?" the chauffeur asked, mouth agape. "This is like something out of a movie."

"Did you ever hear of James Bond?" I asked, my heart swelling with pride at Sir Jon's resourcefulness.

"Of course." His brow furrowed. "You don't mean he's a secret agent?"

"The real deal," I said. "Knighted by the Queen, even."

Amazement lit his features. "You don't say."

A footbridge appeared ahead and Sir Jon halted there, resting the bicycle along the railing. He kicked off his shoes and removed his jacket, setting them neatly next to the bicycle. The people crossing the bridge gave him barely a glance. He was only another odd Cambridge resident.

"What's that bridge called?" I asked my companion. He gave me the name and I dialed Inspector Ryan to report in. Sir Jon was making a move. What that move was, exactly, I wasn't sure.

Persephone's punt continued to sail along, headed right for the bridge. Sir Jon strode back and forth as he waited, estimating where they would cross underneath.

At first I thought he was planning to leap into the punt, which would be a very risky move, but then I saw him remove his trousers. Was he going to jump into the water instead?

"What's he up to? Swimming's not allowed in this part of the river," my companion said. His head turned toward the sound of sirens on the south bank. "Are they coming for her?"

"I sure hope so," I said, fingernails pressing into my palms as I watched Sir Jon climb onto the bridge railing. I held my breath as he cleanly executed a shallow dive into the river. He landed right in front of Persephone's punt, which had to slow to avoid hitting him. As for our punt, we were closing the distance rapidly now.

"Halt," Sir Jon's commanding voice boomed out. "The police are on their way."

Persephone's chauffeur glanced down at her for instructions. "Go on," she said, making urging gestures with her hands. "I've certainly paid you enough."

"What's all this?" her chauffeur said. "Move aside, man. I don't want to hit you with my punt."

Sir Jon's answer was to swim over and grip the side. "She's a killer," he said. "Do you want a charge of harboring a fugitive?"

"A killer?" The young man dug his pole deep into the river bottom muck, bringing the punt to a halt. "Are you sure?"

"Pretty much," Sir Jon said. "As you can tell, the police are arriving. So maybe err on the side of caution?"

In addition to the wail of sirens, flashing blue and white lights were now visible. Within seconds, several police cars came into view, racing along the adjacent street while avoiding the other vehicles hastily pulling over.

Sir Jon pointed to a landing on the south bank. "You'd better pull up over there." He let go and the chauffeur began poling obediently toward the shore.

Persephone didn't take this betrayal lying down. She stood

up in the punt and moved close to the side, bouncing to make it wobble. "I'm going to jump in unless you stop."

"Ma'am, it's my license. Sit down."

But Persephone remained on her feet, her arms windmilling. "I'm innocent," she shouted. "It wasn't me." Then she overbalanced and fell over the side in what seemed like slow motion, landing in the river with a mighty splash.

Her head bobbed to the surface, her arms flailing. "Help! Help! I can't swim!"

"She should have thought of that before, right?" my chauffeur muttered as he steered us toward the bank. Officers were now disembarking from the vehicles, and I spotted the familiar figure of Inspector Ryan in the lead.

Sir Jon swam to Persephone. "Calm down. I've got you." After a minute of her thrashing around, he managed to cup a hand around her chin and start tugging her toward shore.

Officers, including Sergeant Adhikari, helped the pair onto the landing, water streaming from their clothing. At Adhikari's command, blankets were wrapped around the swimmers, who had both begun to shiver. Meanwhile, other constables were clearing the area, trying to keep curious onlookers at a distance.

"He tried to drown me." Persephone's shrill voice rose above the clamor of voices as I climbed out of the punt.

"That's absolute garbage," I said, hurrying to join the group. "Sir Jon and I were chasing you, Persephone." I turned to the officers. "She hit Fiona Fosdyke with a sculling trophy and took off. Sir Jon, Violet Marlowe, and I had just arrived at Fiona's house when she ran down the garden and hailed a punt. Plus we found the keys from Aunt Violet's Cortina, which almost hit me Sunday night. Were you driving, Persephone?"

"You can't prove any of this." Persephone's lips might be blue from the chilly water but she wasn't going down without a fight. "I was just taking a nice morning cruise along the river."

"Actually, Inspector," a constable said. "Mrs. Fosdyke has regained consciousness and identified Ms. Brightwell as her attacker."

Hurray. Relieved that Fiona was on the mend, I wavered on my feet and my chauffeur had to grip my arm to steady me. I smiled at him. "Bet this is the most exciting tour you've had in a while."

"Definitely." He stared around at the scene. "Student antics have nothing on this."

"Don't go anywhere, Miss Kimball," Inspector Ryan said. "We'll need a statement."

Glad I had his permission to linger, I said, "Whatever you need."

"Why did you strike Mrs. Fosdyke?" Inspector Ryan asked Persephone.

The poet's eyes narrowed, her expression growing crafty. "I found out that she killed Myrtle Marsh, my dear friend." Tears welled up and she sobbed, a piteous mew. She slid a glance at me. "She also had Violet's keys, which means she tried to run Molly over."

Oh, brother. "You mean, *you* killed Myrtle," I said. "You stole my aunt's knitting needle and stabbed her. My uncle saw you." I wasn't lying. Uncle Chris had seen her. Maybe not committing the actual murder, but physically present in the alley near our back garden.

"Miss Kimball," the inspector warned. "Let us handle this."

But it was too late. My accusation had unleashed the floodgates. "I did kill Myrtle. I had to." Persephone's lips wobbled and crocodile tears spilled from her eyes. She clasped her hands in entreaty, as though seeking sympathy from the watching crowd. "Years and years I put up with it. Her demands for money, her threats of—"

"Exposing your plagiarism?" I said, earning another dark look from the inspector. But it was worth it. "You stole Joan Watson's work. I can prove it." I turned to Inspector Ryan. "She even had the nerve to sign into Clive's bungalow presentation as Joan Watson. Then dump the other needle there, to frame him."

That crafty expression slid across the poet's face again, as much a confession as any words would have been. "Wasn't that smart of me? When I went over to Myrtle's flat after the reading, I saw him lurking about. He's got secrets too," she said.

He certainly did. "But you didn't get in that night. Why not?"

Persephone made a scoffing sound. "George was doing something in the hall. Changing a light bulb, I think. I had to come back another day." And Kelsey Cook had run into her that time. No wonder Persephone didn't want her picture taken.

"Now we know who ransacked the place," I said to Inspector Ryan. "And tried to pin blame on Aunt Violet." Fortunately Persephone hadn't found the blackmail evidence.

The poet shrugged as if to say, *What's a girl going to do?*

"Are you getting all this, Sergeant?" Ryan asked.

Sergeant Adhikari nodded. "I'm recording. Shouldn't we caution her?"

"No need," Persephone stood tall, an effort for a woman about five feet in height. "I'm making a full confession and throwing myself on the mercy of the court." She stroked her long braid, her expression now noble. "I've suffered for my art and I'm not ashamed to admit it. Years and years of extortion. But if I'd given in, what would the world have lost?"

"Drama queen," my chauffeur muttered. Sir Jon rolled his eyes.

"My new book coming out only increased her demands," Persephone went on. "She wanted *all* my advance. Do you believe that cheek?" She paused as if waiting for a response.

A man in the crowd shouted out, "That's highway robbery."

"Exactly." Persephone continued to toy with her braid. "So I arranged to meet her for a little chat." Her gaze fell on me. "The knitting needle was too easy. I'd been by the shop earlier but you were all busy. And there it was, the perfect weapon."

Busy getting ready for *her* reading. And to repay us, she had skulked around, looking for a weapon to frame Aunt Violet with. Then killed Myrtle in our garden.

"That's premeditated murder," I cried out. "I hope you got *that*!" I said to the inspector and his sergeant.

"We got it." Inspector Ryan eyed the crowd of onlookers, which had continued to grow. More than a few held up cell phones, filming everything. "I think we'd better move this operation downtown."

Persephone's shoulders hunched as if she were going to resist. Downtown there wouldn't be an audience. She would be alone in a cold, poorly lit cell, her last performance over. Never again would she hold a group of people captive with her every word.

And I wouldn't have the chance to ask a final question.

"Persephone," I said. "About Joan."

She whipped her head around.

"Did you kill her too?" Painful emotion tightened my chest, making my voice croak. After reading Joan's journal, watching her talent flourish, I felt connected to her, almost as if we were friends. Or might have been. Now the only role I could fill was that of avenger.

An odd light glowed in her eyes as she shook her head. "No, it wasn't me."

My heart sank. Maybe it had been suicide. Discouragement about her work. Heartbreak over Gregory. Feeling lost and alone and out of place in Cambridge.

But Persephone was speaking again, her tone almost dreamy, reminiscent. "Myrtle did it. She told me after I found her tossing pages from Joan's journal into the fire. Joan was going to turn her in for trying to blackmail Ruth."

Inspector Ryan and Sergeant Adhikari exchanged glances, stunned by the revelation of a second murder, I guessed.

"So Myrtle added sedatives to Joan's wine?" I guessed, earning a nod of confirmation. "Why didn't you call the police?"

Persephone covered her mouth with a hand, trying to hold back hysterical laughter. "Why? It wouldn't bring Joan back. And besides, I had the poems, didn't I? I had to look at the big picture." She lifted her chin. "Joan's brilliance and talent would live on through me."

Now *there* was a creative argument for stealing someone's work. I had a final question. "But how could she blackmail you, if you knew she killed someone?"

Persephone sighed deeply. "She didn't do anything for years. Not until my first book was published. By then, all the evidence concerning Joan's death was gone. It would only be my word against hers." She bent her head, wrists crossed in front of her body as though already cuffed. "Plus she used a bottle of wine filched from my room." Which meant Persephone's fingerprints had been on it. Clever, clever Myrtle.

"All right," Inspector Ryan barked. "That's enough. Caution her, Sergeant Adhikari and take her downtown." He pointed to the constables. "Clear the crowd, please."

My chauffeur slipped me a card. His name was Fergus. "Call me if you need a punt, all right? I'll meet you anywhere you like." He laughed. "Talk about a thrill."

"I can't guarantee this level of excitement every time," I said. "But thank you." I tucked the card into my jeans pocket, thinking about the relaxing boat tour I'd been dreaming about. Maybe make it a picnic with Kieran?

Sergeant Adhikari cautioned Persephone and snapped

cuffs on her wrists. Then, as the poet continued to spout dramatic lines, two officers walked her toward a nearby cruiser.

Realizing that the ordeal was finally over, I couldn't hold back a yelp of joy. Aunt Violet and dear George had been cleared. And we'd found Myrtle's killer—and Joan's.

CHAPTER 24

"We sold the Oz set," Mum said, setting the phone down. "The buyer will be down from London tomorrow to pick it up."

"That's great, Mum," I said, looking up from the social media post I was composing. After the exciting events of the day before, life was getting back to normal at the bookshop. Puck was on my lap, Clarence in his chair, and out in the lane, pedestrians strolled by, checking out the window displays. "We can treat Uncle Chris and Charlie to dinner tonight." We were meeting at the Magpie Pub for fish and chips.

"We can, but don't spend that money yet." Mum's joy dimmed slightly. "Well, he did say he will need to inspect them first, make sure their condition is as stated."

"It is." I glanced up at the colorful row in the secure glass case. "We checked and double-checked everything, remember?" I'd been as anxious as Mum to make sure our evaluation and price were accurate. Selling the set would go a long way to paying Clive off. He'd probably have to put the money toward legal fees, though. The police had arrested him yesterday for bribery of public officials related to his building projects.

Aunt Violet came into the bookshop, carrying a tray holding a teapot and cups. "After tea, I'm off to see Fiona. She's resting quietly at home."

"I'm so glad she's okay," I said with a shudder. "It would have been tragic if she had become Persephone's second victim."

"Why did Persephone hit her?" Mum asked. "Did Fiona guess she was the killer?"

"Exactly right," Aunt Violet said. "Fiona had noticed a few little things that didn't add up the night of the reading. Persephone was supposed to join her and Ruth for drinks but never showed up. She claimed she was revisiting old haunts on foot. And when she did arrive at the hotel, she was not only dressed oddly, but acting flustered and rather excited. But all she told them was that she bumped into an old friend."

With a knitting needle, I thought, my stomach turning over. Uncle Chris must have seen her right before or after the murder, it sounded like, while she was wearing the coat and a hat.

"All of it is coming together," Mum said. "Show Aunt Violet the news article you found, Molly."

Instead of being behind the camera, Kelsey Cook was in front of it for a change, next to headlines that screamed

"Her Last Bright Performance" and "Who Is Joan Watson, Mystery Poet?" Kelsey had shared her story about trying to photograph a reluctant Persephone, not the night of the murder, but right after she'd gone into Myrtle's flat and taped up the family tree so the police couldn't miss it. As evidence against Aunt Violet.

Aunt Janice had been right. Someone, namely Persephone, really hadn't liked Aunt Violet. But why? What had Aunt Violet ever done besides sell lovely old books?

Then I understood. "Aunt Violet, I think a notebook of Joan's must still be here somewhere. The one she gave Tom. I can't think of any other reason why Persephone would have tried to frame you. She wanted you out of the way in case it was ever found. But even if it was discovered at some point, who's to say Mum or I would make the connection? It was Joan's journal, languishing in Daisy's dusty attic for decades, that helped me put two and two together."

"You might be right, Molly," Aunt Violet said. "I've been wracking my brain trying to figure out why she would do such a thing. Persephone and I were never close but we always got along." Her eyes twinkled. "She spouted poetry and I listened. That's all she ever wanted."

"I can certainly see that," I said. "She made her murder confession into a performance." Videos of her speech had popped up online despite police efforts to contain them. But since Persephone had pled guilty at the hearing, they weren't affecting the investigation. There wouldn't be a jury trial. She was going straight to sentencing.

We heard whistling from the kitchen, announcing George's arrival. "Good morning, ladies," he said. "Am I in time for a cuppa?" He was standing with his hands behind his back, which I thought was odd.

"Always," Aunt Violet said, indicating the teapot, which was still steeping. "How are things going with Myrtle's flat?"

George pulled out one hand, holding a mug. He had come prepared. "Excellent, excellent. I've got a new tenant, starting next month."

"So you're done clearing out the place?" Mum asked. "What a big job."

"You're not kidding," George said. Now he brought his other hand forward, revealing a manila envelope. "Found something interesting, I did." He opened the metal tab. "The police already have the originals, but I kept a copy. For you lot."

What was this? More blackmail information? Something else about the Marlowe family tree? George handed it to me. "You should see this first, Molly. You're the one who put all the pieces together, like."

A strange chirp burst from my lips as I leafed through the sheets, photocopies of handwritten pages. "These are from Joan's diary." With exclamations, Mum and Aunt Violet came to look over my shoulder.

"Yes, they are." Looking immensely pleased with himself, George picked up the teapot and began to fill the mugs.

"But Persephone said that Myrtle had burned pages . . ." I began to read, and all quickly became clear. "She probably did, anything about turning Myrtle in for trying to blackmail Ruth and Catherine. But these pages . . ." They detailed Joan's growing suspicion that Persephone was overly interested in her work. The clincher was a poem by Persephone printed in a local newspaper that Joan felt was awfully similar to her own work. She'd even written the two works side by side, showing the similarities.

"Oh, George," I said. "I'm so glad you found these. The last piece of the puzzle." Rather than let Joan's family or the authorities find them, Myrtle had kept them for future use in blackmailing Persephone. And who knows? If Persephone didn't cooperate, Myrtle might have tried to accuse her of murder. With Persephone's high-profile career, even an unproven allegation could be damaging.

After tea, Aunt Violet left to visit Fiona, a bouquet of flowers resting in her bicycle basket, George went home, and Mum and I got back to work.

"Mum, there's something I've been meaning to ask you," I said.

"What's that, Molly?" She didn't glance up from the computer, where she was working on the shop's accounting system.

"You and Inspector Ryan. Sean. What's the story?" I'd been wondering since the two of them had left the pub together. Or at the same time. Either way, she called him by his first name.

Mum pressed her lips together. "It's nothing. Really. He was at the pub and we started talking. About something besides Myrtle. That's all." Her cheeks were flushed, putting the lie to her words, but I decided to let it go. For now.

"I think I'll tackle the rest of Tom's books today," I said, letting her off the hook. "Who know what other treasures we might find?" We'd already sorted through the first several boxes, with the Oz set the main prize. The rest of the books were now in the children's section waiting for their new owners. With the exception of *The Strawberry Girls*, I was keeping that. I had also called Iona York's publicist about scheduling a reading, but hadn't heard back yet.

"Go ahead," Mum said. "I'll hold the fort."

"If you need me, I'll be upstairs," I said, taking my phone. "Send me a text." I smiled at the incongruity of this, communicating by text in a seventeenth-century building. For centuries, our ancestors had to shout up the stairs.

With Puck at my heels, I went up to the unused bedroom where Tom's things had been stored. During my first foray up here, I'd discovered that some boxes held personal effects brought over from his house after his death. Those I was leaving for Aunt Violet, should she ever want to go through them.

His children's book collection was my aim, and it was extensive. Box lots from auctions, single precious volumes, a hodgepodge of this and that. Like any avid collector, he'd grabbed bargains and rarities whenever he found them, not worrying about what to do with them until later.

Now it was my job to organize, value, and sell them all. And keep a few of my favorites, perhaps. No, definitely. "Ready, Puck?" I asked, rubbing my hands together with unseemly glee.

Today I sorted, going through boxes and pulling out anything of value or special interest. The less-valuable books stayed together for cataloging later. This Christmas I planned to do a push for classic children's books. We'd have nice selections at every price point.

I'd gone through a dozen or so boxes and was thinking about a cup of tea when I discovered one marked Trinity in a scrawled hand. Uncle Tom went to Trinity. Maybe . . .

Footsteps tapped on the stairs. "Molly?"

Kieran. I flew to the doorway. "I'm in here." My gaze dropped to his hands, holding two mugs of tea. "You're a godsend." I gestured. "Welcome to my lair."

He handed me a mug, staring around at the stacks of books. "Is there a hoarding show featuring book buyers? If not, there should be."

I snickered. "Easy. This all belonged to my uncle." After taking a long swig of tea, I set down my mug on the windowsill, the only level surface not holding books.

"I was just about to look in this box." I showed him the notation. "Probably nothing but his schoolwork, I bet."

"You never know," he said, looking over my shoulder. He pointed to the item on top. "That looks like a great old book."

It was a volume of Lord Alfred Tennyson's poems—gorgeous, leather-bound, and most likely quite valuable. "You do have an eye." I placed the book gently aside and reached into the box.

Similar to Joan's college artifacts, there were a lot of notebooks. Lecture notes. Reading notes. Draft papers. All written by hand in the days before computers or even electric typewriters. At the very bottom, I found what I had been seeking, hoping against hope that it still existed. A notebook with Joan's name written on the cover. Inside, page after page of poems—

"Molly. Come quick. You need to see this." Kieran had been wandering the room, poking about while my fickle cat trailed behind him.

Hearing the urgency in his voice, I carried the notebook over to where he was standing, Puck in his arms. On top of a bureau, an ancient atlas lay open to a map of Cambridgeshire.

"I thought this book looked cool," he said. "Old county maps." He pointed to a sheet of yellowed paper with faded sepia handwriting. "That was inside, right there."

Leaning close but not touching the fragile page, I picked out the relevant words. *Testament . . . Thomas Marlowe Manuscripts & Folios . . . Inventory . . . to Samuel Marlowe & his entails . . .*

"The missing will." I kissed Kieran, a long intense smooch of gratitude and joy. "The one that proves Aunt Violet is the rightful heir of the bookshop. You found it."

"I'll find whatever you like if you do that again," he said. "What's that you have there?" He nodded at the notebook tucked in my elbow.

I snuggled under his shoulder, Puck purring at this cozy arrangement, and opened the cover to show him. "Joan Watson's poems. She gave this notebook to Tom to read and critique. She died before he could give it back to her, so it was saved from Persephone's clutches." I closed the book and held it to my chest. "This is a treasure." I would read the poems later, slowly and with care. And with any luck, Ruth would publish them. Joan Watson would get her due at last.

Kieran kissed the top of my head. "I actually came by

to see if we were still on for our picnic on the river. I didn't expect to end up in a treasure hunt."

"All in a typical day at Thomas Marlowe," I said. "Manuscripts and folios and the pursuit of long-lost literature." Puck purred louder. "And cats."

"Don't forget the cats." Kieran rubbed Puck's chin the way he liked it.

This is home, I thought, as we—man, woman, and cat—stood close together in a book-filled room under an ancient roof, in the very heart of a glorious, storied city.

THE END